EIMEAR McBRIDE

THE CITY
CHANGES ITS FACE

GW00579012

faber

First published in 2025
by Faber & Faber Ltd
The Bindery, 51 Hatton Garden
London EC1N 8HN

Typeset by Faber & Faber Ltd
Printed in the UK by CPI Group (UK) Ltd, Croydon, CR0 4YY

*This is a work of fiction. All of the characters, organisations and
events portrayed in this novel are either products of the author's
imagination or are used fictitiously*

A CIP record for this book
is available from the British Library

ISBN 978–0–571–38421–1

Printed and bound in the UK on FSC® certified paper in line with our continuing
commitment to ethical business practices, sustainability and the environment.
For further information see faber.co.uk/environmental-policy

2 4 6 8 10 9 7 5 3 1

In memory of Christopher, Yat & Reuven, with thanks.

AUGUST 1995–DECEMBER 1996

Now

The city changes its face as I tap at my teeth. Rain going delinquent beyond in the street and all over him, closing the door.

Sorry I'm late.

And in from the night. The winter on his body making inroads to mine. Cold lips white. Under fingernails, blue.

Why're you sitting in the window?
Waiting.
For what?
Just for you.

His smile then. And I smile back.

Well   let me just get this wet coat off.
Are you soaked?
To the skin.
You should get changed.
I think I will.

But first my cheek under his wet palm. His wet palm on my hair.

How are you doing?
Fine   you?

The spareliest of nods and

All right too.

Then kiss my mouth. His. Kiss again. The smell of his damp hair and rain on my hand.

I'll get dried off   then cup of tea?
                    Yeah   I'll put the kettle on.

But my eye goes through him for his state of mind, and that quick glance – turned eyebrow itch, turned to yawn – is gauging, I think, when he thinks I can't see. How is she? Fine. Or she seems okay. Good. Tick. Now? Fine. Good. Tick again. Out of care, I know, but dismiss as whim his carefulness of me. Sidestepping it so, and out of real interest, ask

                So   how was the show tonight?
        Not bad actually.
    Many people in?
        Full house, far as I could make out.
            And many round after?
        One or two.
            Anyone there you knew?
        Thankfully not!
                And the others?
                    Were all heading out for a drink but   I didn't fancy it.
                                I wouldn't have minded.
                    Wasn't really in the mood. Besides, it was pissing down, so . . .

But already halfway down the hall. The frozen lank of him cutting the corner to vanish off into our room. I glass flaw tap. Time to relinquish the street. All those rushers in their dashes from the gutter spouts of taxis. It is downpour Camden. Drenching city. And night, like I like best.

– 2 –

Which is all to say, we are here again. Him having gone round in the subsequent time and me having gone round in it too.

So unfold my legs to put feet on the floor. Quick shift my stiffened body into his brought cold. Let the curtain drop and the streetlight maraud where it wills beyond the pane – wide beyond and across those civic realms where all, but we, reside. Even to where I saw earlier's white sky through. Above the lent chimneys and further off too to where the tube must be. Remember that? I remember it. Pigeons and gulls play-acting adrift but winging through dramas of their own. I think I watched them long. Now I leave all that out in the flood. Instead, make along the distance of his voice. Lino stoney-ish beyond the worn carpet I cross. Eye on the, ear on the. Move now, this moment. And call after

Why didn't you jump in a cab?
I would've, but there were none to be had   you know how it is when it rains.

And I do, in this place become so like home that it, improbably, is. Armchair. Sofa. Phone on the wall. Bills in his name. Letters to my own. A photo of his daughter. A photo of us. Fairy liquid on the windowsill. Plastic washing-up brush. Streetlight gleam from below and more black sky above than I can see my way through. Nothing really but a brick box on the top of the town. Bedrooms though and a bathroom. Palatial in comparison to our formerly inhabited cram. And ours, I suppose – ish – by the month. Some entrenchment implied in the postcards stuck up, in the heap of kicked shoes – my sandals in there although it's winter now. By my long-cold tea on his long-lacking shelves, and the books and the books and the books. Sideways. Longways. I am trying my best with an alphabetisation, which is not helped by the One more there and Stick that in the gap. So many writers with fixes for the grips we need to get. No. Neither bother with reading like that. Both, by osmosis, staying well out of it, favouring wild worlds instead. Now though, the same wild's been walked in. Trail dripped and trod on. I kitchen-roll spread and sop it up until my socks wring too.

Jesus! You brought half the Thames in with you!
What?
The floor's swimming.
What'd you say, love?
You've dripped everywhere!
Sorry about that.

His regrets too loud because he can't know I'm already there, hanging round the bedroom door.

No need to shout.
Oh! I didn't hear you coming down.
Well, at least your voice's holding out.
Yeah. Thank God it is.

Tapping the top of his chest. Near blue in the chill of his near nakedness. Glancing to my arm but concentrating on my face. Me folding it over, pretending he hadn't and him turning quick, also, away.

Those cough sweets did the trick. That and taking care in the third act.
I liked it when you did it louder.
Me too but my vocal cords weren't so sure.

Then fishing in the wardrobe until a hanger goes crack.

Shit!

Pulling a broken one out.

Here   give me the bits.

When he passes, I knit the cracks. Fit. No good now though, even dosed with Loctite, so I see-saw it back into twigs.

Mind, Eil   you'll get a splinter.

A last gristly snap. Abruptly so violent I wonder at it myself. And chuck it. There. With my inner curse – you're broke, so be that and lie, unmourned, in that Sainsbury's bag lining our bin. A plane passes over. A train shakes from underground. With unusual indiscretion, his eyes wander me down, asking after all the things he'd like me to clear up. For want of willing, I am flip.

Those hangers were a swizz!

Leaving him a single option then – to shrug and pull dry jeans over long cold legs. The circular silence revolving itself until he does his fly and I foot-flex to cramp.

Ow!
All right?
Just my foot.

Damp still on his neck. Dark hair on his stomach. Desire begins. For me. For us both? Immediately spurned by his dry jumper's yank over. Compounded by a bid to wrangle totally free. Here's our new world.

Did you see that bill?

Which?
It was there before – the council tax.
I haven't seen it.
Bollocks!

Down. Searching on his knees. Wet jeans pooling the floor.

Here, pass those up, Stephen   I'll put them with the basket.
I'll do it   fuck   it was there this afternoon.
Just pass them.
Don't worry   I'll do it.

But I still go to go round him and our bodies touch, if only may-be chin to hip. Enough though he moves all the way back. Snap and

Just leave them, I said!

And clicked then so quick to some impassable him. The instant sorry in his eyes mere annoying accompaniment to the intransigence everywhere else. But here the matter is, nonetheless. On the tip of both tongues, almost destined to be said, or set upon, if we choose. I want to. I really could. Resentments assemble and ready in my mouth. Accusations of. Allegations of. Incalculable wrongs. I have so   Then it blinks and gets unsurer of its ground. Attempts a quick myther. Is forestalled. He shifts in himself. The moment goes over and

I'll put the kettle on.
Ta.

Again. I have said this again. 'I'll put the kettle on.' So do it then. Depart this brink. Leave him to search for his bill with the tail-end drip of hurricane worrying down his back. And fuck him. And it all. And all of that. Don't even wait for the Wait! I know will not come. But know too that neither are battle lines drawn. Rather, in a minute, he will come where I am. Prop himself up close by, start to be kind, and I will give readily in. To an idle comment. To aimless chat. Then we'll skirt this dulling despondence we've recently learned how to share. Its dampening pace. The clog it makes in the air, which we knock against or occasionally stub toes off. However, before that minute arrives, there's still this. Annoyance. I shake it by the scruff. Stomp the hall. Fill the kettle. Slap in the plug and bang it down hard in electric revenge but

but   ever and always singing its song of

I'm waiting. I am waiting for you.

First Summer

Flitter litter across the bare bed. Box-lugging bruises up your arms and chest. Laughing though, through your cigarette. So that's about it then, let's go! Old heat now in this soon old room. Yours for the last time. Next week someone new. Nevermore for us and we pity the fool. No. That's only me. My body still covets what it was. Not yours. Not one bit. It is lax impervious, while mine insists we Look around one last time. Look around for what? At everything that once was. And because it never will be again. You are Mmmm. You are unconvinced. Won't you be a bit sad even, to never be here again? Never see it? After everything? Nope, can't say I will, I'd put a match to this place if I could! Don't say that! But you won't indulge me. Will barely loiter as I aspicate our past with Here's the spot. There's the place. This the window I looked out from when. Busted bedsprings. And farewell, sink. You just flick your fag end out the front. The last fag you'll ever smoke, ever in this room! All right, Herodotus, enough, come on! No, I Wait! And gaze into the evening dust until my sentimentality's thoroughly routed by your lack of. Jesus, come on, Eil! Which is fair. You've far further back memories than me of here. And they are   And they were   full with bites and rifes and   Let's go now, love, it's really time. So, spell unbinding, I dramatic Farewell! Then follow on out and down the stairs. But as you turn your key – last time too! – I am obliged to observe the earth staying on its axis just the same.

Now

The clack of the kettle as its sole duty's done. I investigate for fury but, on finding none, consider clearing the breakfast bar now. The dish piles are getting out of hand. We're clearly outwaiting each other again. Most often it's him. But this time, it seems, I'll be the one to break first. Very firstly though, I make the tea. Spoon-standingly strong. Two. Bit of milk. No thought for the hour or that I mightn't sleep. Post-show skeins in him anyway before tiredness gets in – adrenaline tapped, probably, and slow at draining. Lately, besides, sleep for me's become a thing for shrinking – with its runnels of dreams gnawing into my brain, pretending they know what for. Look at you, he says mornings, Were you at it again? Implying I've spent the night hours replaying the lists of diseases I might get or failures I may yet commit. Worse, the existing shames I cannot escape. As some kind of warding off? he asks, but I only answer Yes, if in the mood for regret at the sight of his concern. Oftener I brassy No, for want of better deceits. Either way, my tiredness spirals and he always knows it. Just like I know all my revisiting yields no good, yet do it anyway.

Mind if I turn the heating up?
No   I mean   go ahead.

And a tangle of hand at the nape of my neck. Freeze balancing out the affection in it, but I do not move away. Take the touch and what I can get. Lucky the actress he kisses each night, who probably does not care a wit beyond timing it properly, I assume. I assume.

> Thanks for the tea.
> No problem.

And his long fingers go round it. Heat bringing them bluish to white. Nicotine-stained to the knuckle. Brown between the top joints. Years of hard work in getting that hue. Pulling and drawing. Blowing it out. I miss it and him at it as well.

> Don't mind those dishes now. Come sit, Eil   I haven't
> seen you all day.

So leave thoughts of his smoking and kissing in the sink. Hop up instead on the high stool opposite.

> Did you tube or bus it back in the end?
> 274 but it broke down, so I ended up walking from Euston,
> hence the lateness   and the soaking.

Tip my fingers to the tips of his.

> Jesus, your hands are still froze.

He looks to them. Under his lids. Still, fuck it, I see and, before he can withdraw, cover them with my heat. Warm hands, cold heart. We all know what that means. But he just lets me. Good.

Yeah, I wouldn't be surprised if there was snow.
Too wet for it to lie.
I don't know   it might freeze.
        But   you're still glad you took it?
What?
        The play.
Yeah   it's good being back in the theatre again.
Different?
    Maybe   a bit   do you mind me being out every night?
        Sometimes.
            Sorry.
        Don't be   it's fine.
Well   I like having someone to come home to from it for a
change.
    But is that ever   annoying?
        No   why would it be?
            Just

And the past goes stutter, reminding me of his Come here, as I
barefooted up the bedroom wall. Uncivil in our new room. Upside
down and hanging off. In the mirror behind, his bare shoulders
above and my hair all the way to the floor.

            Just what?
Knowing I'm   waiting   if you'd rather go out.
        I would never rather, so don't think that. I'm just   tired
        when I get back.   I always want to see you, Eil
        sometimes I'm just ffff

Then seeing how he means it, and much, it's all right to pass on
into further domestic.

Are you hungry?

Starving.

I don't know why you don't eat before.

I do   just not too close, so by afterwards it's   late.

And still not a pick on him to stave off that while it eats at me, his nightly famishment. As if more hunger's in there than I've ever managed, even on my leanest day. Even in my only bread and jam from Kwik Save. Like tunnels endlessly construct beneath his skin and while awaiting their purpose keep riddling him with more, and yet more, gaps to stop. Right up until I want this, I really want this, engulfs. A wanting greater than anyone could possibly content. I dwell on the coulds of this hazard, now and then. On how the slyness of his thinness is only a blind for those vast diggings within. He knows too I know, and so why I am, eternally, wishing he'd eat – to, at least, start finding his fill.

What, Eil?

Nothing.

No   what?

Nothing. What do you fancy? That's all.

I don't know.

Up he gets.

Let's see what there is.

Between this then, and the lingering by the fridge, I would happily bet we are now on a countdown to cheese.

– 11 –

First Summer

High white van scraping under trees. Driving like you know. I do
know actually; you've just never seen me do it before. When'd you
learn? Years ago, it's handy, you should learn. Sure Stephen, I hav-
en't a car. Well, maybe I'll get one and teach you? God, I've no
interest in that. A decisive No then? That's right. Fair enough. And
it is too. This much is enough for me, feet on the dashboard and a
smile from him snatched between Amber and Go. So for now, I'll
just Clyde him to Bonnie me, smoke waltzing from our mouths,
slipping in through the traffic and ready, and ready to

Now

Cheese sandwich.
How did I guess?
Should've gone to Oxford.
It's their loss.
The world of telepathy would've never been the same.
I'm a woman with many contributions to make.
And I don't doubt that's the case, but would you reach me out
the piccalilli please?

So now I'm mistress of piccalilli and slices of bread.

Toasted?
No, ta.

Going for the knife and piece plate himself.

The very last clean one!
Congrats!

Christ.

What?

If you're waiting for me to wash this lot up, you'll be waiting
a while.

Oh, too grand for it, now you're in the West End?

I've been in the West End plenty. It's just your turn. I've been
doing it all week!

Sure what was I doing when you said to sit down?

True. Apologies, madam.

Apology accepted.

Still   that was experience talking.

You shut up!

But I like this skitting about as his bare foot rocks me back and
forth on the long-legged stool.

Don't make me spill my tea!

Don't yourself!

Slurping. Then buttering. Piccalilli-ing. Cheese on top.

And what did you get up to, Eil, while I was out?

Keep still. The pages flitter over in my head, arrange and rearranging themselves. It's got so much further, but I'm not there yet.
Undotted. Uncrossed. Although those aren't the risk. I'm just not
arrived at admittance yet, to anyone, even you. So pull away from the
sheafs, with their chaotic reach, back to here and its precarious real.

Not much   read   went over some lines.

For the Priestley?

Yes.

Go in all right?

I think.

Do you want me to be on the book?

No, thanks.

But you're   ready to go back? You feel you are?

I suppose.

Well, that's good.

Full stop.

Or not.

So   you feel like your concentration's coming back?

Yeah   it is now   I think.

That's   got to   feel better.

Yes   it does.

But a hooked pause now sits before a difficult next. And where are international incidents when you need a hindrance? Never coinciding with an awkward instant, that's for sure. I can tell though, it's coming, by the way his fingers curl. Just the moment before   and then   it officially begins.

Speak to anyone today?

Wasn't really in the mood.

Go out at all?

No.

Eily.

Sure you got soaked.

I know but

I just don't want to. Don't fuss.

I'm not fussing, I only   I worry you're on your own here a lot and

You're at the theatre.
But what about seeing your friends? Alison? Danny even?
I don't feel like it, Stephen.
I know that but
And neither do you   be honest.
Yeah but   I'm working and besides
You're twenty years older, I know!
I know you do, Eily, but
And yet still a fuck-up!
As we both know   but

A douse of silence on top of that. Shit. I'd scrape it back if I could turn the page. But no, and winnowed, as we already are, by mistakes, I suppose I must swallow this too. I can say awful things for which he never holds a grudge. But even for me, Fuck-Up was a fuck-up. And crass, although his fingers look supremely unbothered amid their halving of slices of pan. Good, I think, Eat. Fill up. Then note the fingers curl into his palms. Pausing for thought more than effect. Effect's not really him. Regret, however, is suddenly high on my list. So I smooth the knot vein on the back of his hand. Press, in reparation, the run of blood through his veins and invent something kinder to say.

I love that   the shape of that vein.
Eily, I just   I worry about you.
I know   but don't.

Doubt remains around his eyes, so I press it again.

Really   don't worry   it doesn't help.
If you promise me that you
I promise   all right?

Because I can't let the end of that sentence arrive. Swallow. Swallow. Right down to dry.

Okay then, love   I'll try.
You really don't need to worry, Stephen   I swear.

He doesn't believe me, but enough's been said for his fingers to reopen. To relax. To dive back into action, fast, and gather all edibles in one great sticky salvage. Then that sandwich's hour has come.

First Summer

Dropping boxes, one and two. Sweat, more than sentiment, gilding this threshold, but none the worse for that. Just in! Room. Rooms. Ours. Length and light. Sitting room. Hall. Bedroom for the mattress. These alone, this stuff and us, but plenty for pioneers. Astronauts almost, on our approach – if only five minutes traversed from down the road. But for you all this normal is so alien, foreign, that I hanker after snaps to play. I have none though – parallels. For I can't stop being at the start or seeing only as Next what you look at with wonder. For me, this is only a new flat. Other plug points. Different sinks. For me, new's you, this you and me, this you and me and here. But for you this is the balance of your past going sunder. Plus the getting of a witness and a co-conspirator in whatever flounders shall be. Doubtless those'll be many in our inch along as uncommon people who hope, beyond all reason, for the unlikely best. Do we accept? We accept. And all of it. Excepting none. Que sera, sera.

So we took and turned the key. These new rooms going groan for learning – window latches, floors and ceilings. Today and night we will. What doors need shoulders? Which taps go drip? How loud this stretch of Camden and rowdy this street? How little we cared for each of these potential annoyances then. And, it turns out, never really will although, right now, that remains to be seen. Instead, between the future and our boxes stacking the kitchen, the print of the shabby lino got mapped. Square to square, by your knees and my back. Again and again until it rubbed nearly smooth. I do I do I do I do think everything's going to be fine.

Now

Bite.

             Good sandwich?
       Cheese's a bit stale.
         I thought it looked a bit curly.
            Oh well. I'll just get some more tomorrow.
         Piccalilli still okay?
              Yeah.
          It's nearly done.
             Remind me when I'm going out.
       Are you going somewhere tomorrow?
Just round the corner to get a few things in. Maybe take a turn around the park if you fancy it, Eil?
         If it's not raining   I might.
          Okay.

And press my thumb into the crumbs on his plate.

            Want some?

Offering share of his terrible sandwich that I wouldn't touch for love nor money.

           Oh no   God, no.

And cock my snook.

> Well, don't knock it till you've tried it.
>> That's what they say.
>>> And I agree   with the traditional caveats.
>>> Obviously.
>>>> Obviously.

And smile at our own blackness. Swig for swig of our teas. These chancier moments are actually easiest. Prodding a little. Showing we know the past but aren't stuck in its say-so. Not any more. Like it's never had dominion and, although it's had it all, here in its shadows can be a nice place to play. To rearrange. To claim Here we are, still, and mostly unharmed. Saying and saying it, even if it's not true. It's a life, however anyone cares to think, with every possibility for happiness permitted, no matter when we're blind to which way. Thunk, then thump. His stool rocks me back to now again. Too easy here, on the leeside of the sun, to trip, topple and fall.

> Did you catch Grace in the end?
> Just before the half.
> What time was it there?
>> About eleven, I think.
> Morning?
> Yes.
> Did she not have a class?
>> They're already off.
> Oh, right. So what did she say?
> The transfer's gone through now   officially.
> Well, that must be a relief.
>> It is.
>> How's her mother taking it?

Shrug and a lip twist.

    She'll survive.

There. Showing only a little rise at what's owed off the back of the past. He keeps those grudges low down – though they nip and can strike – from a born inclination to leave all that behind. And whenever a little, like now, hangs out, he's quick to snip the loose thread.

    I'm sure she'll be fine   it'll just take a while to adjust.

But this excess of equanimity makes even me cough. Whoop. And cough again.

    What?

Giving me innocent eyes despite, surely, being far from. Mustn't he want to go wreaking? Or maybe I want it because that's what I'd definitely do.

    Nothing.
No, what?
    Nothing, just it's ironic the shoe's on the other foot.
It's not like that, Eily. There's nothing to win.
    Because you already did?

A laugh and reluctant, lopsided lip lift.

    Eventually   I suppose.

Then I have what I want so can flip it away.

And what else did Grace say?

She's looking forward to seeing us next week.

When's she getting in?

Thursday night. Half nine, I think.

You won't be able to meet her this time.

No   but I might ask Rafi if he would.

I'm sure she's fine to get the tube.

I'm sure she is but   you know   I'd be happier if she had a lift.

The insistence of fatherhood getting me again by surprise. Yet will fade, I remember, to commonplace across the days she is here. So discard the thread and go from there.

Excited to see her?

God, yeah   August seems ages now.

Will she make the show?

Last night.

That's great   she can go to the thing with you   after.

So can you.

Mmm   maybe.

Doesn't have to be a big deal. Just stick our heads in   say hello and

We'll see.

Eily.

Stephen.

Okay   but have a think?

I will.

Cheese falls out. He puts it back in. Bites more off than he can chew. Has trouble with it. Then bows his head to spare me the view. Fingers on lips. Chew. Chew.

Does she know?

Chew. Hand staying in situ, followed by a nod on repeat.

Uh-hm. She does.
What exactly?
Only the essentials.
Good.
Well, I thought you might not want
When did you tell her?

Chew.

Just after.
Right after?
Pretty much   she could tell there was something up.
What did she say?

Chew. Swallow. Swipes last crumbs from his mouth and gulps more tea.

That she was sorry   That she hoped you'd be all right.
What else?
Nothing really.
Really?
I don't really remember, Eil   I was pretty preoccupied
at the time.

Fingers dance the Formica with their own roll of sound. I've gone closer to this than I care for, but now   since I'm here

Who else knows?

Don't even know if I want to know that. And know anyway he rarely tells what can be left. To anyone. Even to me. Still, the question's asked, so

Well, obviously the cast know   at least some of it. Rafi. Grace.
                No one else?
        Only whoever you've told yourself.
            The school because   you know I'm supposed to be there.
                And I'm sure you will again, Eil   soon enough.
            That's why I'm prepping the Priestley for next term.

And look to each other without saying it. Will I be there? He hopes, as a hope of improvement. Of me acting again. Back to art as to life. Resuming myself. Or how I was. But I can't think much of drama school now.

                Anyone else?
                Alison.
                Of course   but
                No   that's about it.
                So   not your mother?
                No.
                Why not?
                Why would I?
                I don't know   might help?
                I doubt that very much.
                    Okay   I just thought

I don't want to know though, so snap that shut.

Since when are you so misty-eyed about family stuff?

See him take it in and step right back.

That's fair enough   that's fair, Eil.
Yes   it is.

First Summer

Tilt. Cigarettes, and plastic ripped from mattress dips. Mind yourself! Should've probably done this first. Too late now so let's call
it inducted. Ah yeah, we'll call it that. Wound all round my wrist.
Stuffed into bags. Venus of Bubble Wrap, me – doing your accent.
What accent's that supposed to be? It's clearly Sheffield! Is it fuck!
Ah, you know it is, shut up! And just laughing us both, either way,
as the boil outside makes sloth of in here. What unpacking must
get done. Let's do it! Yes! Quick! But useless together in the face
of this inescapable, organisational imperative. For we are lazy and
gone shag weak. Lacking the discipline or character for one true
great unpack! Because I'll not move, despite the sweat. And you'll
not move me because you only ever say yes to any old offer to
fuck. And the fucking's all good, all fucking day. We even got to the
evening on just sandwiches and tea. Then in pagodas of our boxes, after forks of sweet and sour, we played mandarins on duvets
strewn in peaks upon the sofa. And though the far world crept
towards us, looking for invites in, with the phone still dead and no
post yet, we were an atoll of our own. In the midst of the city but
on the outside of time, if only for this little while. Screened from
the futures we could not yet see – or my share of them anyway.
Your future didn't reach so unknowably far, only to when London
would swap for Vancouver. Not that you minded. You've had plenty endless future before and never liked it so much, you said, as this

foreshortened now. Or how it was getting lived. And how different we were in those hours and minutes. Ones we'll never repent of or want back again. Freely given, shared and taken. Just starve-eyed urchins at a groaning table who could not look away. Instead we squandered our time properly, on the finer things, for as long as we could. But eventually, brutalling up from the food and the fuck, the great unpack resumed. Ah don't, Eil! What? Move – don't get up yet! Stop putting it off, and don't think for a second you're leaving it for me to do while you're away. That hymn of conscience galvanising you then, just like an I-knew-it-would charm. Bollocks! All right! Here I am! Creaking up. Buttoning your fly. Manhandling a box of novels. Will you be all right, Eil, while I'm away? All cursory but threaded with underplay. Ah Stephen, don't dump it there! Sorry, then where? Over there in the corner. Okay, but will you, Eily   be okay? Of course, it's London, what can go wrong? Plenty, believe me, so double check the locks before going to bed. Ah, come on! No, promise me? All right I will, but will you? Will I what? Be all right, Stephen. How do you mean? Over there, in Canada. And then your face. I don't know, Eil. I'm hoping for the best but I . . . I'm not sure what to expect.

Now

I dice round fingers again in his crumbs. Not too many. Maybe enough for neat-freakish piles – if I was of a mind, which I am certainly not. Such interests extend only to the piccalilli on his thumb so, to rub it off, lick my own. Do it then. Scrub. Work my nail in round his. Leading to the smile, a little tired, from him while surrendering to a harmless

   Ta for that.
   So did you find the bill for the council tax?

I did.

Where was it?

Down the back of the drawers.

Must've been a draught when you closed the door.

Yeah   probably.

Gulp. Down. He makes short work of that tea. Now, backing from the stool, he'll lope to the sink. Rinse his mug. Dump it to drip. Swipe crumbs from his piece plate and repeat. I reflection-watch it be exactly this – grease-spat glass notwithstanding and thwart of the light. Brightness above. Darkness without. Then a strained chew of his lip. In-camera perhaps but still boding ifs. If he. If she. I wish I. Shit! As he loses the rinsed plate to a slip. Just catches it too, before it breaks, but in the pane our eyes meet. So my seeing his doubt is also seen by him. Looking at. Looking at. Waiting for. What? Anxiety denied in the form of a laugh? A kiss and great reassuring sweep off my feet? Fat chance of either of these. But my kingdom for any fix to this trap we are both staring at, yet so careful not to spring. And although we are rife with knowing this thing, how soon till we both look away? I'll not. I keep looking. Look and look again. Then he just turns. Please stay, I'd scream but don't even say that. Or Please keep looking at what we are both looking at. Keep on looking until there are fissures and cracks, because I'm all for the shatter and what might ride in on its back. I also don't say that. Then turn too from conflict, with its many tempts. Wait! One last ditch where I   but relent and mostly just fancy a drink.

Do you fancy a drink?

Is there anything?

Not sure   maybe a beer?

Well, if there's one in the offing.

Let me see.

Hoist on over from my stool to the fridge. Half a ring of Holstens. Here! Chuck his. Ta! Caught and cracked. Drinking long glugs as I help myself. Loitering a little in front of the shelves. Grey eyes drifting our gluts of titles. Now and then, cocking his head. Beer cooling, and no more than a sop to the mad but I'd say we've both earned that. So follow along with his line of sight. Loads, his of old, interspersed with mine. Mix the books, we elected the summer we moved in. Side by side, his scruffed Kafka now with my new Sarah Kane – from an afternoon of standing tired-legged in French's. This is who you wanted, Eil, wasn't it? Let me get it for you. No no, don't. But still, he did. I'd go back to that past, in a flash, if I could. Our whole first summer and right to the next. Not without knots but definitely without wrecks. Except starting again is an itch with no scratch. Better to head towards possible nexts, with their aims of forward, or at least absence of stand-off. From where he is stood though, across the room, how to offer him invite in? What 'Come into my parlours' have I learned? Mainly his and mainly to make me laugh. Don't know if I'll manage that. We're too lost in our detours, and so totally map-less, that funny'd probably stretch us to snap. So what's next'll have to emerge from this obstructive past, whatever else I might want to do.

It seems so long ago now.
What does, Eil?
That first time you phoned Grace   from this flat.
I suppose it's   what   a year and a half?
If not a bit more.
I remember it being pretty near to when I went over.
Was it?
Maybe even that week. Took forever to get the line
connected up.

Did it?

Drove me mad   using the phone box on the end of the road.
I don't remember.

Always trying to hold on to pound coins?

Oh yeah, but did it really take long?

Weeks!

Didn't seem like that to me.

You didn't have a long-lost daughter you were trying to
speak to.

No   I suppose not.

First Summer

Other stuff merited notice, probably, I just never thought of it.
Only when the man from Cable & Wireless showed up did we realise it was purely track of time had been lost. That, out there, life
in its many facets was still waiting for us to return. But amid his
mealy-martyring about missing sockets, or crucial leads, was your
sharp I don't care, just sort it, mate! Then I realised the realising was
only mine. You'd been waiting this whole time, distracted perhaps
but waiting all the same. Meaning, from that landline epiphany on,
life in its many facets was here.

I did not know those gears though, or how to move, and could
not work out what you knew. Here it comes. Ratchet. Set for
change. Click. Me there inside the mechanism. Tock. Then tick.
Up you got. Set. Ding ding and off! While I rose unready, hovered foot to foot. After the Cable man left, you said you'd call her,
first. Of course you did, and why wouldn't you? Except. Somehow it gave me a land. So to unrush all my blood, I offered to
hang our unpacked clothes. Clothes, remember those? But you'd
already turned away. Steeling. Composing. Closing over the door.
Going to the kitchen in your old robe. I listened and didn't listen.

Didn't want to think I would. Knew I couldn't not. Couldn't tell if you'd disapprove – having closed it over, not tight, after all. Then pondered too the novelty of putting something on after what had been days and days. So I did. T-shirt over. Knickers underneath and, thus wrapped in my decadence, leant in and an ear. To? Your falter at her first Hello – a Gracie, is that you? The way her name was said and how Hello love, it's your dad, brought another broke road to its end. Along with So now our landline's in, you can call me any time . . . any time at all. Over-tipping, I banged my toe on the unbuilt bed. Fuck! Hopped and tried not to disrupt closeness being made. Still, my bished body – unused now to lone – itched to see yours again, for a moment. So it did. Looked out. Looked up the hall, towards it in the kitchen where it leant against the wall. All kind with the receiver. So happy at her voice. Yes, I'll see you very soon, it's really no time now. Weight on your left hip, as you lit up. On your right, as you exhaled, while I watched from the dark. Saw you heard every word and, if I'd asked for repeats, know you'd have had her by heart. And where was I or could I be in that? Jacobean tragedies not much resolved by young women in T-shirts. Or young women at all. But. Then. Oblivious to my ruminations, you looked for where I was. Saw. Becked me up. A finger come hither all it took, and I took you up on it. Happy to. Eager. Pulled into your pit. Cheek against your hesitations, hearing your toil to get it right. And beating through your ribcage, every response to her voice. I strained for it but couldn't quite hear. Felt my knicker trim found by your fingertips. And twanged a little, I think on instinct – like fig leaves had just made their debut. Then, doubtless for thought of her, as swiftly withdrew. And I was handed the phone. Grace, I'm passing you to Eily now. Expelling me then, from the hideout of your arm, off you went, to get more on.

I took the receiver, wondering what? Her Okaying, as you wandered off, without even casting back. Trusting we'd be fine? Or to goodwill? Prematurely, surely, but still. Here be gulfs – perhaps you thought – may as well wade in.

Hello, I to her, and she Hello'd then. Nice to meet you, Grace. And you, Eily . . . as well. Beat. And wait. And who'll be next? Her – ha! – with You're all settled now, Dad said? Yeah, but the phone line's only just gone in – adding, as a gift – which makes you the maiden call from this flat. Happy phone line then! she said. And I liked the ice-breaking of that so stole further. It'll be nice to call your . . . father now . . . whenever you fancy, I'd say? Which did sit strange on my tongue. Your father. Her father. Yeah it will, but . . . we'll have to work the time difference out. Oh yeah, Vancouver's nine hours behind London, is that right? Eight actually. So what time's it now? After midnight! Oh, Jesus! Both us starting to laugh. Does he know? I don't think so but it doesn't matter – when it rang so late I knew who it would be. Oh, did you now, needles but keep it inside me. Weird how she's already forecasting him well, even after a decade of nothing at all, like she's some old hand at him down on the level of blood. Daughters guess their fathers, I suppose, though what do I know about that? I'm just caught in their current now and can't swim against. Appeased by its purity but unprepared for its strength. I need to get a grip. And, after all, you remain where you've always been, stood in the gap between me and those places where the past runs in. Holding and helping me hold the line. So now that your history's showing its wares, I should . . . I should . . . I should and do say Sure then, you already know him well. Do you think so, Eily? And she seemed so thrilled I extended it to You sound just like him as well. Really? My mother says that but she means it . . . you know . . . less positively. And I've education enough in that wild mess to dig no further, especially when we've gone for friendliness. Well, I mean it as a compliment, Grace. I know, she said, and That's nice to hear. Which drew us right to the end. We hadn't broached the strangest thing but how could we yet? Enough we'd exchanged some things and sidestepped cause for complaint. I thought. I hoped. And kept to myself what I could suddenly see – that I'd never be so simple for him as she'd be belonging, as she must, to that other side of him which was, of course, the other side of you.

Cued up then, span and neat, the wanderer returned. Eyeing my efforts, tugging your T-shirt down, giving me a corner of smile. Bloody cheek of it! But I said only He's back, I'll hand you over now. Her suggesting that we'd probably talk again soon. I'm sure. Nice to have . . . met you. Phone met you. You too. Here. Bye. Give and take. Still smiling your own thanks when the floor went shake and I panicked back into you Fuck! What, Eil? What's wrong? Didn't you feel it? The whole flat just shook! That's only the Underground below us, love, haven't you felt it before? And I couldn't say I had, but wondered if that was the result of being so much on the flat on my back? A speculation I could not, just then, air. But What happened? she must also have asked because then there was No, nothing. The tube passing under us just gave Eily a fright. There's more shudder up here than in the old flat, that's all. Comfort given. Problem solved. On the outside of them though I missed those old walls and all the time shut in. Stock in their sturdy. Private with our past. If I knew, if I'd known, would I leave them now? But we were both set for leaving so there's no way to tell. Jammed tight in with the here of it then, I took the bait of your smile. And smiled it back. And, for want of interest in causing other wrecks, went to the window to look. Day. Another. London city and world. There before me as you were. I still see you as I saw you and long to be you, as I was you, all the way over again.

Now

Going by his side, I flick through that time and wonder how remembering it's doing in him? Very active or not? Either way those eyes

just keep drifting books, as he sips at his beer, and thinks in himself
of things I can't quite guess.

How many times have you been to Vancouver now?
     Three. It'll be four   after January.
  And then, I suppose, you won't be going back again much.
Well, Grace will be here and it's not like I love that flight.
     Long.
  And a fucking killer on the legs.
    That's what you always say.
      Because it's always true and   anyway
        What?
     I don't like leaving you.
  Stephen   I'm always fine and I will be too   this time
as well.
I was just thinking   maybe you'd like to come with?

I just give an eye roll and fun it off.

    What, to meet your ex?
       You'd be with me and Grace and   so what if you
       met Marianne?
    She'd know how old I am.
  She knows how old you are and, even if she didn't, do you
think I'd care?

But really it's the other thing which now I have to ask.

      Does she know?

Which turns him about. Neither Kafka nor Kane interrupting
that subject.

I haven't told her.

   No?

    Why would I?

   Has Grace?

    I don't know but   I'd be surprised if she has.

     Why?

I think part of their truce is   not discussing me.

    Haven't things   improved there?

    A bit. I don't ask though, so I only know what Grace says.

But you and Marianne are

    Fine. We can pass ourselves but, you know, she isn't a friend.

     Fair enough.

Any more of these left?

Him shaking his empty. Going to the fridge. Looking for another and, on finding there is

     You too, Eil?

    I've still some left.

Glad of the beer fur running under my skin, getting into sore muscles. I like the leeway it lends them to ache and to still be fine. Right. Push a spine to tidy in a book. Then a whole row. I swear it's the tube, shuddering under, shuffles them out – my only remaining notice of it now as it races beneath my feet. More noticeable his long legs going crack as he settles in the armchair.

    Jesus, Stephen, that doesn't sound good.

     I know   it's like I'm falling apart.

Does it hurt?

    No it's just the sound.

  Must be getting old.

   No way back from forty, Eil.

    Too bad for you.

You're laughing now but, before you know it, you'll be staring it down as well.

  Ah, it's a long way off yet.

    I thought that once.

   Still must be better than your thirties.

That remains to be seen!

    Oh, come on you've got Grace and your film.

I'd like him to add me in, but he's just eyebrows up and a nod of agreement. Why are all our journeys so hard? To be fair, he's smiling more now than before that first flight. Happier in the memory – all ifs long gone poof! I remember myself then as snagged between the torturing wait for him to leave and the thought of his being away.

First Summer

After the Grace call, misgivings settled in. Their primary nip being who'd return in that skin, the one I never wanted changed? Feeling it as I passed the shirts you'd badly ironed. Getting worse at the zip of the case. Continuing on through the Tickets? Passport? Money? I endlessly incanted until Okay I have them, Eily, I think I've got everything. And then the time was right there, no longer coming. Not a single other night or day or hour in the future. The whole of me urging to faint, or shout Pax! Just to keep You were going though, and right for it. So I was left to a stammer of So . . . so then I'll . . . just wait? Would, apparently, as you grasped your case with a practical I'll see you then, in a week. Can I not come to the airport?

No, it's late, and you don't want to be alone on the Piccadilly line coming back. Actually, I do. Eily. But. Eily, don't, you're better off staying put and . . . I don't want to be worrying about you, which I would, all right, love? All right. Bastard world flashing Let Go Of Him! Let Go Because He'll Go Even If You Don't! Come here to me though, is what I got. So I went. Arms and arms around with lingering intent. Tipping the sierras of your bony spine, wondering how will I do without them? But, rigged for pragmatism, by then you had already gone. Remained with me in your body but out the door in your mind. Already striding off into Camden, soon to be followed by this same skin and bone. An old trick of yours I knew from before. So knew too to just take it and watch to the end. Bye. I love you. Had it said back the same. Meant as well, I was sure, but that was the end. On out the door and the door loudly shut. And all at once then the flat was so fucking hot – for a place this suddenly empty and soundless. Left alone, I stood in the midst of our stuff but suspended in some third act of yours.

Now

Remember too though that that was AGO. Here in this night, all cycled forward, I cross to sit down by his legs. Stretched just a little. Rest my can on his knee, circling the cap where it indents in. A sympathy of bodies, and if at sixes and sevens, now mostly kindness and tiredness between.

> God   I'm done in, Eil.
>   I can see. It's been a long week.
>   It's been a long run and, with the film and everything, I'm
>   kind of running out of steam.
> Not long now though   until the break.
>   No, but running it out is difficult.

At least tomorrow you can stay in bed.
I'm not moving before eleven!
Well   you've nowhere to be.

Hitch though, where I'd not anticipated it. A small rock tossed in the shallows and from a distance.

Did you really not go out today, Eil?

Baulk. Ripple. Ripples. Segue and siege. I   am reluctant for admissions and what ruptures they'll seed if   if   I say what I was at. No. Not ruptures. Questions without clear answers as yet. Jesus. And not mysterious. Only private. That's all. Still   it's a rare word between us and will last   until? I don't know but assume I will tell it sometime. Then stare at my notebook under his chair. Unremarkable cardboard but I also   wonder   when I might get that far? He's waiting though so, as a less troublesome answer, I let its insides become some sort of truth. The kind that will do   for now.

Actually   I did, I   just forgot.
Oh yeah? Where did you go?
Kentish Town.
What? Really?
Yeah.
That's great   why didn't you say before?

White sky malevolent. Vast and immune. Above. Above everything. And some starting at finding myself, from back then, now all dissolved into air. But I'll maybe not   let on to that.

No reason   I forgot.

Twisting to me then, for eye catching. That's what he's at. Glimpse it from the corner of mine and know he'd like to be let in. However, my eyes have other things to busy with and from which they'll not be easily deterred. For example, that rug over there. The frayed-up curl where it flicks. More pronounced now even than it was last week, and a trip hazard if ever there was. I toe-tap it like that vein of his hand. Veinlike, it compacts then plumps again so that'll be a matter for tape.

Eily?
What?
Tell me?
I just forgot.
Okay, so now you've remembered   how was it?
It was good.
I haven't been up there in ages   maybe not since you moved.
Me neither.
So   was it changed much?
A fair bit.
Did you go by the old flat?
Yeah, but the front is being rebuilt and the Blockbuster below is gone.
What's there instead?
A grocer's or something   I couldn't quite see.
I must walk up some time and take a look.
Really?
Of course. I often think about that flat.
Do you?
I don't know why you're so surprised. I mean it was kind of a memorable time   wasn't it?
I suppose.

Well, don't do me any favours!
I didn't mean it like that   of course it was.

And I give in, to ensure there's not the slightest of slights. From the look of him though, I'd say that was a fix. Wily. So wily and credit where it's due, he's engineered my eyes right into his. But I wonder if he understands I think You've got me looking at you, but I know it's you who's looking at me? Tallying it together, probably. How is she? Fine. Good. Tick. Now? Fine as well. Tick. Or sort of. Or wavering. Or   whatever. These palliative circuits are no surprise, quack, and easily undermined by my looking away. So, I look away and return to the admission of Kentish Town, as seen this whitish afternoon in my head. An inner goad whispering not to, but why is that? Surely, my earlier silence was just a matter of tact about a strange hour I spent imagining there? Yet it does seem to cleave to the tongue, glue-ishly almost, so perhaps that's a sign? Why did I even say? I should've scratch-needled on about staying in the flat. How I stared out the window until stark weather mad! And ignored what I know are his not unreasonable fears – that I am styliting it up here. Hermit on a pillar. Sealing myself for acts of I know what. Calculations boil over each night at this, in the dwindling moments, before he gets in. Always trying to think of better answers to give him. For I hate to serve in the cause of blame – his, although he'll do it anyway – because I've whys and wherefores to answer myself. Plenty. It's just not the time for them yet. This is only the time when he'll fish for evidence and I'll say whatever I choose. But, with my eyes drifting from his, it's only seconds surely until Five   Four   Three

Go on, Eily. I'd love to hear more.

Two One Go.

Okay.

But how will I do that, ragged and rolled over, as I was, by that glass and parky day? Try one word at a time as each image remakes and lines up with its match from the past. So.

Now, Imagined Earlier

I stood in a place I was once known and knew and, from that same spot, touched time. Then it ran like a tipped spill over the edge. Liquid and visible. Middle of the day. Eyes ranging from the concrete up into the sky. Blue always in that past. Nowadays white and blind. Old eras opaqued or elaborately rimed with a dust beyond polishing off. I blew on it anyway. Brushed past by strangers but aiming for intimacy with those good times and bad times again. Memory repacking around still-live veins, goading dulled clots into liquification. Active. Activate. Activation. Then I saw it.

Then see.

Yes, the drain there where I dropped a key. Further, the tube. Nearer, the library. Greggs. Blustons. Costcutter. Owl Bookshop. Proof, if only in hearsay, of my former occupance. Of a time when I moved through this place, said and did. Sensibly sometimes and often its opposite. With conviction too, but alongside a self ignorant of how soon it would have passed on. Also of how I'd always remain, in part, alive in that time. Gliding invisible although the updraught was gone and only particles swirled through the air. That first, never finished, version of myself that haunts the old haunts of was. Today my eyes followed where the past led. From there to here. Same some ways. Others different and unexpectedly. But before that pricked too deep, a 214 passed, leaving me once more in the street. Boring and literal but realising how even this live moment strives to its finish – whether I will it or not. Every moment but a crease where time bends itself before, finally, folding right in. So, at that very fold, I left to make my way home. Leaving all I had once left, again, where it was. An experience of afternoon not easily told and definitely no simple hop off the tongue. How to say all this so? But whenever I'm lost I go to the body again because the body's always waiting for me. Alternatively, show the notebook. Let him see what he sees. Beyond the past, on into meaning, or the page where meaning might get made. Where I unsafely know, yet still dream myself, as though each has hope of becoming true – by the next punctuation, perhaps, if not now. In the meantime, remember pressing until the words break. How that breaking reveals what language they'll make after their inelegant transferral from me into the world. Then, how I shook the biro. And put it down. Dry enough to rip.

Now

His knee. In his now near kneeless jeans. Piths of black hair. Rough knee skin. Chill at the rip. From the night? Or my can? What a waste of examination when, for countless times, I have catalogued all of him before. But purposes, like bodies, serve themselves and today's is only resetting to safety again. I, however, have lingered far beyond when my answer to his question should've ricocheted back. So now he's looking for what I've been looking at. I must arrange what it was – without owning only to fright at the vastness and passingness of time. Yes. Flippant it for everyone's sake, and don't weigh myself under water calling Help! Which, anyway, he could not, being himself a whole half of the sea. No. I'll work it the other way with a light touch and curlicued penwomanship. Excise the void. Fuck existential angst and slide only the most temporal through.

It was just weird, that's all. To think of us then.

What about us?

Not just you and me. Everyone. The Mrs. Danny. The Mrs Boyfriend.

Yeah   he wasn't so bad.

Danny either.

I suppose not.

Really?

Let's just say   I'm fonder of him now than I was.

Because he's so great in your film?

Doesn't hurt.

Playing you.

In a fictional version.

I believe you   thousands wouldn't.

And so the smart aleck returns!

I could fall into this banter. I could do it all night because now a hair couldn't be passed between us. However much I go there though, the body isn't right. I can know or unknow that truth all I like, but if I place my hand where it can only mean invite, he will refuse to pick up the slack. That's where we are at. And I know where we are at, so I say the other thing. Or maybe it's just on my mind. Or maybe I'm not so great at telling straight lies, especially those he's not asking to hear.

It freaked me out though as well.

What did?

Kentish Town.

Why was that?

I don't know   a 214 passed and suddenly I wanted back.

To live in that flat?

No   I don't think it was that.

What then, Eil? To where?

I was so turned then. Head facing back. I was so for anything
and yet couldn't say what. Felt myself going fleet. Back to where
indeed? Maybe it *was* back to then? With its antics and wiseness
to all angles of next. Being of the. Who was the. Even the drugs?
Again, it's a maybe but I'll not tell him that. I'm not after raised eyebrows and I don't think it's really right, really that, anyway. Maybe
more the lure of my former certainty. How I knew, later, after, and
convincedly, what shape life would take by my mid-twenties. How
lately's derailments have put a stop to that and made dank wallows
of once hallowed designs. Made hollows in me too till I'm half
drill-riddled with unallowable truths. Like the new thing that sits in the
corner of my eye? That mouths itself to existence so readily now? Except   if
I've not told him, how real can it be? The notebook, with its cover, and the
life within? Sssh. Shush it and better not. Admit to a weird afternoon where time within me crashed. Lung-whelmingly so, like it
was waters I swam and, drowning, woke from with flailing hands.
But how I still returned to here, with its sound sense and breatha-
ble air. Yes. Easier to make the answer I offer a mere I remembered
when. Besides which, the bus was soon gone and the wickedness
of that white sun also revealed other treacheries of Kentish Town.
World that I had loved so long. Now I won't love it at all. So, piss
off 'Become a Somerfield', I remember what you were once too.
And with that decided, I return

Sorry. Say again?
Where did you want to get back to, Eil?
I don't know   to how much simpler I was   perhaps.
I don't remember you being simple.
How do you remember me?
Well   I'd say   you were more   hard work.

Lovely!

But hard work I couldn't resist.

You can't unsay it now, backpedal all you like.

I don't want to backpedal, Eil. In fact I'd add, there was nothing

What?

You wouldn't come out with. Nothing you wouldn't ask.

So I was nosy too?

Undeniably.

Right. Like how?

Like 'How many women have you slept with?'

It was a valid question.

Maybe but   I'd never met anyone who didn't know not to ask.

Really?

Yes   who just asked   and expected an answer.

Now I'm mortified!

Don't be   you were   lovely.

Lovely?

And new   a person like that   like you   to me.

You mean a fucking eejit?

I didn't say that   and besides   it worked!

Worked how?

Well   we're here, aren't we?

I suppose.

You see? Then it wasn't so bad.

Wry advance into glances across this bridge. Eyes meet to mock audit our various hits. Find we are nick-wounded only, so smiles linger a sec. Then he drinks more of his beer while I rest my cheek on his cold leg – which I find I am allowed. And the night isn't so far gone. I'd bloom at its promise if it weren't for Kentish Town – the dread it caused, sitting above. Maybe I should go further back?

Because, whatever my memories of it, he'll have his own and I bet they're resurfacing now. What might they be? The miles he trod up there to see me? To sprawl on the sofa or knock on the glass, prevaricating into a future more implausible than obvious. There on the pillow, asleep in my bed. Life filing down his ambivalence, in spite of himself. Whiling us towards where balance might strike – despite any railing against or unbearable lightness. Or maybe I romance it too much? He doesn't, wouldn't. Never thinks like that. The hike here took too long to have forgotten escaping his past. Besides which, we're here, aren't we, like he's just said, and I am convinced of his honesty whatever else. Those words ring inside me anyway as true, refuting we've veered off so far it can't be returned to. Not when neither willed nor wanted this. When it all just arrived in unexpected hitches and then more awrys followed suit, like tectonic shifts when the Underground shook. So what? The world shook. It's shaken before. And haven't we just been poking at each other now? Prodding? Provoking to laughs? He's so close I will the beer to work wonders this night. I still hoard memories of when change was little more than that and lay coiled in its doze like some quiet cat. Claws in but on Wait. For now.

First Summer

I woke up. Flies. Flight. Morning. Dream sweat. The chatting of magpies. Where from? Regent's Park? What do you think I   but I was by myself. In sheets alone and shivered by it –a back left cold in the dark. All night since the going, the real going and gone – although I don't think the flight was till five in the morning, whatever use that news to my spine. Made no matter soever to these environs, which maintained their water tricklings and heel clacks on the stairs. Outdoors already aware, growing loud with street speech. Truck sweepers' spray and the vacuates of buses across the ankles of impatient queues. Dioramas of rush hour except here, above, where I lay by the alarm clock I'd chosen not to wind up because   summer, et cetera. And because what fool aspires to waking into What will I do? All only placing distance, of course, before the arrival of how you were not, really not, there. Instead I gave into imagining where you were in the air. The skies of London. The skies over Vancouver. Or no, not quite yet. So let my knees turn me over and up I got. Crossed to the window on un-hoovered carpet and looked high. Leftwards. And there. Jets or vapour trails tracing where you might've gone beyond. Ally Pally? Hampstead Heath? Or way over the Atlantic, passing Iceland or something? Not that I knew much of those tracks. I was just keeping you close in a contrivance of imagined goings-on – consisting, admittedly, of how long-haul flights looked in films. Not disaster movies though. Didn't even think that, and also pressed skip on you striking up chat with whoever you were sat beside. I didn't hesitate to deny them your smile or the easy-goingness that's your favoured lie when out and about in the world. People always so charmed by how you keep them away. Liking your eyes but not knowing how they, even lowered, see more than most eke from a stare. Reading not only them but everyone there. The man of the boy who had to learn. Wouldn't have minded a spot of your reading right then. Guess what I am thinking of now? Christ. Already? Don't be at that. Reminded myself I was fine alone and not remembering you pressed on my stomach. Your mouth in my hair. No. Think folded paper sickbags and legs aching with length. Or you seeing past your reflection to the white and blue below. Otherwise, calculably, deep in a book. Thinking of your fingers, I arrived at my body's burning to smoke and went from there to cigarettes. Lit one while considering if you'd ever gone so long without? Of course, you'd bought all those patches. By now you must be really slamming them on. Finicketing peel with fingers. Smoothing them down. Annoying for anyone sat beside. And what about the tic by your mouth? Would it return, when you got there, if she started to ask? What could you tell her? Or want to? I wouldn't think much. More like, with the years of heel cooling suddenly stopped, now's when you'd be pondering practical stuff, like how you should be with her? I wondered too. Cautious? Unwary? Sorry for the past? Yes, certainly, you'd be sorry about that and asking her about all you'd missed. Finding her again. That's when it hit, once there, would you ever   be tempted to   fuck it   tempted to remain? No. Definitely, definitely my thought, not yours. Still. What bad things can't come true? No. No. Not this, with the whole of a week to go. That way madness lies. So I lifted eyes back to watching the sky. How trails turned to clouds. Got so intertwined that one big huff would wipe them away. I didn't though. Distracted myself instead with What's it like there? Summer too? Just a further off summer. Further than the Caucasus, say, and, map-wise, much to the left. But from whichever direction, beyond my best stretch. Where you'd tread through accents unknown, alongside foreign feet, through alien gates, then onto their strange streets and more far-flungedness yet. Exaggerated somewhat to condole with myself and forget that, for you, their strangeness would hold something precious. Closer than I could share. Closest blood. Nearest family member – not counting your half-siblings, which I was not. They were many. She was one, and the only one of her type. In a diamond isolation where I'd be out of sight. All the way back here in London. In this bed. On our sheets which still hold your smell. The crumbs of your toast. Where your tea spilled when you rolled me. So, to keep those things near, I announced to our room I was happy, completely, for you. Which I was. Nose just   out of joint   somewhat. Fuck!

Then got hold of myself for the loads more to come. Breakfast would help, I decided, as well as tot up the time. Negotiations between carpet and brick still the same, wherever or however you'd be. Cupboard and wardrobe. Toilet and sink. The sight of yesterday's socks stuffed down the mattress. Well, I'd have to do something about that. And if I still only knew somethings, you also only knew part. Taking comfort from a lack of belief in predestination, I dropped the net curtain and went.

Did some living. Bought a bag of pasta at the shop. Alphabetised our novels. Some. Looked for a summer job. Arranged a pint with the lads. And made it to the pit of the afternoon, aided by chicken noodle cup-a-soup. By three though, I was thinking of your body a lot. And of the split ends I nicked then flicked onto the rug. Let light in everywhere too, whereas you were more shade. What glorious revolutions your travels occasioned! Reading then, with curtains left wide, I baked until after five, when sunburn ran up my legs. Didn't even notice the heat until rub became scrape and suggested the hour for lotion drew near.

Later again, I listened to London tick back down. Mix of marketgoers going as the clubbers crept out. Camden taking its moment before re-revving up. But I, above, was on the outside of that, wolfing down Pot Noodle. Getting out the old black and white. Twiddling for reception and persuading myself *The Poseidon Adventure* was a fluke. Besides which, it was a boat and the seventies anyway. Moreover, I guessed by now you were there. Had already stared from a cab at the new of Vancouver. Had already smiled at a receptionist as you checked in. Even unpacked perhaps. Showered? Would you give me a quick ring? Or consider it too late? Or would you only call her? And I wished that you wouldn't. But took another book from the shelf and made other plans. How I'd read myself loose of my pathetic hanging on. Or at least back into different times, when different Englishmen did other stuff. Better being helpless to them, than the one of my choice, and pitying the English girls who'd had none. For a while it was enough. While after, less. While after again, just slumped down into sleep. And how stilly I slept.

Reminding myself down there, somehow, I did not want to wake. Also feeling inside it how hot that first day alone in August was. When the hours went around with heels dug in. Resistant to change, both sleeping and waking. And how I dreamt of branches. Growing fastly. Out of control. Upwards. Into pearling air above. Entangling chimneys. Dislodging slates. Out from where I was, to unknowable lengths. Then, from beneath, the ringing. Wake Up. Wake up. Eily! Wake up now!

Now

> Jesus, your leg is still froze.
>> Yeah, as I said   it was cold.

I am loath to leave his knee to get a blanket though, so cover it over with my palm.

> Such warm hands, Eil.
>> You always say that.
>> Because it's always true   one of the first things I ever noticed.
>> How hot my hands were?
> That very first night in bed. The room was so cold and we were   at odds, I think it's fair to say.
>> At the very least.
> I still remember their heat   when I put my arm around.

I remember that lonely moment. His hand on mine. In the dark after I'd started to cry. Way back now in earlier times before the commoner occurrence of quilt above my head. The airlessness under and curling myself all over his ribs below. Sleep soiled. Night dulled. Intimations of sweat. There, behind my knees. At the in of his elbows. Falling between us. Hands passing all sorts. Comfort. Heat. In its own good time, love. Once we let it. Then did, on repeat. This has not only been imagined. Nor would I mind that history riding again. And, as God loves a trier, you never can tell, although it seems a while since God bothered with us. So long I wouldn't even mind the Holy Ghost lending his chicken claw to this. Or fluttering all the skipping cogs back into sync. I am tired, and know he is, of all this getting there. Almost. Then just   slipping from where we'd both rather be – loose of the hard hours of these last weeks. But failed grips remain failed grips, and even chance barbs sore. How long have we been at this? And how much longer until

No.

I refuse that, right down at instinct, and besides, everything he's saying is kind.

First Summer

Flat out and hot boiling, centre of the mat. Ring Ring. Somewhere here. But far near or far off? What's even eligible to be making that noise? My brain did it slowly – unrolled slowly to up. Here's here. And it's now. The phone's there. So, at last, I stirred to its plastical chime and made sense of distance in my dozed mind because, if it's ringing, it must be him. Then I was up at that. Spry as any deep-sleeping eighteen-year-old might – nineteen in a few weeks all right but, by any measure, pretty spry. Wrench-wresting dead legs. Uncradling it and Hi Stephen? Is that you? And you then Eily? It's not a great line   is that you? Of course it is!

All torpor blown by missing too much. Right through my whole body and yours so far off. But wakeful enough not to make a phone scene, I sedately enquired How are you, Stephen? Then hung on your hoarse I just got in, had a quick shower, ordered some tea.

And I loved that tired voice. It was nowhere near me but I felt it just the same – its usual manoeuvre and beat under my skin. How was the flight? Pretty fucking long. So how are you, how are you feeling? Jetlagged mostly, I think, but   I don't know   I suppose I'm here. And I could hear all around you the size of that room. Echoes off its shallows. A reverb from windows. The insulation of adjacent other rooms going endlessly on, offering other conclusions to other women and men. Us merely one cross-reference, on this line, living out what grain of world history came next. And, for us, it was the grain in which I asked Are you nervous? And the grain in which your answer was Yeah   but tomorrow I'll probably be worse. Is that when you're meeting her? That's right. What time? Around eleven o'clock. Do you know whereabouts? Down in the foyer – her mother's dropping her off. Do you think she'll come in too, to say Hello? I don't know   I. What? Can't believe it, Eil, that I'm really here. That all those years have passed and   now she's seventeen. Last time I saw her she was only   well   you know this anyway. Then I thought of all the other men on your floor, probably contemplating young women in ways more annoying. Or obvious. Or insane. A daughter last seen twelve years ago won't feature for many. Maybe not any others at all. Thankless to be so original though, especially over there on your own. Not that I'd be of much use, with my far flimsier flitch of experience. What distractions could I offer as a party piece? Lame jokes while opening your shirt with my teeth until you started to laugh? Well, I could at least have done that. Or willingly lain there with you, in the dark, as you re-dotted the dots of those twelve years without. I would've, if you would've and not preferred to pilgrim alone. Not that I don't get the reasoning, but I wish I was with you now. The simplest so is simplest said – not always of course, but in this instance. Stephen, I wish I was there with you. Me too, Eily love, but   another time. And knowing you meant it, I soldiered on into What do you think she'll be like? Silence. Wait silent. I don't know, Eil, which seems such a weird thing to admit given we've exchanged letters for years, but   I wish I knew her more. And then I thought Oh no, I've caused you pain down this shitty phone line. Because every nerve of your waiting, over all that time, must sit exposed now the end's finally nigh. So don't fucking poke.   I   can't imagine her, Eily and I've spent so long doing just that that I   I   just   I don't know what she'll be like. I just want to see her as she is. Stephen, I KNOCK. Hang on, love, that's my door. It's probably the room service so   I'll just   No, go on, get it, I'll wait. The Bakelite clunk and. Footfalls away. Me imagining your bare feet on the carpet in there. The work of a latch. Just a minute, you said. Then opened. Then.

Silence.

Then.

Nothing.

At all.

And attentive as I am, I don't hear Where do you want it? or Where should I sign? – not that I've ever stayed in a hotel, but I watched it back in 1980-something, I think. So, in my mind's eye, that's how it must work.

But.

Then.

A thing.

A catch?

A cough?

An

A

            Oh   oh my God   Grace   isitreallyyou?

For an age, for an hour, for a minute or two I couldn't hear beyond the muffle and was trying so hard to. Staring right into it. Sick with the wait. Wishing to be there and not witnessing like this. Overhearing though, whether I wanted to or not, some vast suspension of disbelief in your voice that I did not recognise. Had not heard before. And I'd heard all your voices – or so I'd thought – from the finest of times as well as the awful. But actually never quite this.

Oh   oh my God   Grace   isitreallyyou?

I couldn't hear the answer, although there must have been one because   you didn't ask again. Except   then I realised   you were crying. I knew it. As I knew one damp hand secured your towel while the other probably gripped her. And I went from here to there. To that room where she was, perhaps, crying as well. But, interloper that I was, I couldn't be sure. Inventing. Guessing. Eavesdropper. Spy! I should've hung up and yet found it impossible. Even to move. Never mind press the thing. Could only participate, if surreptitiously, in this long-overdue cumulation. Surely it must've been for you both. Two sparks striking from a past of cannots and don'ts. With me, unelectric and surplus to requirement, just hanging nosily on. But if I imagined sight, I couldn't the sound. Only the image of water dripping down your back. The image of her face against the palm of your hand. But I knew, in a moment, you'd have enough. Would step away from her body to straighten yourself, then reach far into your deep wells of detached. Its impassivity long being the greatest weapon you have and, even in the worst – as I've no need to learn – the one you favour first. All of which she couldn't know. Yet. And then there it was, down that bad line.

A breath.

The first of you becoming your private self, inside your private body, once more.

A step.

You withdrawing into the room, where I still was, and on the threshold of which she still stood.

A word.

Stay there, Grace. Let me get something on? I was only just out of the shower.

And I heard her nod, if only in my head. Heard you cross back to me. One knee on the bed. Then fumbling up the receiver Hello? Eily? Yes? Sorry, it's   I have to go   she   Grace has   just shown up so   she's here and I should

I know. Go. Call me later, all right?

Okay, love   I'll   talk to you soon.

But pictures kept making inside me to match with your sound. The beige room and dark door. Tall girl in the hall. Your wet hair pushed back and Stephen, I   No. No. You'd already gone and couldn't know how I'd hurt my ear on the phone in case you hadn't really hung up. Hung on until the buzz disconnection droned me into your distance and the dead click assured it was true.

Abroad then, in Canada, you were in that room. Somewhere in Camden I was in ours alone. But I chose it. I choose it and I'd choose it again. Chose to replace the receiver and look around. Streetlights right across the borough gone on, and so the night had come! And what if all action was yonder with you? If all I was was half sunburnt and Pot Noodle perfumed? Well   so be that too. Time remained on the go and the same went for life, whatever seras would be. In that spirit then, I tuned back to the street. Saturday night below and already active in its various states of hell. Tidals of. Roars of. But also its heavens and me alive there in its midst. Sometimes snatching at eddies. Other times in its flow. Always tugged by its current. And if the stillest time was now, really, before every tide turned, I could not know that yet.

Now

So I run my nail against the grain of his jeans. Lay my palm on the fray.

Well then   here's some heat.

The cold of him going live beneath the warmth of me. Even I can tell that.

Actually Eil, that's really good on my knee.
Superpowers at last!
Apparently.
I'll thaw you out in the end.

Going clang with its incidental double edge. Will he pick it up? No. Just traces my fingers, then chooses to leave it there. Meaning I can't tell what's with us or against. But I like this touch and have a sense he kind of likes it too. Go on. Go on so, I goad within.

You know you've got a hole in the seam there, Stephen?
Really? Big?
About an inch.
Huh   never noticed it.

And bends himself over to see. Uneventful but a little more between, so worth the eking out. But I can arrive at no obvious next. If I stay still though, will we stay like this? Close as got by weird attempts? I don't know. His long fingers lift to the ends of my hair. Also trying? Maybe also as help? Twirling in through what's left of a wave. Earlier's plait so tight it started a headache and had to be undone. Worth more now, anyway, between his finger and thumb.

> I like it when you're curly.
> It's just bumpy from a plait.
> I know. Just   saying I like it.
> Do you think it looks a bit pre-Raphaelite?
> Yeah   stretched out in the bath you'd be a right
> Ellen Terry, Eil.

Lips giving too to a laugh as I fold hands across my chest and gaze into romantic realms beyond.

First Summer

I was in the cold and how cold it was, waking again to the early. Phone hanging, uncalled. Staring at its greenness, there on the wall. And wondered if I could have slept through? Doubted that but imagined her with you. Having a coffee. Or rather, you tea. Probably you'd take her out for a meal. And if you did, that'd be a Chinese. If I knew anything. But I didn't know, and wouldn't have guessed, the boardwalk you were lingering along right then, looking out at the harbour and bay. Looking out while playing out the dream and game. At last in the flesh, instead of thought, as before. Did the wishes of years surface in those long-conjured talks? Did you notice her teeth while she laughed at your jokes, remembering when they first came in? Later you told me you did. Feet up on the stead of our bed, saucer of fag ash balanced on your chest. Eyes though, fixed there, at then. Showed me photos too but like searching for cracks, little hunches of what the future might let leak back and asking always Will we be okay? On that morning I knew hope was cardinal for anyone who'd ever had to entrench, even to the damning of their present – as you had, with your drawn-out wait. Why do it? – the reasonable might've argued from their reasonable perspective. Advocating you let the past let up and let go. Grieve. Lick wounds. Accept. Move on. But confounding all that, you'd stayed in it instead. Stretched yourself in a glue trap, all glistered with pain, waiting for the rip in your skin. Alive, even after it did. Then continued waiting, with all those missing welts. If you could do that, what was my small interval of wait? Although I told myself this, the mute receiver jabbed. Reminding me how you alone knew what sleeps in my body, in our bed, and can hatch from the night into nightmares in my head. As I know yours. Have long known them. But if that's so, how come you've become the island while I'm the one with the sea all in me? Recast by this tie to your other girl's   what is it? Just to your other girl.

Then the phone did ring. And every day after it. Filling me in with as much detail as long-distance permits. There was some I'll tell you more once I'm home. But enough She took me to this place and I found something you'll love, to make up for the trim. Certainly enough to know that missing was my only cause for concern. Even that last evening, before the next day's flight. After my I wasn't expecting you to call again, I still got I've just said goodbye to Grace and I wanted   no   really needed to hear your voice, Eil.

Now

Long finger-spun ringlet unfurls on my cheek and wonder what he thinks of when he thinks of it? Of Grace's hair and the even less curl in it? Funny, how on that night I imagined it long and lank. Exactly as it proved in the months to come. In the photographs after. In the descriptions often given. So often I can't remember any more if I do remember or it's just become what I know? Maybe he's thinking of all that. Or maybe he's simply saying he likes it. If so, I'd do well to take a leaf from that book. I can drive myself halfway to Bedlam in a blink – and not the new one, the original down by Liverpool Street, thronging with the stark staring mad. Even when I am searching for OFF, it's an elusive thing – a feeling-around-in-the-dark type of switch, which I have no true talent for. I'm more wind up and keep winding, right the way to snap! Which is why, unbeknownst to him, this may not be the best time for

What are you thinking about, Eil?
Nothing really.
No   say.
Just remembering that first time you saw Grace   again.
What about it?
How I heard it   accidentally   on the phone.
That must've been weird.
It was.
I don't even remember what I said.
'Is it really you?'
Really?
That's what I heard.
And what else?
Then you cried.
Yeah   I remember that all right. She just gave me such a shock.
What did you think when you saw her?
Honestly? Fuck! I'm not ready for this. And then, I'm not even dressed.
I'm sure she wasn't fussed.
Wasn't exactly a dignified reintroduction though, was it?
It all worked out anyway.
Yeah, thankfully it did, but   why're you thinking about Grace?

Not her so much as about how stuff can still happen   even
when you're alone.
  I suppose that's true.
 Although that was pretty fucking dramatic   when you think
about it.
        Yes   sorry about that.
 Wasn't your fault, Stephen. Just   how it turned out.
        So   is something dramatic happening now too?

And realise I've tripped my own self up as his eyes slope over, in
cautious alarm, searching for signals he's failed to discern. Wise to
those eyes though, I offer only

            No. There's not.
              Really?
            There's been enough drama, don't you think?
          I do, but   that's no guarantee, is it?
              I suppose not.
        And you know why I'm asking, so if there was   you'd tell
me, Eily, wouldn't you?

How many matters under that? Worst of which, the midnight
horrors he was left mopping up. I wish I hadn't been quite so   but
I was. So now he must ask things I realise he'd rather not.

            Stephen, there's nothing to worry about.
              But, Eil
            I mean it, there's nothing like that   Honestly.

First Summer

To the day of your re-arrival. My last night's expedition now through. Lairy stag nights entwining those hours with endurance as I travelled each province alone. There for tired. Now for bed. Here in changed sheets I endeavoured to wait. Impatient mind sleepily lifting itself by galvanising your rate of return. Hurry at the airport. Leg it to a plane. Reverse race what vapour trails brought you away. Packed with unknown treasure, and doubtless tales, still came those unwelcome early galleons of sleep – which I shook from by stepping down non-existent steps. Or discovering a dead arm that needed its mate to work pins back out and blood in. But awake or asleep, waiting all the while. Waiting for, waiting for you. And I missed it. Fuck. In the somewhere off dawn. Your key turned, must have, in our front door. Bags must've been left before you came down the hall. My first steal to aware being a whispered Eily? I'm home   sorry   didn't mean to wake you, love. Against the hall light. Prevaricating my reach. Wait, I should shower first, I stink. But I did not give a shit. Just offered myself to you. Here you are. You're really here. Searching you for differences too but finding none there. Same, how you looked at me through your too-long-again hair. How you touched my cheek. Then my mouth. And kissed it. And straight after, got down to business with Get off that T-shirt. Slid fingers to breasts and cued by my hands all over the place. Nails already in your back. Mouth at your neck. Hitching by the hip into pelvis to pelvis. Ow! Take it easy on that – it's been half ready for hours so it's aching a bit. You should know better then, shouldn't you? Definitely but   I couldn't stop thinking about you. Charmer! Vamp! Actually, you don't smell so bad. Well, you smell fucking great, Eil, I could smell you all day! And your new fag smell over old sweat, felt against mine like it'd never left. Just like it knew mine exactly the same. Just as I wanted. Just as you'd said and I believe it now. So get your pants off and give me a break! Creak. Belt buckle. Jeans heeled to the floor. Eily, I. Come on, get them off! I missed you, love. Getting back against. I missed you too, Stephen, so much. And quick with the feeling we'd better get quick to it before the sun showed up – due any minute. So do. Only holding. Barely a kiss. My thigh over your thigh for simplicity's sake. Fuck and. And there it is. Clamped to by want but so stricken by miss, it was over half a gasp from the start. Bollocks! Oh no. No, you keep on. Can you? I can   for a moment. Okay okay okay. Go on. God, Stephen. Yeah? Yeah   there it is. Slip and finish. Feeling already the sheet's a mess. Both laughing and Sorry, that was rubbish. Nah, did the trick. Well, I'll sort you tomorrow, properly, I promise. And I will hold you to that. Breathing like I couldn't quite, into your neck.

That's better. Much better. I can't believe you're really here. Ah Eily, where else would I be? I didn't know then or like to think. Besides, we were right on the edge of a sleep so deep I soon forgot it began. Only how, once we got there, we fell right in. My nose in your armpit. My crown under your chin. Lullabyed off by the last dregs of night bus revving, crossed with one-legged pigeon chur. Bodies having already what dawn bodies could want. Comfort. Rest. Breathing quiet. Satisfied that the answer to Where have you been? was Away but always coming home to you.

Mingled, hours later, I woke into the day. Already being looked at. Hey. Smile. Oh, hey. Right, I'm getting in the shower before anything else, okay? And that was okay with me. Content to lie, pushing out the kinks, eyes drifting to your exit, stiff with the travel and sleep. Although I wondered what your else might be? Then I heard the shower and you ffftthhh through your teeth, evidently having forgotten how slowly it heats. I sat up too and contemplated making tea. Decided to so, after, it would be ready and you'd just get back into bed.

Made mugs. Made toast with jam on it. Made haste when I heard you flush the toilet. Made sure I got back before you did. And succeeded. What's this? Tea and toast. You're a fucking star! Wet hair and nothing on. A whole half slice in your mouth while working your towel and glugging back the too-hot brew. Fuck! Careful, it's hot. No shit! Jetlagged? Yeah, I can hardly see straight. I'd say it'll be a couple of days before I'm right again. Have you much on? Not today, but tomorrow I'm supposed to be meeting Nick. Film stuff? Nod. Just a quick catch-up. He's had a few thoughts for locations. Just London, isn't it? Yeah, but the actual shooting requires being a little more specific. Ha ha, yes I know that, I just thought you'd use the Holloway Road. We will, where we can, but there is the peri-od element too. Late seventies? Yeah, so it's changed since then, which we have to take into account. Fair enough – watching a long drip escapade down your left – Missed a bit there! You towelled it up. Then pulled me to my feet. So what have you been at this last week? Nothing much, this and that. Pining much? I thought about you occasionally all right, did you think about me? Once in a while. Fucker! Smile, and an arm slap for that. Ow! Okay! I thought about you a lot! Every day in Vancouver? Even more every night. Fronting to front then to get to kissing your mouth. Tea to the fore. Jam a little back. So what was that else then? What? You said you were going to have a shower before anything else. Oh, that . . . no, I just meant. But across you, abruptly, a startle of guilt I had not been expecting. Stephen? What is it? Cold going down me. What happened? No, no, nothing like that   Eily no, really   I mean it. So what's the matter? As all the light I saw around you went strange.

Now

His nod then, like a reluctant accept. But the suck in of thin cheeks suggests lack of faith. Eyes searching about mine for spots of deceit. Finding none, though his thoughts must still alight and alights on

You know, love, it's all right.
What is?
Whatever's going on   it will be   all right   eventually.

Oh, will it now? So must I take, or not, this singular balm? It's all right. It'll be all right. I swim in its sound. Breathe its waters and swallow its charms while its pin-prick bubbles buoy me up – at least until blood hits the surface and my ears go Pop! I am not, nor will I accept to be, the only one of us in difficulty here.

First Summer

Releasing you, I stepped back from not yet knowing what. Fast-emptying lungs making ache out of talk. Eily, don't look at me like that, it isn't . . . it's not . . . But forthright legs took me back to the bed. Got me up against the wall. Knees to my chest. Started preparing balance against every traitorous thing, from philanderous thoughts to philanderous doing, and faced the face I'd been dying to see but now had tales to confess.

All right, Eily, I'm just going to tell you, then you can say what you think . . . and you mightn't even think anything of it so just hear me out, okay? Loosed somewhat, I What is it then? You turning but, on afterthought, turned back again. Okay . . . okay . . . so Friday . . . night, just after we spoke, I was packing when there was a knock and . . . And? It was Grace. But hadn't you just said goodbye back at her house? Yeah, after the world's most awkward nut roast with her mother although, actually, her little brothers were a laugh, ten and . . . Stephen, get on with it! Right, yes, the point is, we'd said our goodbyes so I was surprised. Before I could ask though, she just said Can I stay the night? And she looked so plaintive I said Come in. But I was thinking there's no room! Only the

bed and not even a sofa or   Please, she said It's been so long and
I remember how it was when I was three or four. So I asked what
she remembered? She said Not a lot, but I remember you reading
to me at night, how you'd fall asleep beside and it felt so warm . . .
Grace, you're seventeen, I said, We can't pretend now those years
between haven't passed, and what about your mother? But she
she said What about yours? Sorry, Stephen, she said what? Gracie
said What about your mother, Dad? I want to ask about . . . what
she did . . . And you know, Eil, I'd been waiting for it all week.
Maybe not for something quite so   specific, but when she didn't
bring it up I just thought lucky escape! But then   there it was, and
asking to spend the night and   I said You know what happened
and that's enough. Then she asked Does Eily know . . . all of it? So
I had to say Eily does, but that's different and nobody else ever has.
Dad, you don't have to keep it secret, she said. She's part you so
she's a part of me as well.

Fuck, Stephen, I   fuck!

But already you were up, blindling out into the corridor, fast as
you could. Wave-warding me back as the bathroom door, luckily,
gave. And over you went. Your length doubling while everything
ingestible ascended, tea, toast, jam, bang into the bowl. And again.
Jesus, Stephen, are you all right? One more. Rubbing your back.
It's all right, it's all right, get it all out. Which you did until there
wasn't one retch left. Flushed then, boneless bodied, sank to
sitting beside. Head in your hands. Hands on your knees. Mine
sinking down. What was that? Something you've eaten? No, that
was   that's what happened then too. When Grace said that to
you? Nod. It was awful, Eil. She saw every gag and just kept saying Sorry. I kept waving her out but she wouldn't go. Stood and
watched me from the door. Yet another excellent memory of her
father. Stephen, you worry too much about that. You've found
each other again, that's all that counts and I bet it's all that matters

to her. And then your hand took mine. All right, so what happened next? Well, obviously, eventually, I stopped. Got up. Washed my face. Rinsed my mouth. And then? I said You can stay if you like, but you can't ask about that again. She is not allowed in any room we are ever in. She isn't a part of me, or you and that's how it has to be. What did she say to that? She said Will I ever be allowed to ask? I said Maybe one day, perhaps, but not yet. It's enough that you know at all. And? And she understood what I meant. And she accepted it? Yes.

What happened then?

I ordered a pizza and we watched the telly.

And Grace?

Yeah, she ate a bit and, after a while, fell asleep. I watched on through to the end of the film. Then I turned off the light.

And did you sleep?

What do you think?

That you probably didn't.

Yeah   all the old fear just came back, that she could still be in me.

So was she?

She wasn't. She's been rotting in her grave these seventeen years and thank God for that.

Now

But what is going on, Stephen?

You know what I mean.

I don't think you mean what I do when it's me asking.

Don't I?

No, you definitely don't.

All right   so what is it you mean then, Eil?

– 63 –

Allowance, like indulgence, but lip half chewed in. Hoping sur-
render will afford him some swift corner turning. Can't flick off
annoyance though, now my dander is up.

        Don't!
    What?
         Do not.
            Eily, do not what?
  Play oblivious to what I am talking about.
      Fuck's sake! I was only trying to offer some   comfort or
    Well, I don't need a pat on the head.
Fine   Sorry   I didn't mean that way   I just meant

Him casting across the floor. Behind his eyes, all work. With playing neutral now impractical, how best not to argue? High road?
Low road? Which'll he plump for tonight?

    Okay   I do know   of course I know what you mean.

Ha! Capitulation, apparently. But already knowing that trick, I
jag a finger on in.

      Yeah   what about it?

Off guard. On guard. He gathers quick. Or maybe not gathers.
Tells the truth.

   I   I just think   as far as sex is concerned   it's a minor
   problem right now.
     Is it?
  In the   grand scheme of things, it is.
    I don't see it like that.

> That's because you won't deal with
> What?

Oh. Will he push? He won't push. That's a mess neither want. And, like cued up, he moves on.

> Anyway, it's hardly the first dry spell, Eil. We've been here before.
> When?
> You know when.
> You mean last winter?
> I know you remember.

So now it's my turn to tell a truth.

> You mean   when Grace first came to stay?

First Winter

I stood in my best behaviour, willing myself towards a clue. That, I recall. And brooking the wait. Their slow progress from Heathrow a scourge of delays. Watching action in the street below overlay, overlaying, building up, with each supplementary five-minute check.

That dustman's cart here – three hundred seconds later, there. The plastered woman barely upright, then puking in her hair. Adidas-ed bands of whooping mod men. Near. Then further. Then far as I can see. Almost beyond the Odeon. Each face singular to me and a cause of effect. Sure you'd stand out though, guessing she might. Deciding a How's it going? wouldn't quite cover it and that the future could split on such hairs. Those hairs. Hers and mine, crossed. My window-self unravelling into vistas of fright that

I could not help returning to, however wan and whey-faced she might reflect. At least, these days, that shyest one no longer looks back. She's now apace with the ways and wiles of Camden Town. She falters not before daughters. She cares nothing for hairs. She is in full possession of a hardier self. There has been substantial renovation, and not without cost, but without it how could I bear standing here?

Eily! Love? Are you in?

I remember your voice from the hall. Hearing it while stood by the breakfast bar. Going frozen and being shocked because hormones, usually, took up the slack but   not then. That night it was loyalty alone shook a leg, commanding Out you go. So out I went to where you both already were. You, keys in hand, with, inexorably, her. And just like you. Up to your shoulder. Taller already than I'd ever be. Nonetheless, I tried to toe-dip into worldly because, comparatively, I was a bit more. Because I. Because I had you. And for all she was, she didn't know how, after your quick kiss, your subtle squeeze of my arm communicated a terrible wish for what awkwardness there was – which was very much – to somehow work out fine. It might not be beyond us, you'd said – finger-cross hoped and heathen prayed. But I was more set on holding my place in what great grand ructions might come. Serenely, if possible. Obstinately if not. And she. Well. Raised her hand a little up and said only Eily   hi!

Now

Change of face. Both of us. Change of guard on his introduction of this. Moods abandon their posts as no reason to fight. If we're to go in, this is him opening the door to it. And while I know to tread softly, wherever we tread, when he steps in I step on in too.

That's right.

No   Stephen   this isn't like that.
    Really?
  There's no comparison.
     Of course there is.
   I don't know how you can think so.
     Well, I do.

Which is the moment eyes open – mine – to the extent of this. For if he so easily invokes that thorny Christmas, this, us here, might be worse than I thought. Try catching his eye but he's become the one, won't. So insides fall, and palling begins.

First Winter

Then there she was, all absolute, in our hall. Wearing, like she'd earned it, her version of your smile. And your eyes. Upright in your frame. Flesh and blood pulling rank on our more improvised relations – if you wanted to see it that way. But all her wanting seemed only for me to be friendly back. All your wanting obviously also wanting that, while my wanting mostly set itself towards getting through the next hour intact.

So all the bags sat there around her, smaller than your, feet. Both pairs of shoes lathered in Camden sleet and forlorn as I was, beneath my shoulder chip, Hi, I said back. Because I should and couldn't not. Then added, because it really was Well, this is weird, isn't it? Yeah, she said, from behind your smirk. Infecting me with it because my saying so had made the ice go crack. So I smiled. And you smiled. And she smiled back. And someone – you – said What the fuck, I'm just so glad to have you both here. What the fuck! What the fuck! The quickest cut through of quack. Then she and I, identically – and what-the-fucking back – leapt in the deep end on the off chance we'd work out how to swim. And did.

Hugged awkwardly. So didn't drown at least. Doggy paddling, if not pretty, still gets the job done. Also good to take the same side against those congregations of tut who'd surely be having their say. Glancing to, though, I remember all the feeling in your face. Almost not knowing what to do and, to help hide it, I bent for her case. You, going for the other, mouthed by my ear Eily, thank you for this. It's fine, I said, but thought of how later you'd take my skirt off. Cover me and find into me. Then how she'd be gone – at least for that little fuck-stretched while. I had only to bide my time. But already threading below, even in that thought, was the strange beautiful thing we were venturing towards; turning this, our strange beautiful estate into a mere common place as fast as we possibly could.

Now

If he shares my presentiment, he does not reveal. Having been prodded this far though, he'll now say what he will.

> How is it different, Eil?
>   I can't believe you'd ask   that was only
>   Go on   say it.
>   Nerves   maybe?
>   Nerves?
> Or shyness.
>   Hardly, Christ!
> Wasn't it?
>   Eil, you know what it was   both of us did.
>   Even if that's what it was   you got over it pretty quick.
>   Yes, I did. So stop worrying.
> But you're not getting over this   what happened.

Wind knocked from sails then, he tired rubs his face.

> Are you, Stephen?
> Eily, it's just
> > Are you?

And he can look off where he likes, but there's no other place.
Just our breathing in here and rain out on the glass. Distance none,
except inside us, so he sees he has to say

> I don't think it's useful to think of it that way.
> > But I'm over it.
> No, you're not. How could you be?
> > I am, so you should just
> > Eily, what happened is more than a   get-over-it kind of
> > thing.

Then here we are, once again, at the feet of an unbeatable So
that's it then.

> So you'll never?
> > Stop it.
> No! Answer me. Never?
> > > What's the point of this?

First Winter

That night I lay in the last late drift, having recused myself early
to allow for catching up. Now though – after lights out and front
door locked, beyond checking the sofa bed was ready in your office,
some apparent hugging and Night then, love – came you, quiet,
into the dark.

Hey, Eily. Still awake?
Yeah, just closed my eyes this minute.
Okay then, I'll leave off the light.

But stealthy shut our door like a child might wake and soundless came on in. Jumper tugging. Shirt off. Belt. Up on my elbow
though, I am all quiz.

So how was it? Are you glad she's finally here?
God, yeah. I've been   missing her.

Shoes too then. Fagged rub of your face before lank joints
creaked in beside me on the bed.

How was it for you? You seemed to get on?
It was fine   I think we did.
That's a relief I didn't want this to be   weird.
Bit late for that, I'd say!

But half laughing in my hand and you also did.

Okay   so   not weirder than it already is.
I don't mind weird.
Well, you say that but
Stop worrying, Stephen. It's going to be all right.
Is it?
It really is.
I hope so   she's lovely, isn't she?
And the image of you.
You think?

He already knows but is so pleased that I allow one repeat.

   I'd know her off you anywhere, right down to that smile.

And savour you trying to hide yours now.

   Well, let's hope she inherits nothing worse!
      Ah, she should be so lucky.
   No, don't say that.

Then you got to your feet. Got on with getting undressed – just as she was surely also getting, somewhere on the other side of our wall.

      Tired now?
   Completely fucking wrecked.

Trousers floor-stepped from. Socks as well. Pulling up the duvet where I lie – already in the nip, and inclined.

      However   you are a sight for sore eyes!

All rangy night chilled, sliding in beside. Taking me, and my willing, in your stride but I but I

      Jesus, you're a block of ice!

As the long froze shanks slipped between my thighs

      Warm me up, so?

But your cold electrocuted through.

Ah, you freezing bastard!
Guilty on both counts!

Fuck though, you knew me inside out and my useless partiality to the foolings of your mouth. Slightest on my throat, even hardly on my breast, and I am eyes closed hopeless, sharing warmth or whatever, right up to – and beyond – the nth degree. So you did what you knew. And I knew already tonight would not be the one when I'd rise above.

Will you warm me up now?
I'm not convinced   yet.
Now?
Well
Now?
Do that again.
So   now?
Yes   more   whatever the fuck you want!

And I was gone so far, so quick, I'd not a single comeback left. Only flitters of syllables trailing to laughs. Mouths fixing shifts to further acts of Here we go. Always and again. Want touching only once before done with asking. Ready bodies chasing for swiftest there. And though the race was in quiet, we were tough compelled. Not least because finally I had you to myself. And then somewhere through the plaster   ZIP!

Wait, Eil.
What?
Hang on a sec.
Why've you stopped?

I just   thought I heard something.
What?

Whisper.

Sorry, I just thought I heard   through the wall

Listened us both then, but me the most, with my body only wanting yours.

Heard what?
I don't know.
It was probably just Grace.
What?

Oh shit, oh shit for, shit for brains. Too late as the hand slacked its task between my legs.

Don't stop!

And pressed my bones back up against where the long fingers now hovered suspended.

Ah Stephen, come on. You didn't hear a thing.

ZIP
Then her case unzipped again, calling on the withdrawn fingers to reach and point.

There.
What?
That was it.

That's her unzipping her case. She probably has stuff to get out.

    But I can hear it, Eil.

      So what?

Well, that means   she can hear us.

    We'll be extra quiet then.

        Eily I

Don't you dare. I've been waiting all day.

Touched your mouth with my mouth, until you loved it again – trying hard to turn stop into go. More. And you let it. Fingertips returned. Allowed them to wet and suggest your body in. Lifting to spur   but then ZIP again   and then   then nothing at all.

    What now?

    Nothing   just

    Stephen, what?

    I don't think I can.

    What do you mean?

Turned my eye from yours, to down between. Still thinking I'd gospel swear to what I'd feel. But laying on a hand found no you were not. Instead, all around you the space had grown large and your body, in an instant, gone to sleep.

    Don't you want to?

      I do   I just

        Then let me

    Eily

        How about with my mouth?

Obligingly I pushed the duvet, but you

Don't   that's not what it is.

And rolled onto your back, leaving me forfeit. Down in the ins, I ground my teeth but, on the outward, possessed myself of patience and tried another tack – a little light work of the wrist.

> Just let me   I know I can, I
> Eily, no, I said!

Then swept off my plague hand and turned yourself all away.

> Sorry   this is just tricky for me today.
> No shit!
> It isn't to do with you   honestly.
> Yeah, I fucking know that.
> Don't be angry, love. Tomorrow, all right?

All right? All right. And so much of it. Turning back-to-back, I refused your cold feet. Let them go warm themselves up on   no. Of course not. But I could curse all I wanted in my head. That said, and now I was so silence-reigningly rejected, I could actually hear her too. Shoving stuff around. Stifling floor-creaking movements, yet definitely, definitely there. That your ears were so attuned some-how made it worse because how interesting could it be, whatever she was at? Undressing? Night-dressing. Flapping the duvet? Lying into the mattress's dip? Spreading. Sprawling. Bedside table lamp switch. Then I noticed, there and here, sounds getting merged. Her and her father's matching long legged clicks. Twin yawns recycling air up from their skinny ribs. If you were listening, and you were listening, did you also hear it? Your pairing. Or was it only me? Or did you lie there only half taking it in while her, as a little girl, was what you imagined, and let the night cultivate that? The neat of her smallness in your crook. The ache from a summer's day of shouldering her about. Ducks fed. Ice creams eaten. Beans on toast served. The shit playgrounds of eighties North London unearthed and explored, only for her sake, while telling Knock-Knock jokes. And being her dad. What a father you must've been. That's what I lay imagining. Except no need to imagine for there she was, incarnate on our sofa bed, making it now every body for itself. I could have made it that. But turned to stare instead, into the back of your neck. Hairline. Tea stain. Vertebrae intact. And longed to kiss its other side. Was left though, rent with a desire to bite. Don't bite. Don't. That won't help. Then traced your pale skin, lay in against and took its cold into warm mine. When there was no objection, put my arm right around. Through the wall then, and your ribcage, I heard her cough. Just a little throat clear, but you didn't mirror that. Only breathed for yourself and she was again alone with herself, unsynced from your overlapped time. Which should have soothed but made me want to grab. Before I did, however, your fingers found in through mine. Pacifyingly. And I was pacified. Or enough anyway to let slip

I'll miss you tonight.

And got back, for my troubles

I know, love   I'll miss you too.

Now

Not really the worst night, that, as nights go. Far worse were already abroad, out in the great To Be. Tonight shaping up as one such, maybe. What purpose so, in remembering it? Because now it seems to stoop over the end of every bed? Sit in every room we are in, displaying itself. Casting aspersions. Forecasting distress. What more can it do though than it already has? Behind it, that first summer. Before it, what now is. But with so many nights queuing for remembrance, why tonight for this? Some kind of signal sorrow? A presentiment of end? Well, if so name it, fuck it, and let it in. Let everything in. Except. We do not agree and do not both see that night as related to this. I know why he's trying to, and while tricky enough, it was hardly as complex. Nowhere so knotty as this. Besides which, I'd rather keep on this line.

> The point is   it's pretty significant, so never?
>   Stop it, Eil.

Never?

>   That's not what I said.

It was   sort of

>   It wasn't, and it's not what I meant.

So what did you?

>   I suppose I meant   not being over it yet.

Yet. Yet. As in nevertheless? Or yet as in until the present? Both forecast another night throughout which neither will relent. And as his eyes go to my arm, I tug a sleeve over it. Two can play at hide and seek.

First Winter

Then there was morning to help us bridge to the rest and slot this upskittlement into our everyday selves. Pyjamas anyway pure death to elegance and grace, and Grace herself bleached jetlag pale. Our street's late-night row-ishness unhelpful as well – as well as starting early enough to affect those who wouldn't have minded another hour lying in. Still, stiff limbs stretched and smiles were made. Night thoughts compacted and night itches contained within my solicitous

Morning, Grace, how was the sofa bed then?
The bed was fine. It's the time change that's washed me out.

Tick. Over to you. How long had you been up? Then a tale of thinking you'd heard her, early, moving about. And apparently had because I can see there's been plenty divulgences since which I, it seems, slept right through. Tock. Yet another shift for me to assess. What had been shared between, or understood, by them? Such time was their own, of course, but by the curl of your mouth, I guessed magic had been carried within. Evidence – the now shared glances and joking. An inescapable history of that great moment writ before my eyes. So I sighed, smiled, sofa sat. Made sure my knees were tug-covered by nightshirt. Then listened in to you offer more breakfast. Anything on this wide earth she'd fancy, so long as it was toast with spread. But then, out of pity or by way of redress, you also made me tea. And insisted I eat. Kissed my cheek. Shy about it before her, it seemed. Still, you did it all the same. And she sat too. Sofa'd with me. Also nightshirt tugged over her knees. How modestly we, showing our breeding, waited for your service there. Not really. She was full of exam, so curiously opposite to the restraint of   her dad. You. How had we found this flat? Was it always that busy on the street? How did I like living here? How did he?

Dad, how do you?
Sorry, what was that, love?
Like this apartment?
I like it a lot. It's handy for Eily for school. And for me for work because   Camden's pretty central so   d'you like it, Gracie?
Yeah, it's cool.

Probably a whole lot smaller than you're used to.
   Well, they say size isn't everything!

   Fuck! I almost   and your face at that. No idea where to look.
Only swallowing a Mmm before turning your back to fumble hot
toast from the grill.

   Ow! Shit!

Grace, aghast, registering what she'd just said, turned stricken
eyes towards mine for guidance. But I was lost to laugh-smothering
behind my hands. Penises! Jesus! Worst possible

   Christ, Eily, why did I say that?
     And to your father!
       Oh my God!

Then the laugh got her too, something awful, and both faces
went to our laps. Shaking in stitches so hard till she choked and I
was left thumping her back.

       All right?
     Yeah, just need to get my breath.

And you at toast-buttering like it was life dependent. Head
down and just willing for through.

         Stephen!
          What?

But wouldn't look, which only set us even more off.

Sorry!

She
You
                Don't worry about it.

From my schooled side eye though, I read what I noticed – you, almost unheard of, embarrassed and not knowing what to do. In every way opposite to your usual unbothered. Unflustered by anything – nakedness or sex stuff or dropping food while eating. So generally accustomed to your own ill repute that everyone else stays free of the hook? Except here. Now. With her. Something struggling in you somewhere. So, regretting my part, I got up to go fix. Put my face in your back and arms round your waist.

       We're terrible! We're sorry! We'll behave ourselves.

Rather than a raised eye or laugh though, my hands got loosed and I was slipped free of. Grace got the smile, and toast.

        Here.
        Thanks, Dad.

Still, she scanned you sorrily for signs of reproof – of which there appeared none. She was excused. Sat next to. Looked over with care. Crumbs brushed even from the cuff of her nightshirt while I was left to devices of my own. Across the room and witness watching. Remembering the other cuff brushings of yore! But either way, left I surely was, listening in to your

        Right! Now we're all calm, we should decide what to do.
           About what?

The day, Gracie. Where do you want to start?

From my exile I

Oh, I know! How about

Furrow. Stop. His interest only extending to whichever London she wanted.

I haven't really thought about it yet. I've just been looking forward to meeting up so, Eily? Any thoughts?

Her net cast to include me. Not quite getting yet how I'd been saddled with what should've been her guilt. Or perhaps she did, because I wasn't laughing any more and suspected I was the interloper here. Fuck it   I stepped back and

I'm going to leave you to it   I   have lines to learn.
    Really? You're welcome to
Nah   besides, he's already shown London to me.

Only a nip. Then offered my smile to her facsimile of his – Pretty much all she needs now's the cigarette – and took what comfort came from her return of it.

Well, we'll see you later then.

Went. Went. Gone. Catching the last dregs as I fled

In which case, Dad, I'd really love to see the

No. Didn't matter. Shut the door. I was not theirs. I was my own and thus stepped smartly from that ride. A noble-ish exit suggesting intact-ish pride. But if I give you the day, will you give me the night? ran around underneath. Implicit, I thought, hopefully. And that first part had been taken up, definitely. So only ever say what you mean. At any rate, I'd removed myself from between you and all that lost time to regain.

Now

Yet, Stephen?

A reasonable question asked as the jump in my guts made me want to reach for a pen and slog all this out on the page instead. But. No. Then his answer.

That's what I said.

Here in the flesh, with blood in the offing, not ink.

It scares me when you say things like that.
I'm not trying to scare you.
What then?
I'm trying to be clear. I'm not over what happened and I know there is no way you are.

But my mind elects to scribble over that part in favour of

Then when will you be?
I don't know   I don't know   whenever I am.
So you're just going to hold it against me   forever?
I'm not holding anything against you, Eil. If you feel guilty, that's another matter.

I don't.

Good I don't think you should, but

What?

Nothing exists by itself and   we've both been here
all along.

Bald truth in some ways and yet   not at all   because I've been
so busy with fooling it round into other ways to see. Droplets of
sentence, but now's far too early to   better hedge with attack.

Have we?

What's that supposed to mean?

Far as I can tell, I'm the only one here.

That's not fair. I've been here   through all of it.

There are more ways than one to be by yourself.

Jesus, Eil, I'm sure there is but   how the fuck would
I know?

What?

How you feel? Fucking telepathy?

I

You tell me nothing, no matter how often I ask. It's like
getting blood from a stone to find out if you've even left
the flat.

I don't want to talk about that.

No shit!

Yes   no shit!

So what is it you want? How should we deal with it?

I just want   to go to bed.

Then go! Don't wait up for me. How many times have
I said?

Not like that. I mean with you.

What?

With you. Remember? We used to do that   all the time.
    Not this again, Eil.
 I even remember you liking it.
    Don't.
Don't you miss it?
    Sex?
 But not just
   What then?
Being close   this not being is strange.
  Yeah, it is   so   talk.
    That's not what I mean.
   Then let's leave it   I'm too tired for this row again tonight.
    Well, I don't want to fight either but

Too late. I've hit my edges and am falling through time. Apparently willing to wring guts from mere disquiet because of course, when in doubt, chase the tail. Although if I catch it where will we be then? Bitten. As I well know.

First Winter

Better back to deep that afternoon when, dilapidating further our lino, I paced your return. Home from journeys and flush with tales that'd make much, for her, of our London world. I presumed where you'd show her and, once there, what you'd say. You'd taken me those byways so why not take Grace? But I cursed, to myself, all I'd willingly flog just to be those new eyes with you again. Seeing once more as I saw then, through the material heat of your attention. And not just those sod ends of city but the odd ends of you, preserved as you'd once traversed them in your own sealed ago. Noting bookshops. Tower blocks. Pub stops. More. Except you'll doubtless be obscuring some history from her. A necessary blind to all the other, the under past I've seen.

So I thought:

For her London, doubtless, will sit high above the waist. A cleanliness atoned for with jokes from Boswell or tales of the Krays. Smatters surely of When I first arrived, back in the seventies. Or, apologetically, When I was new here. As is right and proper. As should be. And while I never pass the Lamb and Flag without a wince, vis Grace's singular rights, she never will. Such a pretty place this, the pretty Bucket of Blood in this pretty changed world and your pretty divvy of it up. So, what's the special balance stricken for her? Ambiguous truths and a warily worn mask? All unalterable facts secreted within fine-graded gags? Or just swallow your past's every unsavourable surprise and hope they won't surface again? You do know a thing or two about dodging questions and were, after all, accomplished at compartments until I pulled out the drawers. Plus, she hardly knows which histories really exist, no matter about her mother's gossip. Or so I think and so I wish and know that you do too. You'll not want her stood, like me, at any fraught reveals. Or wobble-legged among the aftershocks, waiting for peace. She is Sunday best. I am bedsheet creased where the belly is dark and damp-lick rich. Where your body tells me and I tell it – as well as what we whisper between us in the dark. Terrible things to outsiders' ears but, to us, just ourselves no matter where we are. Those are stories she's heard but isn't made of, in the marrow, like you and also me.

As my wait trod our lino, that was it. All the previous trickling. Settling. Ordering itself between the varied strata of what all three of us were about to become. At least a clear and welcome division of labour   perhaps? Or reprieve from, and a guard against, unwelcome overlaps? We'll see. Places please now, ladies and gents! The second half is about to begin.

Then I thought So what if she's out with him – her version of you? I'm the one always present. Looking forward to key sounds and the coming in. Was before. Still am and know you enough to put money on lunch in Chinatown. Will you have done St Paul's? Or maybe Brick Lane? Somewhere nicer? To the West End? Of course, she's been to London before, which probably means no Marble Arch or Tower of. Galleries? Could be. Or separately, for later in the week. Southbank? Nothing there, so I doubt it. Unless maybe for tickets? Yes, you well might, for some other matinee, night, or the weekend. So, Foyles? Definitely. Money also on it. Buying her books, any she'd want. Then telling her. No. Not telling her about that but, perhaps, remembering – although how many afternoons in there have we spent browsing since? That first one though, with its intemperate kiss, recurs often enough to be the most rebuilt of all my memories. One I always favour. Sometimes only to re-glimpse how unprepared you were for what might, and did, eventually become happiness. At the first Foyles kiss, however, I was oblivious. Analytics interrupted by the blood in my ears and the arch announcement of We're closing up! While your raised eyebrow belied any hint of pang, along with All right, jailbait, let's go! All fluster adjusting, I just followed out, misreading adroitness into the twitch by your mouth. I'd no way to know then, but I'd recognise it now – your fear of feeling too much cutting through. She wouldn't and can't, having not known you before. I, though, have seen it take you so many times this last year. Creeping in through your body and prompting up from unaware some stray emotion you've neglected to secure. Hiding it by laughing but not fooling me. You know that I know, yet try anyway, and I see through that as well. And what's more, I can fathom what I see. Just how unquietly you coexist with even the littlest happinesses – which is something she'll have to learn for herself.

Never mind. Never mind at all. Mind instead the metal turn of key in the door. And the pair of you in, weather bringing, to the hall.

Eily? Eily, love? You in?
Just putting the kettle on.
    Hero of the people!
    Don't I know it!

Commotion! And you smiling at me like there'd been no taut morning. I was glad to see it. Just a father with a half-smoked cigarette. And a daughter who, from a Sainsbury's bag, drew biscuits.

    Dad said you like these best?
    Gingersnaps, yeah, lovely thanks. Go on. Sit down.

So to sitting and settling. Arranging those many long limbs.

    Wet out?
       Getting. Probably rain later on.
       Just as well you're in in time.
          You're telling me!
       So   where'd you go?

And   oh   what's that? A little guilt, with lowered lids, on your part.

       What?
    Actually we   Grace wanted to see
       What?
             Dad's old flat so   he took me.
     Off the Camden Road?
       Yeah.
     Why'd you want to see that?
     Why wouldn't she?

No reason but   hardly Buckingham Palace, is it?

 I know, I just   wanted to see.

  Fair enough. I lived there too, you know   for a bit

And I too   a lot longer ago.

  Oh God, of course you did.

 Only at weekends, I think   Dad, is that right?

  Mostly   sometimes more   depending on your mother's
work.

   Do you remember it?

Sort of. Some things. I remember Dad's stack of twenty ps.

 I don't remember those. What were they for?

    Oh, the old meter. That was long gone by your time, Eil.

I don't want be on the outside of that flat. Couldn't bear to be, so, to re-site
myself

   Same bed though, wasn't it?

Your eyes lit at the very mention of.

        I don't remember now   probably.

And a warning beneath your lashes of Don't do that, Eily.

  Amazing, when you think of it, a bed surviving   all those
years of

   Just a bed, Eil   I never much thought about it.

 Except to complain it was way too short.

  Oh, yeah well   there was that.

Comfortable enough for me though   given it was only three
foot. I can't remember it at all.

  Well, you were little and   I usually slept on the floor.

Did you?
In a sleeping bag, remember? Navy, I think.
That's not really   how I remember those nights.

So how does she?

So how do you?
Mostly Dad reading to me.

Your hand out to her hand and her taking it. Grip.

I remember that too, love.

And I want also to be remembered so breathe my oxygen in.

Well, I don't think I'll ever forget the mess!

Groan from you but grin as well, showing safe distance has been
attained.

Ah   I did my best.
Did you fuck!
Language!
Timothy?
What?
Language, Timothy!

And that gets your laugh up, which I know works better than digs.

What are you two talking about? Who's Timothy?
Old sitcom from the eighties. You wouldn't know it, Gracie.

You and me. Alone inside that.

> We get some British shows.
> Really?
> All kinds.

But I didn't care if they did. I cared about infiltration and oust. Not that it was in the air, but   I was on my guard. Or partly, given this morning's apparent alliance. So, with rank curiosity still killing compliance, I preferred more of their flat visit instead – that one where they once, as a family, lived. Not that one where we, in our old-fashioned iniquity, fucked.

> So how did it look then, the flat?
> Covered in scaffold and plastic.
> No!
> Yeah. They're doing it up.
> Luxury apartments?
> I'd say it was always going to go that way.
> Shame.

And I mean it very much. For such rich past to be scoured off. Histories, even – if I'm feeling magnanimous towards the ones there before my time.

> Suppose it was that or knock it. The whole house was a wreck.
> Still, sad to think of it gone.
> Eily   it was a dive.
> It was, but I

Sought some recognition and didn't care if she knew. Just see back to what I see and know what I mean. Was all I was after but got incomprehension. So on purpose, even Grace said

Dad, don't be such a stoic! You lived there long enough.

You just matter-of-fact shrugged at our follies.

I'll leave you two to the sentiment. Far as I'm concerned, it was a dump!

But picking my thread up, she passed it back.

I could still see through Dad's old window   beyond the scaffold.

Siding with you though, I just hardheaded

Oh, right   and what could you see?

She took and tried but she   but she

Actually   nothing. Old paper getting stripped

You just laughing.

Well then, I'd say that's that!

Cigarette stubbed. Ashtray emptied. The finish finalised, and you weren't a bit sorry to see us run to this end. Accepting so, we relinquished. But because we'd provoked the past, it then turmoiled around in various forms of disguise – like your long sojourn linking, as much as dividing, your many visitants there. Her and me. But others too. Too many to count and in ways too lurid to name. Not that I ever would – I'd only been dancing. Making sure you knew her place was hers but mine still bore weight in the room. Which I did know you knew, when it suited me to. When it didn't, it shot me through with longing to be lying on that old bed, in the lawless era before her advent. So either way that old place, with its newly closed eyes, stayed put on our mantles still. That's when I looked up at you, suddenly looking at me. Looking into and reading. And, evidently, deciding the time had come to be man of the moment then.

Right, womenfolk   I'm volunteering.
For what?
The fish and chip run.
Oh Dad, yes!
Eily, I know you're a fish sceptic so   burger?
Please.
Cod for you, Gracie?
Yes.
All right. I'll be quick.
And Stephen, get in some beers while you're at it.
Okay. Grace, what'll you drink?
Beer's fine for me too.
I don't think
Dad!
Yes?
Stephen, she's nearly eighteen.
I know, but still
Stephen   come on.
One then, and that's it, and don't tell your mother.
Dad, she knows I drink.

Both us convulsed again over this. All parentally unsure, you just lit up a fag.

Fine. I won't be long. Behave yourselves.
While the man of the house is gone?

Not rising to it, you took yourself off. And was that whistling I heard out in the hall? Lit a fag myself and cleared the cups. She offered but I didn't need help.

How's the jetlag?
Still there.
Nice to see the flat though?
Sort of   strange   Eily   can I ask you something?
What?
Do you think   he's nervous   of me?
I haven't noticed lie especially. Why? Do you?
Sometimes I think he is, but I don't know him that well.
I think he just doesn't want to make a mistake.
Far as I'm concerned he can't, unless he takes up domestic violence!
Given his childhood, I highly doubt that.
Sorry, that wasn't much of a joke.
Don't worry, he'd probably laugh.
That's what I mean. What I can say. What's too much?
There are so many things I want to ask but
Just ask, and if he doesn't want to answer, he won't.
You think?
I know.
Even for me?
I think so   probably especially you.

Hardly more is relevant from that night. All passed as expected and more besides. Chips were eaten. Innocuous beers drunk.

The morning merged with oblivion as though it hadn't happened. What video to watch alone opened a breach. Some campaigned for *Three Colours: White* but it was *Universal Soldier* that triumphed! Those who lost fell asleep on the couch, while the rest enjoyed Jean-Claude Van Damme. And in a little while

Eily, is he really asleep?
 Yes.
  Give us a drag on your fag?
  I didn't know you smoked.
   Only once in a while but I really fancy one tonight.
 Here, but be quick. I don't want him thinking I'm a corrupting influence!
    You'd have to do a lot worse!
    I'm not even going to ask!
 Well, I am my father's daughter.
     What's that supposed to mean?
 Nothing, I just   accept him for who he is.

You stirred but did not wake at that, or our bit of panto with the fag. Yet, like good evolutionaries, we were being changed. Incrementally, because willing. Consensually, because friends, or offering an attempt to be. Remained on the lookout though, both of us. Noting who got where, or how far with what? Her eyes on my hands during the credits, fingertip drumming it out on your thigh. Absently, because I could touch you whenever I liked, while she still had to wait on your lead.

Now

Prising himself up from the sit, he tosses the drained can into the bin. His body also so obviously it, I half pity him but   not enough not to hang on.

    Don't go yet, Stephen.

Why not? Or   is there something you want to talk about?

    Since when have you been so   obstinate?

Since I've been trying to be a fucking grown-up.

    You never used to be so

So what?

    Direct.

And where did that get us, Eily? Where did it get you?

    That isn't to do with this.

You don't think so? Bit convenient.

    It's not convenient at all!

      Well, if you miss being close to me then fucking talk. Say
      something. Anything. Just stop this impenetrable fucking
      silence I'm supposed to know how to decode.

Thorny to back my way from this. Yes, he opened the door. I,
however, went in. And now he's getting to say everything I've
made silent in the two months since. Since I   Since it. No, it's
my silence too and I will not trespass it. But if I don't answer   will
he just give in? This! So I opt for brazening his anger   frustration   bewilderment? First wave, those. Second, guilt. Third? Wait!
And he resigns.

    Well   maybe it'll be easier once the show comes
    down.

An end for him, but I stay on point.

    No, Grace will be here by then.

First Winter

In from the bathroom first, I sat on the bed. And, after your turn, watched you undress – angled to the dark but with the lit upper deck of a 214 racing your spine. A ribbon of old scars drawing reflection. Then back to the black of Camden beyond – never true black though, is it? Always light enough to see off your trousers and shirt. Uncustomarily folded. Back of the chair. Making audience of me for this as well. Then, adding insult to injury, a T-shirt dragged down over your head. Prompting my needle of

Look at you in your vestments!

Brushed haystack-wardly by your

It's pretty cold.

And further – lifting unfolded underwear out of the drawer. Bluish in the refrigeration light from below. Down where the foxes eat KFC, and night drunks piss, and where morning deliveries will bleep us headachely up from dreams. I waited for want to show in your limbs. Knew I hung on your say-so and was still hanging. Remained hopeful when you finally sat on the bed. Back turned but even so. And then   nothing else. Staring at the floor? Readying yourself? Hard to say. But I waited to beyond when invite had usually kicked in. Beyond too the last pipe trickle from the last toilet flushing. Beyond even hearing her bedside lamp switch off and the mesh squeak of sofa bed turns. Only beyond all these beyonds, I worked to the question

Stephen   you coming to bed?

And, as encouragement, got in properly myself. Legs stretched out. Presented a hand. Which you took and let yourself be drawn down. Lay beside. When I kissed your shoulder though, it was

That's nice but   not tonight, Eily, okay.
     Again?
I'm just   tomorrow, all right?
    Is something wrong?
Nothing for you to worry about.
    What then?
It's just been a bit of a day   I'm sorry.
    Don't worry.
Night then.
        Night then, Stephen   sleep well.

Night night bitch battle body fold and ache. Bloody spurned to the wall by your blanched shoulder blade. Bloody looking at the state of the wallpaper on it. Bloody fuck. Bloody what anyway. Bloody am I too quick to accept your sidling away? Maybe I should try? Or not be a nymphomaniac? As he said   after all   it's been a bit of a day. And so it had. And so I turned on my side. Planned the rest of the fall on my own. You not moving a muscle. But I could tell you were nowhere near sleep. Just laid. Breath steadying. Trying to work on your heartbeat. Blue-lit white skin showing the veins of your neck. I thought then, as often, of their progress. Their deep-dug journeys up from beneath your bones, from under guts or over lungs – not that I knew much about physiological stuff. I just considered the existence of all those mechanics and marvelled at how they stayed on the go. And kept going. And hoped they would too. Bit of a macabre one that, even for me. Then I yawned, just as you did. You turning to appreciate the width of my yap.

Impressive! I think I saw tonsils that time!
Well then, lucky looky you!

And both smiled, like at usual play. No harm in disentangling wherever able, despite the adjustment for the difference of that night. For who was lying next door. For the purpose of the T-shirt. Alert to how this new step – which felt quite like a trip – itched to be spoken of, yet hindered itself, I wondered if there was still more. So said

So?
So   what?
You tell me.

Then all at once, there it was, the tic in your cheek.

Jesus, Stephen   what's wrong?

And though stuck behind your teeth, it was as far as your mouth. I could see it so stroked your face there.

Go on.
She's   she's reminding me of her.
Grace is?
Yes.
Of your mother?

Nod.

And didn't she last summer?
No   all I saw was her then.
But now you're more used to her.

So I'm seeing the resemblance.

Strong?

She's   very like her   sometimes.

Like how?

Her smile.

She has the same smile as you.

Well, it's not like that's something I ever look at.

Weird for me though.

Yeah?

Seeing you there.

I can see how that would be.

So what else?

Similar voice.

But she's so Canadian, and your mother was Irish.

I know. It's more   the tone.

Does it   upset you?

Not exactly, but   I've never had that before. I so
rarely think of her and now   she's across the wall.

She really isn't.

I know, but

And don't ever say that to Grace.

God, no   I'd never

You're not having any other

What?

Feelings.

Fuck's sake! I am not!

Sorry, I didn't

I shouldn't have mentioned it.

Stephen, don't say that.

Just forget I said anything.

But looking at your mouth twist, I saw something else. Fear. And not that you did but that you would. The long legacy of her. Deep in your life. I'd rip it out, if I could. If I could only see clear and past the similar version lodged in me – which swims me now and then. Less of what it might make me do, unlike you. More, of what got left behind. Thinking this, I stayed silent as you turned your head. Its interest presumably taken by the blank wall adjacent and the girl asleep there beyond. I still knew you though and how the past harmed, so whispered

Stephen? Stephen, you don't have to be afraid.

Nothing at first. Then, in your back, some relent, if I chose to read it that way. I chose to read it like that. Pressed my lips to it too and heard you breathe out. Soft like sadness into the room. Then reaching back through the mess, your long fingers found mine. Drew them around and kept them close to your chest. So   a repeat of last night   except   somehow we were even further off. More unbodied. Becoming built of alternative stuff – the instinct for comfort rather than for us to lock every other world out. So there we both were, staring at the wall. One at least, me, hazarding at the direction of travel. The other, you, hobbled by the past's thwart of your now, and not much help at all.

Now

Pointing out Grace will be here when his show closes is scarcely news. But new is his pretending her presence comes with no past.

So what if Grace is here?
   Stephen, it's not exactly   private   then.
   Fine. So   another time.
   Another and another.

Your point being?

'I'm preparing.' 'I'm rehearsing.' 'The show's about to go up.'
'It's the first night.' I've got a matinee.' 'Eily, I'm exhausted.'
I mean, you're only forty so, presumably, you're still able to
fuck?

Cheap, and he will not rise to that. Just a grim shrug and one
brow alone lifting up.

Yes, presumably, but   this is going around in circles so   I'm
off to bed.

Thus he leaves my gone sealed self, with its now dormant tongue,
viewing a bedside glass of water get run. Rim cracked on the tap
proving his agitation, but general fucking off remaining the gist.
Body held rigid, ensuring he will. Purposefully and doggedly. Will
not desist. Locked, however, in a grip from which I cannot seem to
unstick, I go to the night instead. Not any either. Or out of doors. A
revert and return to that night in mid-autumn. My body all commotion. His then rigid as well.

This Autumn Gone

Camden. September. Two months past, if now feeling more. Flipping its
days between nippy and warm. Morning over bodies. Fast wrapped.
Legs and arms. Mine, by itself, in the start of a dawning. Yours, at this
moment, asleep. All dauntless so, I scratched my nose on your chin.
Saw the eyes flicker open and that first morning twinge of knowing
us here together again. No for granteds in this bed. Only a stretching of your frame which carefully kept close against. Options always
open, et cetera. Arms finding me under the quilt

Morning, you.
Morning, yourself.
How did you sleep?
Yeah, not bad.
Third Year starts tomorrow, right?
Yeah, why?
Then this is the last chance saloon!

Yawned shoulder growl. Endeavouring yourself on. Crack of bones settling. Muscles finding room.

What do you think you're doing?
Selflessly offering to wake you up?
So selfless but   I already was!
Then how about

But interrupting yourself – and this was trouble's starting point I know now   didn't then.

What's that, Eil?
What?
What do you smell of?
Sweat?
No.
Garlic?
No.
Then I don't know what.
Well, I like it, whatever it is.

Charm and hygiene then abandoned in favour of lower pursuits. Swift and actively gotten into because the alarm clock could go off any time.

So that was the outset and, while benign, set other clocks a-tick towards your understanding – as well as, by alarm time, my lie. Not yet though. It was a while before any actual lying arrived. Even then, it was mostly the 'Of-omission' kind. And who are you to judge when it comes to that?

First Winter

Leggy through the door glass. It wasn't you though, or her. So

> Who's that?
> Just me!
> Oh, hello.

Locks undid and got my cheek kissed by my slatternly flatmate of old, Danny.

> Hey!
> Stephen around?
> In the kitchen. What's up?
> We're supposed to head into town to have a look at the cut.
> Really? First I've heard of it.
> It's been arranged for ages. I hope he didn't forget.
> Come on in anyway.
> Cheers.

Lanky unwashed, and still never washed hair, spivved over the threshold like belonging there.

> You're looking well. How's Second Year treating you?
> Grand so far.
> Started your solo scenarios yet?

Just before we broke up. Still don't really get it.
  Ah, you'll be flying by Easter, I swear.
    So how's the great world of you, Danny boy?
      Be better once he gets this cut done!
        Want it for a showreel?
      Wouldn't do any harm   plus everything else.
    What? Mega stardom?
      Shut up!

Smoothed his hair in the mirror before rounding the corner.

  Don't worry, he'll still think you're beautiful, I'm sure.
    Cheeky bitch.

Then

    Oi, Antonioni!

Getting you to look up from elbows on the breakfast bar over
burnt toast. Fag already on the go, but eyes quick to smile.

    Danny! All right?

Got up too, proper fondness between them now, to put an arm right
around.

    Good to see you.

And him the same.

    You too, Stephen. How've you been?

Eyeing each other like they're in on something. Then you just smirked and let him go.

Oh, you know, all the better for seeing you!
Don't I know it, man!

Before showboating to me

Your boyfriend still fucking loves me, Eily.
Yeah, I'll watch my back.

Wry smiling, you offered a stool but got back to pragmatic

So what've you been up to?
Just back from Hungary actually.
Holiday?
World War One thing. BBC.
A harrowing, gut-wrenching death?
Gory, yet moving. How'd you guess?
We've all done our time in the trenches.
Yeah well   pays the rent.
No shame in that, Dan.

Suddenly then he flicked to not spivvy at all. To mobilised all over by some awful want to know – or not, if it wasn't worth the pain.

So   how's the cut looking, Stephen?

And though he searched you, he didn't know how to translate. But extracted some meaning, from the slow get back to your feet – which I saw as barely more than a stretch.

Good. Nearly there   I think.
  You'll be finished soon then?
Couple of weeks. Got a bit snarled up on the sound but, really,
it's almost there.
  I bet you'll be glad.
    Definitely relieved!
      I suppose it's a lot to keep   revisiting   every day.
      Yes and no   depends.

Both studied the other then, like knowing more. Those weeks of
filming so concentrated they might as well have happened on Mars,
however much I was told about them.

    Yeah, it was all pretty fucking intense.
          It was, but   that's in the performance.
      Yeah?
    You'll be happy, Danny. I would be.
        And you are?
          Yes.
              Sure?
      I've been on it for weeks and anything that didn't work
      is gone.
  What do you mean 'didn't work'?
      Don't be paranoid.
        Sorry I just   I don't want to have fucked it up.
          Well, you didn't, so, want a cup of tea?
      Is there time?

Sloped grey eyes to the kitchen clock.

Actually, maybe not. We're booked in for three.

Danny up then, still suffering but enlivened somewhat. Put out though, I

>So you're just pissing off to Soho?
>>Yeah, didn't I say?
>No.
>Sorry. Thought I had.
>>Have you even told Grace?
>Before she went out. She said it was fine. Just for a few hours.
>>Oh right.

And my annoyance judged you up then down until Danny, zipping his jacket, pried

>>Who's this Grace?

As the front door closed.

>>This Grace will be me.

Just back, and unbeknownst, arrived in. All laden with the flotsam of Saturday Camden. Shook her umbrella before kissing your cheek.

>>Going out now to see the edit?
>>>I won't be long.
>>I wish you'd let me come.
>>>It's not ready for an audience.
>>Well, he's going.
>>He's in it.
>>>Yeah, I'm in it.

Lucky you!

But used her raised eyebrows as an excuse to give him the once over. As Danny did the same, always and ever calculating.

And so   Grace is?
            Me.
Yeah, I got that, but what are you   specifically?

You, though, went all introduction obstinate.

Come on, Danny, best not miss that slot.

Danny, however, remained on the job.

I can see the family resemblance, so she's, what? Little sister?

I doubled in cackles at that. You, though, reached for his ear and flicked.

She's my little daughter, so don't even think about it.
    No way! Your daughter! Fuck!

Further Danny Dannying ensued, but you were adamant. Hustled him from the kitchen with

Right, let's head.
    Hey, wait!
    Hey yourself, out!

Grace and me followed too into the hall, entertained by their few more rounds of

No way she's your daughter!
  She absolutely is.

And

Why did you keep her a secret?
  One, I didn't. And two, she's none of your business.

And

  Yeah, fair enough but   still.

You so keen to go, and Danny to stay, that neither saw what I saw
– how Grace calculated him as well. Well, well, I thought. Well, truly
her father's daughter in spite of it all. Then you brought it to an end.

    Do you, or do you not, want to see this cut?
      No, mate, I definitely do.
        So then   out!

And propelled him towards it, calling behind to us

    Have a think about what you fancy for tea and I'll give a ring
    once we're done.

Door closed then. Men gone. But, soon as they were, Grace
slipped yet more of you on.

    So who's the mysterious Danny then?
      We shared a flat in Kentish Town, back when I was a
      First Year.

Is that how he knows my   Dad?

But that brought more shenanigans to mind than I'd readily share. Definitely, definitely not for her. All three of us have made that past a pit, into which we've chucked those less noble skins. Needfully, for the future. Gladly too, to stay friends. But, caught out by this, from the blue, resurrection, I made a small mistake.

At first, then   obviously he cast him in his film after that.
Oh, right   which part?
Himself.
What?
The main part   that's based on him.
On Danny?
No, on Stephen.
Is it? He never told me that.
But   I thought you'd read the script?
I asked to and he kept saying he'd send it, but

You didn't, did you?

He never did.

Then the worst affirmatory shake of her head. Shit! A curse on my foot-in-mouthing and everything else!

Sorry   I didn't realise he was being   cagey about it.
So   why is he?
Oh no, that one's for him.
Eily
No way   he's your father, not mine.
You know why he is though?

I   can guess.

I already know about his mother, meaning it can't be that. So what is it?

I'm not getting in the middle of this.

Why not?

You know why not. Come on, Grace.

Fine.

Sorry.

No, I am. I'll just ask him myself.

Yeah, you definitely should.

But wished I'd ways of misleading or places of fall where tacit deceptions might level out pitfalls. Your life was yours though, so I couldn't reckon for it. Besides, she'd already elected another path – one that turned out to have just as much gall though, albeit also for me.

So Eily, have *you* seen the cut?

Not yet.

Why not?

He says it isn't ready.

But Danny doesn't have to wait?

It's not like that. He says it can be tricky to watch a rough cut   if you're not used to it   you know?

I don't like her implication which, if correct, sets us off in the same boat, adrift. Of course, cunning enough, she's already noticed this.

Then it sounds like you're getting it too.

What?

Evasiveness.

Oh   I wouldn't say that.
Really? I think you are.

But, if I can't make her not say it, I don't have to give in, so propose my own

You're just pissed off about the script.
I am, but think about it? Why's Danny off to Soho while
we're left here?
He has nothing to hide from me.
So then why is he, Eily?

Which is a good question to ask.

First Autumn – Filming

I lay awake those nights until you came in. Late. More often though in the a.m. Mostly froze to the marrow, but nerve ends flaring with the rush of past working back through.

How's it going?
I think all right.
How are you doing?
Probably fine.
Probably?
Or else I   can't think about it yet.

Happy though. Dog tired. Eating a sandwich on the bed. Taking my hand too and threading it. Observing I needn't wait up so late while seeming always glad that I had. Then other nights, more askance. Betraying, through your cigarette, unease about a shift in perspective. About noting a sticking point but not taking for granted your right to reinterpret a thing. After all, fact was fact and fair remained fair. Any fending off, by hindsight, unforgiveable to that intractable there. But trickier to deny what you saw playing out beneath hot kliegs. Your own history reframed by your DoP. Your own actions rerunning on the screen but changed too. Necessarily. Because reimagined by Danny and his own logic of why. Becoming, all in all, a different way to see. More. A whole other route into the story. This alternative view, every instinct in you, was itching to run to ground.

Because I know, Eily, that's how things get made. Whatever you've thought or however you've prepared, when something interesting shows itself, that's where you have to go.
So, never look a gift horse in the mouth?
Yes.
Then that's your answer.
I suppose so, and yet
And yet?
How do I do that without letting myself off the hook?

Tiredness stealing from you any vestige of guile. Just asking. Really asking, at that ungodly hour. And from my own guilelessness, it seemed apparent that

Maybe it's time for other ways to see   or think about who you've been? And let the past go under the bridge.

The winding clock of you, though, refused this comfort. While wanting it just the same.

But Eil, that's who I was and I did those things. So who the fuck am I to absolve myself of anything now?

Knowing all this already, I wrapped round your chill skin. Then, with its cold taken closest in, willed you to leave the battles of that much younger man to the mercilessness of his own time. And, failing that, to offer him instead the spec of your newer lens with its wider, deeper field of view.

These were our late, or early, chats each night of that shoot. After which you'd lie beside me in our bed where, at least, was love. And rest. And time for the swarming images in your head to relent a little as you slept.

First Winter

But I already knew the answer.

> Because we've already been through it all, Grace.
> > Except for actually seeing it.
> > Which I will.
> So why not push him?
> Push yourself.
> I might.
> Well, best of luck with that.
> Look, I didn't mean
> > I know him, all right?

Probably better than you is also what I thought but managed not to say.

> I know you do, Eily. Far better than me.

Her knowing I was annoyed, but me knowing she didn't mean it, forcing me to concede

But you're his daughter and that's different. I'll always be on the outside of that.

Both us making so much effort. Yet both, by now, so agitated that God help you, I thought, when you get home. Only a thought until I said it aloud. Her agreement so ready, the anxiety dropped. Laughter got its claws in instead and threw us about. Weird for this, of all things, to have buzzed up into irritant. But then she couldn't understand what understandings you and I pass, without question, hand to hand. In the meantime, and in your projected absence, I advanced another plan.

Fancy heading out for a pint?

And

You know what? That'd be great!

So I scrawled a note to leave on the table.

Stephen, we've gone to the World's End. Come join us if you want.

Then out the two of us went, into a Camden of late afternoon.

Now

I am stood. I am still amid so many nights. Whether beckoned for or banished is no longer of account. What matters are the answers I cannot provide to the questions he cannot but ask.

Therefore this, our latest vainglorious impasse! An epic of tap

drips tuning to rainfall without. High road sirens aiding others, perhaps, but not us. Just crumbs from his sandwich and heating ticking
off. Water edging over his glass as he passes me. Splash. Down my
front. Onto my foot.

Sorry.
　　Don't worry about it.
　No! Of course, Eil. Why would I do that?
　　You just think there's a different problem to the one there
　　is.
　The one that can't be solved by having sex? I suppose I do.
　　It's my body.
　Yes, it is　but I'm the one who
　　Shut up!
　I'm the one who had to
　　Shut the fuck up, I said!
　Eily, this is serious!

But I cannot hear this. Hands over and

　　No no no no stop
　Then fuck this for a game of soldiers. Goodnight!

And I　　having not anticipated this turn, reach for his passing
arm.

　　No, Stephen! Wait!

Just get shook off. And soon as it's clear he will not, the kitchen
elaborates itself into objects of malice. Mortars. Trajectories to hit.
And within this graspy maelstrom it's the piccalilli gets it. Picked
for its circleness but flung for its weight. Doodle bugging the air

before hitting the radio. Knocking. Rebounding. Then down. Shatter. Smash. Everywhere about. Piccalilli and glass. All over the stool legs and lino between. Like a shot through him too. Satisfying. Immediate.

Shit! What the fuck, Eily? Jesus Christ!

Can't believe it missed him – either of us. The stink of it also with its liquidish gas. I repent in an instant. Then only for that. Then know sorrier is probably best. And so best foot forward

Stephen, I'm
    STOP!
Wait, Stephen
No, I mean it. Don't move!

I don't.

Look down in front of you.
    Oh.

Foot afloat in an ocean of shard. Lucky he froze me just at its slice shore.

    Oh fuck!
Stay exactly where you are. I mean it, Eily. Don't move.

Before I even accede, he's got to the kitchen roll and down on his knees.

Hand me that bag there, on the side.
Which? The Cullens?

Doesn't matter. Just something to dump all this in.

This stink-slitting pile I've bequeathed to him or, at least, to his care.

Sorry   I don't know why I did that.

And I am sorry now, even if I am angry.

Could you just open the bag?
Sorry.

Then do.
Him dropping it in. Kneeling back down for more.

Couldn't you have chucked a mug, Eily, like anyone normal?
Apparently not.
The piccalilli too.
Never mind, it was rank.
I'm afraid I can't agree.

But somehow he's laughing now into the gungy floor. Not exactly happily though.

Why're you laughing?
I'm not.
Yes, you are. What's so funny?

The laughing stops.

Fuck all   any more.

And, with continued unlaughing, sits back on his hunkers.

> In fact   this is a fucking nightmare and   so are you.
>   I know   you are too.
>   Yeah   I know that as well.

Briefly we surveil each other for decisive stuff to do but, when neither finds, he goes back to the ooze. And when I stoop, to help, am not even let try.

> Don't, Eil! Just leave it!

His voice taking no prisoners but eyes avoiding mine. And I know why, so I won't touch a single sharp thing. Instead watch him work his way across. Wiping guck from under stool legs. Leaving sticky but making safe. The grey in his hair more in this light than day. I'd like to put my fingers through it again and tease him. Time for the Grecian 2000! I'd say. Him examining, conceding You're telling me! But with craic forbidden now, I track his arm's arcs instead. Out, to in, then into the bag. New sheet, then a repeat of the exercise. Surely his back must be sore? So intent on his movements though, he's got right to my feet before I notice the blood. The half-moons of it stippling out in wide sweeps which, somehow, he has also not seen.

> Stop! Stop it, Stephen! You're cut!
>   What?
> Look down.
> Oh   bollocks.

Dripping, as he lifts it from the floor.

> Careful.

On his haunches now, examining for   finding. Pulling at it.

Doesn't it hurt?
Well   now you mention it   it is starting to smart.

Another go at extraction. Sliver out. Long and sharp. But the whole side of his hand suddenly spewing with blood.

Oh my God, Stephen!
Yeah, I see it. Fuck!

Me remembering, of course and at once, his face at the sight of it. Do I though? I can't possibly and yet   familiarity's breeding   something like I remember this from before.

First Winter

Less hassle than Saturday, getting pints back and forth. Happy though for the help of bodies, and inevitable noise, to scrub unease from my head. Just remember she can't grasp what he and me have and so empathise with her exclusion while – all the while – knowing we're not in the same boat at all.

Oh, over there!
I'll grab them.
Quick!

Got pints. Peanuts. Got free window seats. Got out my Marlboro Lights.

May I?

Help yourself.

He smokes so much anyway, I doubt he'll be able to tell.

Sure he's been smoking since he was a teenager himself.

Really?

At least since sixteen.

I'm not going to worry then – he's hardly in a position to judge.

But see, even in her lighting up, a rearrangement of you. Head to the side. Thin cheek caving in. Elegant fingers dangling it between. No matter my practice of that particular look, their vernacular glamour is not in my blood and, while I do admire it, curse her for having it just the same.

So do you come here often?

What?

You and my dad?

Nah   he thinks it's pretty much a meat market.

Do you?

I don't mind it. We come after rehearsals sometimes – my year, that is.

And Danny too?

Not so much since he moved.

Where does he live now?

Tufnell Park – it's up the road. Why?

Her all off-hand, exhaling, but I've sized her up enough for advice.

Don't go falling for Danny.

Why not?

He's shagged everyone.

You?

Why're you asking that?

The way my dad looked at him.
Believe me, he's not jealous of Danny. That was all about you.

But did you?
Yeah   we did.

Admittedly a preen of one-upmanship – it being, however, distance appropriate in terms of when and where.

And how was it?
Unmemorable, but we were both fucked   wasted   it was all right.
I know what you mean.

And I know what she means by that. A telling me You are not so advanced, so beyond me in all of this.

Don't worry, I won't tell your dad.
You can tell him if you like, what's he going to say?
Nothing. Not that he'd judge anyway. Not you, that is.

But I thought you'd be hurt by the shrug in her voice. Though maybe that was just meant for me?

So was that before you met?
In between, more like.
Oh?
No   it just took us a while to
Be more than a casual thing?

Eyes catching eyes and some sense of a brink. Should I answer? And how? And what would you think? Until self-respect remembers it is also my life. So drank off my pint and said

Yes.

Which it was, between its deluge of sex and prohibitions stumbled across. All those gargling maws we fell into, and then out of. But remember gruesomer details are for keeping within.

How long did it take   until you knew?
Couple of months.
And what was the moment?

But I'm not telling her that, about the long night of disclosure and the scars on your back.

No one moment really   it just   slowly happened.
Right   I see.

How she looks at me though. Unnerving as you can be when you understand more than I say.

So, on that uninformative detail, another pint, Eily?
Yes, please.
I'll be back in a sec.

And I watched her weave the men who made her rub past. Her slow disdain I applaudingly admired. I might practise that too, on my own. But once she'd made it to the bar, I looked instead into Camden. Considered the dealers outside the tube. The odd 29 and rush-hour commuters rearranging raincoats in the street. Then considered when you might be home. How it went? What Danny thought? Why you'd chosen to show Danny first? And if Grace'd also see it before I would? Live wires all. But quickly deadened upon her rapid return.

> Got some chasers while I was at it!
> Jesus, Grace!
> Queue's a mile wide. This way we won't have to go back up
> for ages.

Sound logic there, so

> Fair enough.

Got going then, we, like under strict instruction of faster, faster
and more on top – with more continually reprised until

> Fuck! I think I'm completely fucked.
> I know   me as well.

But at least guards went down about being correct. Vision, froing
too in the smoke, suffered blight while the edges of sayable swung
wildly to left and right. At last least mostly colliding with blur. Then
it was elbows on the table time and holding heads up and

> So honestly, Grace   do you hate it Stephen and me?
> Not really. Maybe a little before we met, but then   maybe
> that was his caginess again. You know   when you want him
> to just say something out but all you get is bits?
>   Yeah   I know it and it   drives me mad.
> So first it was There's this girl. Then She's not just that. Then
> In fact we're moving in. But I could see through it   I could
> tell there was still something else so   I waited and   eventually
>   What? That I was only two years older than you?
> Yes, which to be honest   was pretty strange but then   I

had this thing with a guy his age not like this but   after it I
was   Oh, you know   I see.
    Does Stephen know about that?
    No. Should I tell him?
    Probably not   most people wouldn't   would they? Tell
    their dad?
    Suppose not.
        Then stick to that. But anyway   eventually   he said it.
Yeah and then I knew   it was serious. Also because he'd never
mentioned anyone before. I even looked back through his
letters and nothing   even when I asked.
    I don't think there was anyone   really   like that.
Plenty of the other though, apparently. My mother made sure
I knew all those tales.
        That's a bit   fucked up   is it?
    I suppose, but then   everyone's parents have sex, don't yours?
        Well   my father's dead so I really hope not!
        Oh my God   that's so fucking bleak.

But off into paroxysms, hiding her face. Then two of us in it, like
heartless wenches. A little mastering required before

        I'm so sorry, Eily   I do know about your dad   I just forgot.

I am unbothered and have laughed at so much worse with hers,
although that I do not say.

        Don't worry. I was only being stupid anyway.

Both that pintful now we're condensation hot and the increasingly less tactful at winkling information out, like her asking – and
how could she not?

When did you first know about me?

And saw myself that morning, shivering off the night, with its eventful loss of virginity to this stranger of a man.

First time I went home with him.
     Before or after?
          What?
     Before or after   you know.
     The next morning   why do you ask?
     No reason   just nosy.
Well, on his desk, I saw your photo so, to make conversation, I asked.
          What did he say?
'That's my daughter' but not   how old the picture was. You know, you were   three or something. Then I asked if he was married and he laughed because
          What?
     The state of the place. That room.
     Messy?
       Like you wouldn't believe.
          Gross.
        I suppose   although sometimes I   miss it.
     He doesn't.
        I know, but   he's got all sorts of memories from there.
     I bet. I remember it as well. The night my mother took
     me away.
     Fuck.
Yeah.
     So   what does she think of all this?

But ha ha ha'd she into her glass.

      I knew you'd ask!
    Well   I'm also nosy   all right?
    Which I respect, but   we can't   me and my mother   talk about him any more.
      Because of how she was?
    Because I just want to know my father and do it on my own.

So true and obvious I lose the run or, at least, any poise I'd been pretending.

      Grace, I know what you mean because   I'd do anything to
      know mine.

Then stillness sits down in the middle of this, despite the World's End's roiling heave on its axis. She and I just looking at what's missing from us and those absences showed up much the same. Where fathers were. But then what's been regained. Who's been replaced. Where's been renamed.

      But you really love him, don't you? Stephen?
        I really do.
      And I do too.

That man we've lost and the one we have. Piecemeal between but ample, perhaps. Before more maudlin gags though, interruption arrives in the form of

      Oh fuck, are you two both pissed?

Now

I

Fuck!

Down his forearm and wrist. Me falling knees forward to wrap my hands round it.

Will I call an ambulance?
No. It looks worse than it is. Just let me get up.

More. I let him to the tap, where he holds it. Fingers run red. My panic following in fits. So much of it as well, and all over the plates. And all down the front of me too. Him gritting his teeth. Checking the wound. For afters. Further splinters. The hurt and I

Here, Stephen   let me see.

He shows. Long and sliced very clean. Bleeding like it loves to. A hanging ribbon of skin.

I'm sorry.
It's nothing. It's fine.
I'll get a Band-Aid   a few Band-Aids.
No. Eily. It's all right.
How about TCP then?
Yes, that. In the bathroom, I think.

But I know it's under the sink.

Just sit down and   try not to bleed on the chair.

A Fucking Hell smile between us as he wraps it in roll. Then sits while I rummage the Jif, Flash and marigolds. This cupboard. Bloody cupboard. All lies where it fell and now me smearing actual blood into the lino here also, but

I've got it.
Here, pass it.

Can't open it himself, with that hand fishgutting all over the shop. The TCP bottle now getting bloodily greased and any twisting only making it worse.

Ah fuck!

He hefts forward and drips on the floor. I take it back. Open it. Dab it round.

Does that sting?
Yeah, it really does!

Then, like a magic trick witnessed, his blood runs right down to my elbow too.

Jesus, I think that might need a stitch.
It's fine. I'll just press down on it for a bit.

But it's under my nails and under his own. Also his jeans. Also my cardigan.

Really hope you don't have anything.
Like what?

You know   in your blood.
Well, if I have, you've probably already got it so I don't know
if that helps?

Swipe a toe at it there but it's starting to dry, meaning there will
be scrubbing.

But could you have?
What?
Could you?
What's that supposed to mean?
It means could you   you know   have   something?

Except now he's not laughing. Nowhere even a smile. A second
passes. And another.

Are you seriously asking?

Which I hadn't been but suddenly am because   these are the
years and this is the time?

I just want to know.
Well, you must have reason so   what do you think? Is there
a chance?
How would I know?
Your own blood tests maybe? You've had a few yourself lately
– if you're worried about HIV? Which is what you're talking
about, isn't it?

I suppose it is although I don't know why, from a choice of
so many, this is the needle with which I have elected to pierce.
Must be the blood. Might only be spite. Could possibly be the

banality I'd rather avoid that's so persistently, however, on the tip of my tongue: Stephen, are you sleeping with someone else? I don't want to, but might have to, ask – this despite the logic being No, from every possible angle. Leaving me, therefore, to admit I'm probably needling because he can so rarely resist. And here he is, not resisting again. At least I am winning at that. So turn the idea. Convolute the thought. Keep carrying it though, because his hackles are up and that is its own reward.

I don't remember being tested for that.
They did though.
How do you know?
I was there when it happened. They did a whole battery.

And I really don't. I do not recall. I was so tired then, with the knot of the gown sticking into my back. It was all the body I owned, I thought, round about then. When I looked so much at the wall in order not to look at him. Looking at me. White and wan. But now it's gone, and there's nothing interesting in that time upon which I care to reflect. I don't even know why he is bringing it up. With his hand dripping blood everywhere like he doesn't give a fuck. And perhaps he doesn't. So

If you say so.

Drip.

I do. They tested for everything   as a matter of course.
Do you remember the results?
Negative.
Well   that's good.
Yes.

Drip.

So when were you last tested then?
   About two years ago.
      When was that?
      After the last time I was with someone   else.
   After that Christmas?
      Yeah.
   Why? Were you worried about it? About her?
   No. It just   seemed polite.

Drip.

   In what way?
         To be sure.
      Why?
         You know why, Eil.
   I don't.
      Well   because   there was you.
            And so?
   So after the test I was sure. Otherwise I'd have kept using
   something and I didn't   although now I wish I fucking had.

Drip.

      No, you don't.
   And what would you know about that?

Drip. Drip. Drip. New blood again. More.

   Jesus Christ! It's really going again now. Pass that kitchen
   roll.

I think we should go to the Royal Free.
No!
Don't be stubborn!
Oh, fuck off, Eily. I can deal with it on my own.

Silent then, I pass it and, as he unwinds, count myself appraised that this is not entertainment. That all my fucking needling isn't much fun. No longer for me. Never was for him.

Here. Let me help you.
No.
Come on. I'm sorry. Let me help you, all right?

So he does. And I do do it tight. Enough that, a few sheets in, there seems some respite.

How's that now?
Better   thanks.

But he doesn't want to talk more. Just folds over himself in the manner of the gaunt, and stares into the bloodied kitchen roll, waiting for whatever comes next. My hands, meanwhile, go terrible, thinking they can architect some way out of this. What strategies though? What can I do? I'll

Here   I'll   mop up the blood.

First Winter

All the long of you sliding into the seat. Aware abruptly of multitudes, I focus but retinas won't agree. Grace doing somewhat better, I think. But then is she

Woah!

Half strangles you with hug. You looking so pleased. Her looking so drunk. No one caring how I look which, on reflection, might
have been just as well.

> Dad, it's so lovely to see you. I missed you so much.
> And I missed you too, love.
> Did you know me and Eily have so much in common?
> Which you've discovered through all the drinks you've
> downed?

More than I'd realised, by the sound of it. Certainly enough to
make your reaction slightly mysterious. Think there's irony there
but perhaps also irritated? Hard to conclusively say.

> Do you two even know what time it is?
> What time?
> Closing time.
> No, it's not.
> Oh yes it is, so you'd better come on.

Get up so, to our feet, but dither around. Pocketing fags. Hunting for scarves. For bags.

> Where are your coats?
> They're   they're
> All right, they're here. This one's yours, Grace, and I believe
> this one is
> Thanks!

Fold it over my arm and kiss your mouth. I'd give it loads more but you pull back.

Put it on.
    I'll carry it.
    Grace, put yours on, pet.
        I'm all right too.
            Then, we better hurry. It's about to rain.

Now

Spilled because of me. Made worse by me. Fuck! Scratch it up if I have to. I don't have to. It comes out. Along with the dirt. And I don't do it for long. I'm not really for housework. You a touch oftener but also not really that much. Customarily speaking, we're for fucking and books. The watching of films. Much eating of toast. Smoking of fags. Evenings in the pub. But then there are also down days. Have always been. Marked by a turned head. A silent unwilling to get from the bed. You oftener also than me in this. Bleaker. Sometimes floored by it. But me sometimes too, and then I am stuck in the dark with no keys. With only the worst of my own devices. Until the past recedes and the rest of me comes to again. And I know your point of return so well. Eyes back to half smile. The hold of your head. Best to leave the other to it, when it comes, we've agreed amongst ourselves. Wait patiently until the further shore has been reached, then be a warm body on the sofa – preferably with cigarettes. We've patterned ourselves to these incursions. And we make them fit as they cannot unbe. This now, though, isn't working like that. Maybe because, this time, it isn't intrusion of the past. And because we are both out of our depth when the present is what's going wrong.

First Winter

Wankered so, and knee bending, we sang back to the flat. In the huge rain up Parkway and our street off that. Hanging out of lampposts. You applying coats to backs we only shrugged free of again.

Christ! This is like herding cats.
Miaow!

She and me. Then a chorus of that, through an ambulance whining. And a bath of its spray. Blinked too by its lights. Posing chip-based questions. Their general whereabouts and the possibilities of.

If you get in the flat without any more fuss, I'll consider going back out, but neither of you are coming with.
But I could carry them, Dad.
Or Stephen, I could.
I swear this must be my punishment for
Bad Dad!
Yes, I know.
No. Really you're not. You're lovely. I love you!
Well, that's good to
Do you love me?
Yes, I love you, Grace.
And Eily?
Yes, I love Eily as well, but please get in the fucking door.
Ah now, Stephen, no need to swear.
You are no fucking help. Please just get in as well.

Now

Remember when you had that nosebleed in the pub?

When?

In the Steele's. Right at the start.

I remember   what about it?

Nothing   just   just thinking about it.

Well, those were the days for worrying about blood.

I know   and I didn't at all.

You'll know for next time then.

I will.

Lucky him!

I bet he'll be thrilled.

Yeah, I'm sure he will.

Fuck us. We're always at this but then, the well hand leaves the injured one to offer itself. And I, more than willingly, take. Hold it gently in the silence that winds us around. This touch, despite our skins' bloody mappings, the most hope we can muster for now.

First Winter

Pulled up the stairwell. Or pushed when needs must, and they did.

God, you both reek.

Well, I've known you hammered so don't get high and mighty.

Maybe save that one for another time, Eil?

Eyes suggesting you meant it, but their intensity drink missed – preoccupied as I was by my sudden umbrage. Already hearing you again in the loo down that hall. Bitterly, echoly puking in the bowl hours of your heavy drinking back up.

That night Grace first called you, remember that?

I remember but   not now.

No   tell me about it?
I think Eily's said enough for tonight.

But drinking's woken the memory like struck flint inside. How drunk you were. Bad to me. Less, somehow, of my own transgression after it. More our effortful travel across copious lines to places where bodies should not. And sweet to martyr myself now your tone's got clipped – at least as the drink in me sees it.

Actually, I can tell her if I want.
Tell me!

Drawing myself up to what height my paralytic state will permit.

Well once upon a night there was a man who got very drunk, and he
Eily, don't.
Eily, do!
And he   and he
Please, Eily   no.

And then you didn't have to say more. Your face enough to make drunk sense dawn. Besides, it was only hump at the 'reek' comment led me to resurrect that thing. Which was between us, after all, from another time, and not for advertising in spite.

Ignore him, Eily, tell me everything!

But already my heckles were sobering down.

He was so pleased to hear from you, he just   celebrated too much.

Dad, you got very drunk?
I did.
So drunk you reeked?
He did   and even vomited.
Thanks, Eil.
Really, Dad?
That too, Grace. I can't lie.

But I stopped it then, short of the further dramas of that night. Cast eyes with you and saw there allayed acknowledgement. Then didn't like what I'd nearly done. Better the past remains our own. So as you opened the door, I went on in. It was Grace, gangling after, fell over. Right over on her face.

Oh shit!
Gracie, you all right?
Fine! I'm fine, Dad. Fine.

But so legless she couldn't get them under her again.

Okay then   let's try this.

And you gathered her up.

Eily, will you get her door, love?

Then carried her puppy limbs down the hall. Minding her head. Laying her down. Took her shoes off as she variously groaned versions of

That was fun.

And

> Eily   we should do that again!
> Hmmm.

As you peeled off her socks.

> Christ, you're soaked to the skin. Eily, pass her a towel,
> would you?

I chucked and stayed upright as you rubbed her feet. Pressed
them with your palms, like conducting heat. But I knew how cold
your hands could be. Still. It's the thought that counts. Then a rub of
her hair which, surely, left it in knots. Intentions however, and as
always, the best.

> Right   I'd better

Peeled her drenched jeans off to the floor before falling to wrangling her sopping jumper. Up. Up. Off over her head, leaving her
silver-froze body in damp bra and knickers. This you looked at a
moment. Went forward. Then couldn't and closed yourself off.

> Eily?
> Yeah?
> I can't do this part.
> What?
> Underwear and that   will you deal with it?
> Oh, yeah   fine.
> And get her in her night things? If you can.
> I'll sort her out   you go on.
> Thanks, I'll just maybe   fetch a basin   in case she's sick.

Still, she got a kissed cheek.

> Night, Gracie.
> Night, Daddy.

From some depths of her consciousness, that. The word. Like a stark volt through. And your cough to cover it in no way fooled.

> Stephen, I
>   No   I'm fine.

Stuck stroking her face though. At last kissing it again.

> Okay   okay   night night then.

And quick as quick, scrubbed off with your thumb, the tear you'd mis-spilled onto her cheekbone.

> You sleep well, my love.

Then got on out fast as you could.

Now

And for a brief moment, let the weather do its work. Storm skirling drainpipes below and aerials above. Gale, for a change, on the outside of us. Us and our hands, for once, not being useless. Bloodied fingers knitting. Preparing us to speak. He goes first. Then it's me. Then him and then me again.

> We'd been to see *Nostalghia*   I seem to remember.

That's right. I'd never seen it before.
I remember watching you watch it. You were   transfixed.
It was so beautiful I cried   and you kissed me after it.
You were so beautiful I couldn't help it. I remember that too.

First Winter

Your silver-froze body then as I came in. Wrangling your own sop-ping jumper off while the streetlight gazed in at the long silhouette in its gleam.

All sorted in there?
Yeah   your back's all wet.
I know   and she's settled?

Hand wiping your neck and undoing your belt.

She's fast asleep now.
That's good.

Treading down the soaked jeans. Damp hair on your legs.

Stephen   I
I might just go turn her on her side.
I'd say she's all right.
Well, thank you for helping out.
That's all right. Sorry about before.

No answer though. Just last of your clothes hit the floor. Fol-lowed by a towelling, of sorts. Hair and chest, with your balled-up jumper, before sweatpants and T-shirt took from a drawer.

Get changed, Eily. You'll catch your death.
          Did you hear what I said?
     I heard, and it's fine   you should still get dried off.

Which I started, as you got in the bed. Turned from while my chattered mouth said

          Stephen   I was drunk
          And you still are, so let's   just call it a night.

Therefore, it became 'A Night'. Yet another wedged in the hinge of this peculiar blight. And stood so stiff in it, I worried about arthritis despite being too young for that. Besides, who'd even care if I did? Would you carry me down the hall? Or poultice my joints – if that's a thing they still do? Or would you just stay put, faced to the wall, pretending you were there on your own? Down, down, deeper I went, to the extraneous nowhere of my exile. So, though drink made thought thick, it was a lone, brittle unpick of my freezing wet clothes. Then I fumbled for the nightshirt to, dampish, don. Slid on over to the not-too-much heat of your back. Do you or do you not like? With nothing indicating, I took my chance. Laid my head against. Self against. Arm round your waist. The smell of you comfort but also the menace of how it makes, always has, want. With such times in mind, I spread my hand on your stomach, thinking of fingers and what they might wander. Where I, if only

          Eil?
          What?
          Let's just go to sleep now, okay?

For you knew every signal like the back of your hand. Invented. Instigated. But, this time, would not respond. Just coughed a bit. Turned on your back. Rolled one long arm down on the duvet between. I lay, spied on and ignored the theatre of it until your profile feigned off into sleep. Your feints as familiar though as the dints of your body. Any moment I knew you would check. And Check.

What're you doing, Eil? Go to sleep.
    What are you doing, more like?
It's been an   intense sort of day so let's save this for another time, yeah?

But then so tired, too tired, I just started to cry. Hid into your shoulder. Tried not to wipe. Uselessly because, painfully, they kept wringing out. Heaving ribs up into sobs until, dark as it was – never totally dark – you knew. And turned. Laid one arm across.

Eily, no.   Oh no, Eily   stop   don't cry.
        Sorry   I'm trying   sorry   I can't
    No   don't be sorry   I'm sorry   It's just   I can't
You can't   what?
I'm just   not sure how to
    What?
Manage   all this   you and Grace.

Which opened my eyes. Right into yours. With their confusion but unvarnished truth.

        Will you always?
        I don't know.
            Want to try anyway?
                I

Even in hesitation though, assessment began. Of drunkenness.

– 144 –

Seriousness. The likelihood of a stop. You knowing I wouldn't so you'd have to trust in what brakes you might want to provide. Should that necessity arise. Saw it go inside you as, all the while, the set of your mouth was driving me wild. Wanted you to. Willed you to.

Won't you kiss me?
Eily, I
Just do.

And you did. Soft. Then so hard we banged teeth. Bumped noses and laughed it off against each's Arctic cheek. Found back into it again, quickly enough. That taste of you. Finding you. Inside my mouth. Finding with. A skate of chill hands. Touched me too then with fingers – the best frozen kind. As I slipped mine under your waistband, trying to ruin its point.

Fucking hell, Eil   I've missed you.
Me too.
Let's keep it down though.
Agreed.
Want to get on top?

I was about to hike up there when   Bowk! What? Brayed through the wall. Bowk again! Unequivocal as symphonic vomit hit the bowl hopefully plentifully, next door.

Fuck!

Long loud and awful. Then long loud and awful again. Before it'd even tailed off, you were off me and the bed.

Don't you dare fucking stop now.

Gracie's sick.
  Stephen!
Sorry   I'll just check. I'll be quick.
    For fuck's sake!
      Sorry.
    You're a fucking dick!
  I know   but I still have to do it.
   Oh then, just fuck off and die!
    Bit extreme, Eil?
  Not if you were me.

Let go so, while you got your bathrobe on. Checking first all body tells were gone before leaving me to lie listening in, to

    You all right, love? Been sick?
      Sorry, Dad, I just
    Don't worry about it. Anything else to come?
     I don't think so.
    Well, I'll empty this. Why don't you go rinse your mouth?

Fuckety cunt arse useless shit. Buried my head down in now cooling blankets. Anything not to witness her disintegrated walk. Or the father in you, with her basin of vomit, go by

Now

A sudden less bit of soughing against the glass.

    Is that the rain stopping, Eil?
    Don't think so   not yet.
     Turned out to be a pretty wild night.
     In more ways than one!

I knew you'd say that.

Well then, just be glad you're so safe here indoors!

Upon which he twists kitchen-rolled fingers and laughs into his chest.

Never mind   things have been worse.

Which isn't really saying much   considering.

Maybe not but I'm too tired to be cynical about it and   I'm glad you're here.

Despite the piccalilli?

Even because.

Weirdo.

I know.

Sorry   I'm an idiot.

No, just   hot-tempered but we'll be smelling it now for weeks.

Smiling because he smiles, and thankful of it, in spite of the dark under his eyes and gone pale lips.

How about I make amends by scrubbing off the stink?

Sounds good.

Then it's a deal   how does your hand feel?

Like it might've stopped, but   I won't unwrap it yet.

So, I take this chance of fingertips down his neck. Inlets of blue beneath the lifting whiteness. Then dip of his collarbone and rise of gooseflesh wherever December's breathed.

That's nice.

Head nodding to rest on my hip. Even reticence too knackered for more than relent. No more fight. Just touch and be instead. Stroke his hair and spurn my own alecking about the greys in there. Much as I love them, I don't think he'd care, at least not to hear it tonight. He likes this touch though, so I do. Nostalgias crossing *Nostalghia* in our quietude, but the mist fields of Italy are not what we see. Our past's landscape a pub up on Haverstock Hill. Our view below, Chalk Farm. To Camden. To the West End. To somewhere the river and Southbank after the Thames. Places for us where memory extends into times beyond these present and slipstreaming woes. But oblique also, as London is. Whenever it chooses. Whenever it changes its face. Whenever it turns its attention from answers to questions. From certainties into shrugs. A game of posing its problems in all kinds of sorts, from how did the skyline look before we last did? To, since when has the generation of Camden night been so different? Or how long has Greater London House been painted above where a 29's windows can see? London serves itself with no concession to the lives of those within, and the very best we can manage is to tie our patched histories to it. Inescapable, its indifference, most of the time – even from walls I've been kissed up against. Still, I have loved, and love it so well that it's a poor thanks to complain. Besides which, as always, it offers promise of return. Like hope that stemming his bleeding will reset us again upon more peaceable paths through the night – as several ticks, after tocks, suggest it might. Such easy solutions though, are rarely for us so, perhaps inevitably, London adopts 'Unforgiving' as our course for a little while yet. I hear it in his voice, feeling around for indifference. And know it in how hard my pulse goes.

    If I ask you something, Eily, will you tell me the truth?
        If I can   if I know it.
            Have you had enough?
            Of what?

Of this   of me?

What?

I mean, I knew it'd come   I just didn't think   I thought there'd be more time.

Stephen, it's not like that   and it wasn't.

Isn't that why you did it?

No   I   I

I don't even really mean why   I just mean   the way that you did?

Circuitous excuses fling around in me now. But his ask's so fucking anguished I deny them tongue. Not today and no matter how hard prevarication presses down. Besides which, if not everything, this crumb might do.

It wasn't   and I haven't   had enough of you   not at all.

And like fag smoke held for a long while, reprieve burns in the curl of his next breath out. Muscles discharging a suspicion confined, until now, to unspoken withins.

Do you believe me, Stephen?

I'd really like to, Eil.

Then forgoing elaboration, which I'd also certainly like, he slides out from under my hands.

First Winter

Enough! Fucking 'nough! Get out of the bed. Rip up and haul our duvet as well. You can sleep without. Or in with her. Or go to fucking hell! Now I was the one on the march. Past the bathroom where she was over the bowl. You ponytail holding in some weird revision of old. You and me. Then and there. The Camden Road flat bins. So do! Because what do I care?

Went to, and through, the kitchen instead. Rolled over the back of the sofa and up in the duvet. Here I'll make my stand. Castle and keep. And shut my eyes against more, although the familial activities from behind continued to afflict.

> Go on back to bed, love. I'll bring you something to drink.
> Sorry about that, Dad.
> No, it's all right, as long as you're better now.

Off she went then, and you came up the hall. Ran her a glass of water while I, on the sofa, was not even noticed before you headed back to her room. Settling her yet again! while I stared through the curtains. As scarlet in self as the red night out there. Whoops of other drunks and the gnaw of police cars. Near. Nearer. Then further. Far off. I stayed street attentive until her door shut and you, presumably, returned to our bed. Now a sheet with no body to hide from or against. Pillow but nothing for covering bone-frozen legs. Register. Go on. Register it and

Ah, come on, Eily! What the fuck is this?

Now

Up and across the kitchen to where his soaked coat hangs. I'd stop him but am stopped by the blood on my hands. A view of blood on my cuff and, where still unwiped, it sits in the lino beneath. Whosever's fingerprints in it making mazes and forests. And if I could keep making patterns from chaos, perhaps the night might yet be saved? But then, it's not my blood and he's the one walked away.

Where're you going?
I just

Roots around in his pocket and produces a soft pack of Marlboro Red.

Oh.

Hesitates, first. Doesn't, second. And third, just rips off the seal.

Smoking again then?
So it would seem.

Getting out his lighter. Balling the foil for the bin. Flinch for the many nicotine patches I once helped affix. Both us laughing at his resemblance to a victim of stings. All become a variation on a different string now I suppose. And do I object? Really? Not. I've missed it too, and besides like to watch, as I always have, him in the act. The lighting up, then just leaving it in. Sparing his cut hand but also reminding how legible a fag in his mouth can be, at least to those who can – and I can – read. Pleasure. Displeasure. Opacity. Whole gamuts run at a press of his lips. I've tried that trick too but have never managed it. Him Jesus- ing, mostly when I'd drop one lit. Sometimes on the bed. Once or twice on his chest.

Fucking hell, Eily, no one really needs to smoke without fingers!

I just envied the facility and unpremeditated grace. I shouldn't watch for it now, in the midst of all this, but somehow still cannot resist. Looking. Taking him in. Him steadily ignoring it, for staring at the room. Eventually though, giving in. Meeting my eyes. Then smiling. Fag hanging out the side of his mouth.

What?
You're so handsome when you smoke.
Jesus, Eil   what're you like?
I don't know   a mess?

But, of necessity, action overrides analysis.

Where're those ashtrays now?

There should be five or six, but who knows what was lost in that zealous clear-out – the one where his own evangelism reigned although the why of it was never said. Just did it of his own bat and I let him do that, along with all the other things I'd allowed without making mention of   the fact. No matter. Or no matter tonight.

Bottom of that cupboard, I think. The big glass one anyway.
Oh yeah   that's right. Any chance you'd look?

Indicating the kitchen-rolled hand. So I do the rummage, and find.

There you go.
Thanks for that.

In just the nick of time for his inaugural tap. Ridiculous now to think either would ever give up. We were always on the road back to here.

Can I have one?

Help yourself.

Slides over the lighter and pack and, if he's surprised, does not show that.

Ah   good to see the old Zippo back.

Sitting up on a stool and   where's he been keeping it?

Well   I couldn't chuck it   it was a gift.
From your oldest friend.
David   that's right.

And the cigarette rolls in his lips, meaning I should, though do not, resist asking

Do you still miss him?
What do you think? He saved my life   or at least helped me change it   pretty radically   plus he gave me the only place that had ever felt like home   before here. Him and Rafi. But you know all this.

Cigarette going right the way down and into a feeling he's struggling to hide. God, what am I doing, beyond making a hames of it tonight? It's keeping him talking though. And from going to bed. And, if I pull at it just right, from asking me questions for which I'll have no good replies – that I can come up with right now. Just carry on then, with your feeble plan, and hope inspiration colludes.

Sorry   that was a stupid thing to say.
No, but   it's been a hard day and I can't think about David now too.

I know   I'm sorry you

then just stare where distraction's been willing me not to – the blood on his sleeve and all down his front. Drying there now. Will it ever wash out? What the fuck did I go and do? My eyes have been followed, however, on their sartorial route.

Eily   it's all right. It's just a cut.

I shirk that round inside to see if downplay works. It doesn't and, as symptom, only makes matters worse. So, to continue, I'm left faking a normality no longer present between us.

Been smoking again long?
Couple of weeks.
        When do you?
After the show sometimes   or before   or waiting for
the bus.
Why haven't you   here?
I didn't want to   in case   you know.
        What?
    You were   upset.

Don't know why he thinks I would be, but   considerate and I reciprocate in kind.

Well   I'm not so   go ahead.

Light my own up then and happy draw. Spinning right to my head like months of let go.

Fuck! Isn't it the best though?

It really is.
Let's promise to never again bother giving up.
Yeah, Eil, I'll drink to that!

Take it. Take my chance.

Want another beer then?

Him looking at me sideways   but looking.

Why not?

Delighted so, I go get two more cans out. Set them on the breakfast bar between and redraw my stool up. Already mid 'nother drag
before catching his eyes on it – the cigarette I hold, then on the
memory of why he'd forgone smoking. And just growing so still.
Bit his fag end a bit. Don't don't don't. Please stay awake from your sleep,
I think, though do not say.

First Winter

And then again.

I mean it, Eily, what the fuck?

Making back up the hall and in no mood for it. Me. Or whatever
ruction was keeping you from a warm bed.

Give me the fucking duvet.
No!
Give it!

Grabbing. I yanked it back.

Give me that fucking duvet, Eily!

Pulled it up all the way up until both heard it rip.

Now look what you've done!
Frankly, I don't give a shit. You can lie here and freeze to
death if you want but I've had enough of the antics, so
come back to bed or fuck off.

Then dragged it behind you down the hall. And the door
slammed. I did not expect that. Sobriety rising in the chill around
it, as a variety of sorrys crossed with NO, YOU CAN FUCK OFF.
I got to my feet but so cold on the lino. Grace at least passed out.
You though, with no real drink in you, undoubtedly meant it. And
just as undoubtedly, without that bloody duvet, tonight wasn't
going to work so well out here. Thought then of coats. Yes! Except
they'd just feel of rain. Tablecloths? None. Spare duvet? On Grace.
Could I climb in with her? Too much to explain plus dignity'd for-
bid admitting a brawl. And what would she think of that anyhow?
Blame me, I'd say. I know I definitely would. If I were her and I'm
not. Manifestly not the same. To myself anyway but, come to mention it, what was it you said?

I'm just   not sure how to manage   all this   you   and
Grace.

Bit under-specific in light of all this, but I was sober enough to
see pattern now in the mess. Perhaps small perhaps I could've been
more sympathetic. Could've just let you   off the hook   if only
for a little. Yes   perhaps. Then eff away at myself for impatience.

For always wanting the fore. You though   were very hard to share. And amid that reckoning with myself, I realised I maybe had made   mangers everywhere. All for me and nobody else.   Even your daughter. But is that correct? Not even share you with Grace? No, I had done   so that wasn't right. Besides, I never wanted a father. I'd had my own   once   and I wasn't looking for him again. With so much light between, it was an easy separation. My mind though kept crawling until it arrived at the thought   with me and Grace, is that divide harder for you to see? Maybe that age gap is confusing? Not yours and mine. That's big and clear. Mine with Grace – so scarcely there that is it? It's hard to see? To keep the father for her and the other for me, ensuring never the twain shall meet? That your pulled wires don't find the wrong connect? Because you will never trust yourself. Will always be afraid of her. Fuck!   Fuck!

And bells rung around me like that was true. That's what's been all along   eating at you.   Fuck! Fuck! How did I not notice? We can be daughters or lovers but definitely not both. So   for safety's sake   I'd been   sworn off? Yes, it beats like a heartbeat. And I got up to go tell you. But then thought Maybe not. Maybe tonight's already been enough and what everyone needs is a few hours' calm. Let you sleep. It will keep. And laid myself back down. Pulled a few cushions on, my nightshirt around, and tried not to think of the cold. Took a while. Booze helped though. Then I did, could at last, fall asleep.

Dreams, maybe, but none I recalled before I began floating, in the bluish early, when I woke into warmer than, by rights, I should. Felt a body there.

What's going on?
What? Go back to sleep.

Return of the accursed duvet, along with yourself. Both arranged around me on the couch in what felt like sleep.

What about Grace?
   What about her?
   If she sees us like this?
What if she does? We're decent.
   But the meaning
Eily, it's five in the morning and I couldn't care less.
   Okay, but Stephen?
      What?
         I realised something earlier.
      Great. Tell me in the morning, all right?

More than happy to, now you were there. Aura of the Camden Road three-foot bed in the air. Honestly, I think I preferred it, us together, cramped in. But before the advent of greater contemplation, I went away with it again, for a couple more hours at least.

Now

Sit quiet. Sip and sip. Enjoying the fag. Enjoying the drink. Might almost be, if we stay in this minute, a happy return to form. More. A fall back into the groove of those hours taken as given on sofas. Tubes. In cinemas. Chip shops. Theatre queues. Doing nothing fancy or meaningful. Just passing ourselves slowly through time. Together, however, being the point. For although there's been nothing but proximity of late, the together part's crumbled to fucking shite. The closest we've come, in the last two months, was because there would be questions and the person with the clipboard had to know

And have you, since?

Yes.
How many times?
Once.
How was it?
Fine.
Pain?
No.
Any blood?
No.
So everything's normal in that department?
Well   I wouldn't say that.

Even now feeling it in my face. The awful night I obliged us into making the effort so I could tick a yes for that. Getting it over with, like flies under glass. The furthest reaches we could manage, while still being face to face. So unlike us I hoped it wasn't the frontier of always. But, for fear it was, neither's had stomach for it since. Not to correct. Even to check. Better to glance off ourselves and into separate sleeps. Perhaps a limping sort of death, but with no cold corpse touching at least. Definitely there was two of us in it or out of it   until lately   when all my new writ paragraphs of the past showed something in me had   returned.

> Nice beer this, Stephen.
> What?

To a place where I do want. And do want to check. Or let my body forgive me and his as well so we could be again as before. A dicey-ish slice of territory though. Even I know that.

> Good beer this.
> It is.

Where did you get it?
First night present, I think.
Who from?
Our resident Helen of Troy!
Nice of her.
Yeah, it was meant as a joke.
What about?
Something to do with the North.
She seems a nice woman.
She is.

Fuck! And what the fuck's that? Burling around inside me like I don't know what. Except I do and its only response is

Oh, is she now?

His head cocking and taken aback.

Why are you saying it like that?
Maybe it was the picture in the programme.
Which?
The one with your tongue down her throat.
Which is the play, Eily   as you well know.

But something. What? Funny peculiar on his face. Is he   is he pleased about it? Why would he be? It's only a spot of inane envy.

Well   maybe you don't need to enjoy it so much?
How do you know I enjoy it? You've only seen it once.
Once was enough.
Well, you never mentioned it then.
So do you enjoy it?

It's fucking stage kissing.
            So?
            So?
             So do you?
            No!

For some reason, beyond mine though, his eyes gleam. And I've not seen that mischief for so long I want to follow it down.

            Why're you looking at me like that?
                Like what?
                    Smiling that way.
                I don't know maybe because you're
            What?
                Jealous.
        I'm not.
                    You are.
        Well, even if that was true
                    Which it is.
        It's no reason to smile.
                    Sorry   it's just
            What?
        Something normal   that's all, Eil.
            What's that meant to mean?
            It's just a reaction that's   not hiding anything.

And how should I take this? Furiously, mostly, before my brain can react.

        That's a shitty thing to say.
            I didn't mean it like that. I just meant
        That I'm some kind of fake? Some kind of manipulative
        fucking

– 161 –

Eily, you're taking it the wrong way.
Don't tell me what I'm doing! What are you doing?
 What?
Why were you really back so late?
 Stop it! Before you say something you'll regret.
Why? Is there some secret you don't want found out?
 Wow   and you're already there!

Sitting back on his stool. Eyes alive and which can have I opened?
Fuck! Then I understand.

 Sorry.

But too little, too late.

 How dare you ask that?
 Stephen, I
 After all that's happened?

And now we've upped sticks. Jesus Christ. Things at work here
that are far worse than time. I don't want this, in no way want this,
but we have arrived. At last. At it. By accident, or subconscious design?
Mine? Or his, perhaps? Some cunning at work because, although
I am the one who opened it, he was waiting at the gate. And let's
face it, he knows how to wait. I am the more front-foot impatient,
which leaves me only to brazen it now.

 What's that supposed to mean?
 You know what it means, Eily, let's not fuck about.
 Fine! What am I hiding you're so keen to find out?

Badly played that. He always calls my bluff. And this time too.

Shit! All defences fucked. Because before I can refuse, or even talk, he has my hand. Has turned it up. Has yanked back my sleeve. Has pulled my wrist across. Showing. All of it. And then him saying

    That.
      No.
   Yes. That.
     Stephen, please.
    You asked. So   that's what I want to know   all about.

So here it is. Will I go there again? I could but   it's very fucking hard, that time. Not long ago either. Just this autumn gone. And it's only winter now.

First Winter

All crooked in on you, re-getting from sleep. Nose beside nose and an arm round my waist.

    What're you doing up here then?
   Well, if I let you freeze to death, what the fuck would
   Gracie say?

And squeezed me to make me laugh. Grumped though, and hungover, I was faster to snappish.

   I'm surprised you could tear yourself away from watching
   her puke.
  Love's labour, Eil – from which you've also frequently
  benefitted   as I recall.
   Oh, shut up!

You were foul enough last night so   let's let it go?

As you let yourself slide from the sofa.

Well, you also didn't exactly cover yourself with glory.
             Agreed   shall we call it quits?

Sat then creakily beside, making us face to face.

             Kiss me and I'll consider it.

Which you did. Without luxury and only light on the lips, pref-
aced by a swift check for her first. Arrgghh. To annoy you for it or
be annoyed by? That was the question. But on finding I was, in fact,
unfussed, rolled my eyes and my interest onwards to what I
should've asked long before.

             What did Danny think of the cut?
                  He liked it   had a few thoughts, of course.
                  What about?
             Think he was surprised by some of the choices. You know,
             complained I'd cut his best bit. Where had that close-up
             gone? What happened to that scene? I've done it myself so
             I know how it is, but he got it   once I explained.
                  But he thought it worked   overall?
             He did.
                  And were you pleased with what you saw   yourself?
             That's more complicated, isn't it? How about a spot of
             breakfast?
             Sounds good. Where's Grace?
             Think I heard her before, but no sign yet.

Contented so, I watched you at kettle and cups. Bread in the toaster. Nice trivial us. Barged into though by remembering last night's last thought – about me and Grace getting caught in some loop, the same loop, in your mind. How to say it though? Or ask?

> Eggs, Eil?
> What?
> Eggs?
> Are they fresh?
> Couldn't tell you. Want to chance it?
> Yeah.
> Scrambled?
> Please.

And further rattled my posit as you headed to the fridge. Bury it or mention? Might as well, the devil said, so I went on his nod. Just tipped a toe, at first, before the whole wade in.

> Who else has seen it now, Stephen?
> No one.
> Nick?
> He's the producer, Eil, of course.

As a teabag got teaspooned to the bin. Drips smirching white plastic. Spoon chucked to the sink.

> And   why did you never send the script to Grace?
> What?
> You said you were going to. I remember you saying it.

Production groaned to a halt while your whole body turned.

– 165 –

Face knowing where this might go but then deciding to take me along. And yes, a low satisfaction in that.

I planned to. I thought I would but   when it got to it
    What?
Just couldn't.
    But it's so good   why not?
Ah, Eily the thought of her reading that stuff.
    What? It's beautiful.
    Don't think you'd say that if it was your dad.
        It's not just about those things though, is it?
    You know what I mean.
        She just wants to know you.
        And I want that. But the film isn't knowing me. It's work.
        It's personal to you though.
    It is, but   what if it changes how she feels about me? I've
only just got her back.

And I could see how evasion would be easier than mess. At least for this while, until the first dusts had settled. But   I am not your glass daughter or in need of protection.

    So why haven't you shown it to me?

That gave pause, and that pause roared between, as you found ferocious interest in the bottom of your tea. As I lurched in through memory for what I might've missed in those months of reading, then talking about it. In the time it was made, and the time after it, when I never doubted being on the inside. So now, unwanted as it was, it came.

    You're afraid it'll change how I feel about you too.

Oh God, and your face. That *was* it.

    I don't, Eily, but
  You think I don't understand? After everything we've said?
    No, I do   it's just   seeing it is different.
      Seeing's just next.
     No, seeing collapses reality in on itself and then
         What?
       It can't   I can't   be unseen.
      I know how things get made, Stephen. I make them too.
   I know you do, but
     What? I'm just a student?
  No   just that   you're both so young.
    I'm not Grace! We are not the same person. Or can't you
    tell any more ?

So there it was. Last night's notion as stone. And on the moment of casting, I saw the first snow drift beyond the pane. Harmless. Aimless. But before I could say, there was an entirely other look on your face and

      What kind of fucking question is that?

Straight to the depths. How quick there, you and me. But what truths didn't we know? And many other things. So, step back and retract? Or in for penny? Instinct said to put my whole pound down.

   Are you finding it hard to tell us apart?
     I don't know what you're getting at but I'd be very careful
     now, if I were you.

– 167 –

I don't mean in that way   the bad way.

   In what way then?

I just   wonder if   you don't know how to be more than one thing at a time and   because of your mother

   I don't want to talk about her.

Grey eyes on the still open kitchen door, probably wishing it barred as any fortress.

   I don't either. But   listen   no one wants to cross anything.

  What are you talking about?

  Me and Grace   we know which side we belong on.

     What?

   You can stop   worrying   about that   with us.

    That?

   That something will go   wrong.

  Stop now. Just stop!

   Stephen, I know you get   scared she's inside somewhere

  but   she's not. You don't have to turn that   whole part of you off just because Grace is around and

     Jesus Christ! Enough!

  All right, but   you know what I mean?

Nothing, nothing but deadened-down sound. Outside at least snow. Inside only affront. Then from the left

   Morning, Dad.

Grace in the door. Long, stiff and wrung. Lightening up your scowl though.

   Morning, love. How are you feeling now?

Rounding the breakfast bar to gather her up. Making her the one and only.

Embarrassed   rough.

You just laughed and rubbed the last five minutes out.

Don't worry. You'll be fine.

Let herself be led then to a stool and sat.

Hey, Eily. Why're you on the sofa? Don't say Dad kicked you out?
No! No. Nothing like that.

And glanced to you but got no glances back. My 'You know what I mean?' would be getting no answers. By the look of you too, if I could, I'd unask. Then Grace set forth on her own.

So Dad, I've been thinking.
About what?
About what   I think   you're worried about.

Taking care then, you held it far out. Lit up a fag for the sake of your pulse?

I see. Regarding   what?
Your film.
Oh fuck   not you too!

Relieved and annoyed and all at once.

Well, Eily and I discussed it last night and
  Did you?
   We did so   will you hear me out?
All right then. Say your piece.

The sink leant against and arms folded across. If daunted she did not show it – though checked me for Go Ahead – for which I was grateful and nodded. Then she cut right in.

   I think   maybe   you think I'll judge you.
  And why would you judge me for a film I've made?
    Because   it's based on you.
     Who told you that?
     Eily.
        Did she?

Through your gritted teeth as I fuck! fucked away in my head.

  Don't be pissed off with her. You should have told me yourself.

And that cooled your heels.

   Well   that's probably right but
   Dad, it won't make any difference   I swear.
  I know you think so, love, but you haven't seen it yet and
    Haven't you had enough being by yourself?

If your heels cooled before, now they were froze. And all the silence in you put on a show of stillness. Still as I've ever seen. Feeling nowhere to go. Then finding the window and

God, look it's snowing out there.

White the moment. But she took less than a blink. I saw you
thumb excuses and wondered if she did? You did. You were. Were
about to. Then didn't and just said

['] Actually, that's exactly why, love.

And she looked so like you when that answer arrived. Ready
already with her reply.

Then you've got it the wrong way round, Dad.

Right up to the hilt. I'll give her that. In your favour, you too realised it. Hoist upon it, even! Chewed your cigarette. And uncurled
your long fingers.

    Okay.
     Okay?
    Okay.
        Meaning   yes?
       That's what it means.
    You'll show me the cut?
      I'll show you.
       Both of us?

Without looking at me

    Yes, I'll show you both   but after it
      What?
    I'll need a stiff drink and   a lie down.

But this much sowed quick smiles between you and her – before you faced to the window once more, in apparent hopes of some avalanche as reprieve. Not likely now she had wrung you to this. From my sofa banishment, I was pleased too – although out-argued by her and unanswered by you. How did I imagine my insight would be received? With thanks for fingers stabbed in a past that'll never heal? For perfectly aligning the only two people you'd do anything to keep separate? I have done this to myself. So – with breakfast no longer on offer – I was left to my own.

     Right   I'm off to get dressed.

No reaction. Just flakes shadowing over your face as drifts of Fairy filled the basin. On out I, as behind me, the practical question

     How soon can we do it?
       I'll give them a call about booking a slot.
     Great. Soon as possible, I hope.
       Well, you'll have to take what you get.

Which, until now, had all been mine. You, and that space in you, you carried around that I alone had had rights to encroach. The same space she'd had to wait beyond. But now it was hers, and mine was the time of being beyond the pale.

Now

So I pulled away, but he pinned my wrist there. Cool on the Formica if nowhere else.

     Stop it!
     No.

Stephen, let go!

I've been doing that for way too long now.

I don't want to talk about it. And I don't want you to.

Well, I do, so let's just get on with it.

Then ran his finger its barbarous length. Replicating its every curve and bump. First time, far as I know, he's ever touched it. Definitely first time I've watched anyone look.

Stephen   I

All I want is why, Eil, because   this just fucking scares me so much.

First Winter

Preview theatre. First I'd been in. Stink of mildew. Old booze. Fresh fags – yours probably, from at the back. Where you hung round the door, engrossed in some kind of projectionist confab. A couple of Not that ones, and the clank of cans. Mutterings. The occasional laugh.

Where're the fucking scissors? And why would you need that? Grace and me though, just already sat. Quiet with anticipation but blood loud with impatience. Seat saved for you in between. Which, after some last give-and-take, you took.

Sorry about the delay. Bloody Sellotape snapped.

Before we can ask more about this, or its mysterious properties, you'd raised a hand and said

All right, Chris, whenever you're ready, mate.

And then the lights went down.

Film

INTERIOR. CAFE. DAY. Blue mug of tea. A clockwise-going dessert spoon. Stop. Anticlockwise then. Stop. Clockwise again. Soundscape of caff blurring the distance between us and whoever it is. BLACK.

EXTERIOR. VIEW OF LONDON. NIGHT. As it was. I assume. *Looked at from way up.* A hill? A roof? *Full of itself then,* just as today. *Traffic. Shops. Humanity. Breathing each, in and out. Sirens bluing the moult of yellow lights. Purpling red ones. Giving face to their roar. Streams dividing to byways. Turnings off. Along streets going nowhere. Trimming roads leading west, north, south, east, et cetera, as well as every other place they wish. And so the eye travels. Taking it all in. Indifferent, until the camera sees the hands to whom it belongs. Then disliking itself* dirty fingernails or what? *chooses to pan right away.*

Back to us. In the preview theatre. Now breathing that light. Covertly spying into the notebook open on your thigh. Grace on one hand. Me the other side, as your film begins its trek across our faces, as well as your pen-tapping hand.

> The score's not finished so you'll have to imagine it. Obviously, it will help. And I think the title card will come at this point. Then back to black. Then on.

EXTERIOR. HOLLOWAY ROAD 1978. DAY. Weird beautiful path under snow – except not. Bubbles swept from the floor of a butcher's shop, now expiring out on the street amid threads of its own sawdust and meat. Still beautiful though, and still weird, especially for the Holloway Road. Well, I know that's where it's set. No one else probably would because it's only pavement. I listened so carefully though, every night, that I know too where this shot leads. *Young man walking down the street. Hands in his coat. Fag in his mouth. Stooped until some Oi Fucker-ing makes him look up. And it's Danny looking up,* looking so Danny to me, but also like he is doing his Stephen – sharp way your eyebrows lift. And I wonder, do you realise this? Or don't you read it like that?

Angle up a quick glance to check this theory out but, in return, receive only a whispered

What is it?
Nothing.
Oh okay.

Hard to gauge. Maybe I'll ask later on.

Now, becoming apparent, something's hid up his coat. Weight making him limp with concealment and, actually, not even that well concealed. Interesting tracking shot, that. *He could do with a meal. Sides of his mouth broken down. Raw too round the nose. Warily, if not guiltily, avoiding cop cars. At a thump to his back though. 'Shit!' down it goes 'I said Oi Fucker!' in a clatter of scraps.* Of what? Metal. Maybe lead? Not much, quantity-wise. Lucky prisings at best. *With feigned indignation righting himself, 'Excuse me?' says he,* first time we hear him speak. Good Sheffield accent too. Well done, Danny *but noting the brick shithousedness of his assailant, who's all 'Now then, fucker, what you got there?' 'Nothing.' 'Don't look like nothing to me. You get that off my roof?' 'No.' 'Really?' 'No!' 'Don't lie, you fucking junkie. I saw you.' 'I didn't.' But gets hit a slap. 'Yeah, you did.' 'No, get off me!' Another whack. Hard enough the young man grabs hold of him, not to collapse. 'Hands off, junkie' pushing him back. 'Now you're going to pick that up, every last bit . . .' But, seeing his chance, the young man takes to his heels. 'Oh, no you don't!' and the beefeater legs after, surprisingly quick. Following him too, out into weaving the traffic. Young man getting lorry clipped but keeping right on. Both making the other side. Beefeater even gaining, until 'No! Fuck!' he skid-slips in dog shit. 'Fuck! You come back here, you cunt!' He is left alone with his effing though as the young man makes into the distance, rounds the corner and disappears.*

See you smirk to yourself as you scribble a note which seems to read '1 s off front.'

What're you smiling at?
Nothing, just   thank fuck for that dog! He'd have spilled me all over the road.

But as I think to ask more, you already know and only point me back to the screen.

Young man still running, in close-up, laughing through his bust lip. Holding the bloke's wallet he's somehow managed to lift. Checking over his shoulder. No one in sight. So can revel now in his getaway.

There'll be music here too. Maybe The Damned's cover of 'Help'.
Will you be able to?
Not sure yet. But we'll cut this again to whatever it is – just to make it more playful, you know?
I can see that.

Grace adding

I don't know that band.

And I

It'd be really good.

EXTERIOR. HOLLOWAY ROAD. DAY. He's home free now, wherever that might be. No pursuants behind and ahead only city. The entire freedom of. Except suddenly, and dramatically, not. Stumbles forward like he's run into some different wall. STOP. Blood draining. Eyes back in his head. Then doubling over. Stomach? Chest? I know what though and, I suppose, so must Grace. *Still, a pall in the witness of that pain. Him alone in it too with a body now panicking. Desperate to keep upright. Coughing for breath. Distressed enough that, but for it being the first ten minutes, this could go either way. BLACK.*

Swallow down hard. Say nothing. Prepare. You know where this film goes to and how far. We are barely in the front door so really, get a grip! Meanwhile, you just scrawl another '1 s off e' kind of note and begin tapping the pen on your lip. But already the camera's had enough so cuts to another view.

INTERIOR. DOLE OFFICE. DAY. Dole queue, with its line of loiterers as you'd expect. Girls in short skirts. Older men in caps. Young men smoking, being smart alecks. And him, hands in his pockets, called up 'Next!' to the desk. Dole officer recognising him from the off, apparent in the close-up of his smirk and her sceptical response. 'Nice to see you again, Angela. How've you been?' Her ignoring this and just taking the book he's put down. 'Any work in the last two weeks?' 'I wouldn't be here if I had.' 'Not necessarily true . . .' 'Would I lie to you, Angela?' 'Yeah, you fucking would . . . Anyway' getting herself professional again 'says here you're an actor. What kind of actor is that?' 'As you know, Angela, largely the unemployed type but, otherwise, of stage and screen.' 'Doesn't seem to have been too much of either lately.' 'Dry spell, you know how it is.' 'Or maybe you're just not that good at it?' 'Angela! No! You're cutting me to the quick! How about I take you out back and give you my Hamlet . . . again.' Biting the inside of her cheek not to laugh she, instead, gives him the stamp. 'Lucky for you I'm the cultured type.' 'Oh, I know that, Angela, which is why you always get an encore from me.' She counts the notes out and pushes them across. 'Go on, you chancer, hop it.' Pocketing the notes 'Ta' he raises a brow 'Five minutes?' She doesn't reply, only looks him over, although her expression implies the answer is Probably will.

Jesus, Danny has you down. Almost unbearably.

EXTERIOR. ALLEYWAY. DAY. An alley five minutes later. Them fucking up against the bins. 'I swore I wouldn't do this again.' 'Really? Why'd you swear that?' 'Because these are the bins and I don't even like Hamlet.' 'I could give you the abridged version, if you like?' 'Oh no, don't you fucking dare, unless you want to be eating Spam all next year!' 'So sexy when you're threatening.' 'Just get on with it.' Which he does, while also fishing her pocket for her purse. Stashes it in his own. Then, in recompense, gets so vigorous he brings about imbalance. 'Fuck!' Both falling hard against the bins, toppling them too and ending up on the ground.

This the moment you judge best to obscure your face. Pinched bridge of the nose expanding to a generalised rub of the forehead. I don't even think Grace notices, she's so glued to the screen. But what the fuck must she be thinking? What the fuck would I, if I were her?

And he still finished off before immediately getting back up. 'Where'd you think you're going? I'm not done yet.' 'Yeah, I'm sorry about that.' Just doing his fly, straightening himself. 'Got to go see a man about a dog.' 'Yeah, more like horse.' 'Sorry?' But Angela has no more patience for this. 'No wonder your girlfriend put you out on the street.' Getting up too, working her skirt back down. 'You're a shit! You know that?' 'So I've been told and, I'm afraid, I can't disagree!'

I look at you. You look at me.

> I've heard that one.
> Really? When was that?
> You really want me to say.

Mmmm   maybe not.

Music here too, Dad?

Sorry, what?

Will there be music here as well?

Yeah   there will   to underscore the change.

Me and her looking back then at the screen, which was shifting again. Growing darker. Going down.

EXTERIOR. ALLEYWAY. DAY. Him tracked along, until Angela's long gone. Emptying the purse. Chucking it over the wall. Losing the cheek in his eyes until all his vaunt's gone. Followed by a strange kind of swallow dry mouth? *Then inspecting his hands like expecting a shake. None there though.* Or none there yet? *Quickening up. Looking ahead. As if all that was previous no longer exists and what's coming next is everything.*

Now, yet more in you shifts – concealed behind your note-making at the speed of light. 'Longer on M' and 'D 3 quick.' Then Oh yeah, I know what this is. And sit further forward, all the better to see, while still denying to myself an unconscionable interest in watching you in this act. Well, not you, Danny, but anyway   I know what I mean.

By which time the far end of the alley's been reached, where some friend waits, or just someone waits for him. Ratbaggy too and knackered seeming. 'All right?' 'Yeah. You?' 'Yeah.' 'Same?' 'Yeah, same.' 'Cool.' Exchange gets made and he's already on his way. He has so much to do. But then 'Mate! Hey, mate! Want me to come with?' 'Why would I want that?' 'So I can keep an eye on you . . . in case.' 'Of what?' 'Your . . . health thing . . . you know. I could keep an eye out . . . in return for a taste. Just a little one, enough to . . .' 'Yeah, all right, come on.' And the little ratty scumbag starts catching him up. But hard, with those long legs, for the short ones to keep up. I've known that problem myself.

I think I want to crosscut this with the start of the next scene – just the walking, once the dialogue's finished, but   well you can tell me what you think.

Only I reply, but then maybe Grace doesn't know what you mean? Or maybe she prefers to keep all this as window? A way for seeing in without getting involved? I want to see too, but I am nuts and bolts also. Or   to stay on the inside, have to be? No, I want to know it all and be in it with you – as I am in its aftermath.

I'll keep an eye on it and tell you later on.

INTERIOR. PUBLIC TOILET. DAY. The young man's long fingered hands. Bluish for human skin but, regardless, elegant. Carefully laying instruments out like place settings and plates. Except a syringe – not soup spoon. Matches. Shoelace. And the actual spoon, from no desirable set, with its handle already bent out of shape. His accompanying monologue, as impassive as its logic, is strange and sends grave walking shivers down my spine. 'I don't really need it, it keeps me calm. That's the thing. Stops the heart getting over excited, you know what I mean?' 'Oh yeah, mate, yeah.' 'It's just a kind of management thing and I can give it up any time. It's just for now, you know?' 'Yeah, yeah, I can see that' but sounding more like he is licking his lips at what's getting tipped as if finest China tea. Also, becoming apparent, not a dining room really. Two of them on some toilet floor. Grey lino diamonds representing bogs everywhere. Piss puddles correcting any impression this might be somewhere you'd ever want to end up. Still, and meticulous, the hands continue their work. Medical in their method, despite the environment. Heating. Plunging. Tying off. The fingers trembling a little but not enough to cause spillage or mishap. Justifications, however, start dying off the closer to zero it gets. And he does not show us that moment. Just the POV as it cuts between hands, and the two of them. *Turning into his. Looking back at the cistern. Then at the chain. Then to where the toilet seat should be behind his head. And 'I'll just take that, mate, if you don't mind?' A jerk, while the needle must get yanked out, and the camera grows too tired to look. Slumps to the side. Off down the green cubicle wall. To the floor, with its urinary pools. To the young man's laceless shoes. Then to oblivion beyond the gap visible beneath the door. Going. Going. Going. Gone. With only tricklings and drips from above.*

Me looking at you. You looking at her. Her looking only at the screen. Say something.

      I think it works, Stephen. You should leave it as it is.
      Yeah   maybe you're right   thanks.

Nodding real gratitude over, away from her head. Then eyes lowering again, down the side of her face, wondering what you've done. Or just what's going on? Fixedly though, she does not turn or give you any clues. And the film continues, so I continue with it.

INTERIOR. CHILDHOOD HOME. DAY. (FLASHBACK.) A boy sits at a wooden kitchen table on a wooden kitchen chair. Not tall enough yet for his feet to touch the floor. Staring ahead. Slightly upward. Just a small boy. No music. No sound effects. Nothing is said but, as his mother steps into the frame, his eyes slowly raise and, suddenly, everything is. Unnervingly strained, for his young age, like there are terrible fears to allay. And how do you get a child to do that?

    How did you get that look from him, Stephen? He can't be more than six.
      Opal Fruits.
    Really?
      They're his favourite, so I said if he guessed which colour

I had in my hand, he'd get the rest of the pack. Then I just
raised it really slowly behind the camera. He got it second
take.

And what colour was it?

Red.

Amazing.

Yeah, I like red as well.

No. Him!

Oh yes no   his face is just   great.

And he looks so like Danny.

I know. He was perfect.

Shush!

Sorry, Grace.

Sorry, love.

Soon enough though, I see why you'd taken your eye off. Or
didn't seem to mind that I had.

*The mother's hand raises. The boy gets a slap. Cut away. Straight
away before he reacts.*

Grace wincing to whiplash in fright. You already talking before
you realise. As you do though, hesitation enters your voice and a
wish to unsting it for her.

We've turned up the crack of that slap   just   to punctuate
it. Obviously it's an exaggeration of real life.

She just nods and the film keeps unforgivingly on.

CUT TO:

*INTERIOR. PUBLIC TOILETS. DAY. Pulled back and forth, the
young man manhandled awake. Hands dug into his coat and dole*

money extracted. Then, for good measure, his prone body administered a few kicks. One to the stomach. Another to the head. Ratty scumbag light fingering all paraphernalia else before making off, with some heftier confederate, out the bathroom door. 'Sorry mate, it's just, you know, needs must and all that!' Young man not even looking, just feeling his tongue around his mouth, then coughing a bloody flob onto the floor before passing out again.

Gross.

Well, you try getting kicked in the head.

Playing with me but watching Grace, carefully, perpetually, on the slant. Her unreadable. Barely moving a muscle. No glancing left or right. Less than no interest in the film as an external object. And while it is my window also, I am piqued by a different view.

INTERIOR. TOILETS. EVENING. BLACK. Bleep. Bleep. Medical sounding. Tinny and rhythmic. But disinterested enough to resolve into background the second his sight starts to return. Young man coming to, again. He is here and not yet dead which is a surprise, even to himself. So, choices get made. Sore limbs explore their range while feet begin finding to floor. Hoarse wrenching groan as he arrives at stood up. Trying to orientate, looking about, wipes a piss-soaked sleeve over his bloodied mouth. Steps from the cubicle and, feeling for a fag, initiates his own head for the door. Forward, as if he knows where.

EXTERIOR. ARCHWAY. EVENING. London going as he goes but also rounding on him. Trapping him inside limping coils of illogical motion. Finding and refinding himself back where he was. Or is he? Or is this Archway now? But one more blurred pass of those broke lights. That lad in the Irish pub still looking out. Those bints at the bus stop cackling. 'Look! Fucked cunt's back!' Is that him in the window? Or the drunk with the Woollies bag? Either way, London is moving. Keeps moving. That much he sort of sees. Feels it's refusing its sense then, only to him. Like the city's expecting some rational reaction with which he cannot furnish it. And then there's a low wall. The place to give up. As the camera pans, he even avoids the patches of vomit, and sprinklings of glass, to sit himself down. Smoke his fag and seem to wonder if this is the moment in which he'll die because, after all, why not? Resigned, he closes his eyes, the better to ignore it and just let happen, whatever it is.

BLACK. And, again, that medical bleep.

CUT TO:

The wall, and behind his eyelids, eyes shift as if encouraging that thought on its way.

CUT TO:

BLACK again.

CUT TO:

Oh   and this must be their old flat in Finsbury Park.

INTERIOR. BEDROOM OF THE FINSBURY PARK FLAT. DAY. (FLASHBACK.) 'What're you doing? What're you doing? Jesus Christ. Fuck!' From above, into the camera, a young woman panics. Pushing her hair behind her ear. Near distracted with distress, she strikes the POV, hard, on what sounds like the face. Immediately fish-eyeing it into a less absent conscious. Each cut back and forth after betraying an increase in its focus. Initially, it stays mostly on her. Tracking her movements as if alarmed by her fury. Gradually though, it becomes more self-aware. Grows somewhat less frightened if not much less bewildered. Sits up. Scans the clean, shabby room. It knows where it is. Then where to look. And vertically tilts to pan up itself. Legs. Stomach. Chest. The needle in its arm. Long fingers swift. Deftly plucking out and shoving down the side of the bed. 'Just stop! Fucking stop! I've seen it already!' The thin hands relinquishing. Fingers migrating to the face as the POV prepares to engage with the anguish of the visibly *pregnant young woman standing directly above. But even as it does – and despite understanding the necessity of a rapid excuse – it only produces 'No, wait, I . . . wait . . . I can explain . . .'*

Grace, for the first time, turning her head. Nothing asked or actually said. Or nothing divinable from the back of your head. Turned now to her, I assume, to concede the young woman is Marianne. Her mother or, as she was then, your very long-suffering girlfriend. Weird to have her prised from my imagination and, so blatantly, set into life. Or, if not quite life, some cinematic facsimile of herself. Does the actress resemble her? I shouldn't really ask that. Until later, when we're by ourselves. For now, you nod a mute Yes to Grace's mute request, which she takes back with her into the rest of the scene.

'Don't even speak to me. I thought you were dead. How long has this been going on? No, actually, wait. I don't want to know.' Some scrabbling then, and the POV switched to viewing the young man. Getting right up. Reaching for her hand. 'Come on, listen, I . . . know this looks bad but . . .' 'IS BAD. IS BAD. Is the WORST in a long fucking line of terrible stuff you've already done to me. To US. And this baby!' Arm protecting her belly. Elbow out. 'I know things have been awful but they'll get better, I promise. I swear.' His body's fragility making lies of this already. Then a close-up of her strained face taking his words in. Listening so closely to them. Perhaps even hoping. But, refusing to, reality rearms. Insists she remember their past, then calculate odds for the likelihood of change. And, once the numbers are in, the conclusion's not great. Her knowing, absolutely knowing it, as well as the utter pointlessness of any attempt to deny. Beautiful how the actress does it. All the while staying so still. Done with the eyes and the tense of her lips. Nothing really. No discernible fireworks and yet I feel everything as she does: how her will to believe slowly becomes doubt, becomes hope refused, becomes the unwelcome understanding of what she now has to do. A devasting path to follow the character through. And was it also for you, to do? I'm not sure, but I'm thinking maybe so. Why else keep the camera right in there, examining

her face rather than revert to the young man's perilous state? Why give it all this attention if not to keep us with her? It is more interesting though, not letting him be sympathetic – never mind not the hero. Not letting yourself off the hook.

I risk a look, but you are otherwise engaged with looking over at Grace. So that's another thought to raise later, if you'll be up for making reply?

'Get out. We're done. I'm done with you and everything.' 'Wait, no, I promise . . .' 'I don't care. Go find yourself some other pushover somewhere. I never want to see you again.'

V/O (barely there): 'All right, love?'

Young man casting around. Not wanting it to be true. Young woman really meaning it though.

V/O (a little louder): 'Come on, love, wake up. This won't do.'

His face slowly believing her now.

V/O (loud enough to break through): 'Answer me. You all right, young man?'

EXTERIOR. ARCHWAY. PRESENT. NIGHT. Another wake-up. Another fisheye and he's back on the low Archway wall. Little old cockney lady bearing down. Plastic hair bonnet to keep damp from her set. Shopping trolley leant against his leg and the rubber tip of her walking stick grinding his stomach. 'What the fuck?' 'You all right, love?' 'Sorry . . . what?' 'Not too bright sleeping out here, love, not this time of night.' And, sure enough, he is now under streetlight. Frozen and a little damp. But at least the London gyration's gone at last. Close-up of him realising he should now start gathering his wits. 'Oh yeah . . . no . . . thanks . . . I'm fine.' 'You sure? Don't look it to me. What happened to your face?' Him touching his cheek and, finding pain, downplays the instinct to wince. 'Ah . . . someone mugged me.' 'Well, they'll do a lot worse, love, if you don't get up. All sorts hang round here on a Saturday night. Why don't you get on home?' Although he doesn't know why, he does start getting up. Stiff unfurling. Bones going creak. Stepping into the lamplight. 'Oh no, love, that's nasty. Your eye. Very bad. You want to have that looked at.' 'No really, it's all right . . . I don't suppose you've got a fag?' 'Well' all pleased with herself 'I never said I hadn't. Here.' Passing a twenty-pack of Player's which the young man gratefully accepts. Feels out his lighter. Gets lit up. His whole body, so glad of the rush, remains oblivious to how shrewdly she watches. All five foot nothing beside his six foot three. Twice as wide as him though and infinitely more rosy. 'Not from here, are you?' 'No, up north.' 'Been in London long?' 'Few years now.' 'Then you may not know, the Whittington's just up the road.' 'Thanks, but . . . I'm really fine.' But really not liking the look of that eye, she says 'If you pull my shopping as far as there, you can have the rest of those fags. How's that?' Knowing a bargain when he hears it, he takes the handle. Follows, as she sets off at a lick. Limping though, barely up to her pace. The camera tracking back while they toil up Highgate Hill before the screen goes to BLACK.

Can't help smiling. Nor Grace. Even you smile at it. Beguiling shot. Unexpected.

      I don't remember that in the script.
        Last-minute rewrite.
    Did it happen though?
        Yeah, it did.
          So did she make you go in?
          Wait and see.

INTERIOR. WHITTINGTON HOSPITAL A&E. NIGHT. Brand spanking new. Of course, this was the seventies, not now. *The young man sitting. His eye getting dabbed. Some disapproving clucking. Then bulkily bandaged. 'You were lucky. Quarter of an inch to the left and that eye'd have been jelly.' 'Yeah . . . pretty lucky all right.' But as the nurse starts to clear, he reaches in his pocket to test a theory and, on* discovering he does indeed still have Angela's few quid, the desire to leave accelerates. 'So, are we done?' 'I think you should wait. So does your nan.' 'My who?' 'Wasn't it your nan brought you in?' 'No.' 'Well, before she left, she said be sure you got a . . . thorough check.' 'For what?' But the nurse is not playing this and just raises an eyebrow, which sets him off. 'I was sick, that's all.' 'How?' 'Bit of trouble with my heart.' Her going grave. 'Then you should definitely get properly checked.' But he's already on his feet. As he hauls back the curtain though, she grabs his cuff. 'Then here!' palming him three frayed pound notes. 'She said to tell you get something to eat. So I hope you will.' Young man taken aback, nevertheless pocketing them quick. Pressure in him rising and barely covering it. Danny the living embodiment of shifty. 'Thanks.' Pulling away. The nurse pulling back. 'You don't have to, you know? You could try to clean up . . .' Thus, anchored by her fingers, he must answer, so does. 'Why would I want to do that?' Danny's eyes, through and through, nihilist. And, although from that moment, professionally resigned, she gives it one last try. 'What are you? Twenty-one? Twenty-two? You should give yourself the chance to change your mind.' Cue for him to smile. 'Well, I'll be right back if I ever do.' Uncharmed, she shrugs. 'I hope you'll be able to, but there's not much chance of that.' His forced smile peeling off soon as he turns. That she won't play along leaves him, briefly, concerned. Then he recalls the unexpected few pounds and he's off on the upswing again. BLACK.

Should've listened to her, Stephen.

You're telling me.

Weren't you tempted to, Dad?

You're always tempted to, Gracie, but   I'd further down to go.

EXTERIOR. ARCHWAY. NIGHT. Left, out of the Whittington to Highgate Hill. Lopsided London ahead and below. Laboured breaths *showing, rather than cigarette smoke, obscured by bandage at the edge. The POV plainly uninterested in the view. Only the body's rapid, if unsteady, progress. Buses pass. Shop lights on the footpath. Glow from the pub ahead.*

INTERIOR. THE ARCHWAY TAVERN. NIGHT. Pushed into. Floorboards limped across. All yellowed with fag stain and donkey jacket rough. Young man hauling himself onto a barstool then leaning across. 'Hey Mike, got a fag?' The barman chucking one. 'What happened to you?' 'Altercation with Rat Paul's mate's boot.' 'Could've told you not to get mixed up with that scabby lot.' 'Well, anyway . . . Terry here?' 'Already left.' 'Is he coming back?' 'Couldn't say. Pint while you wait?' 'Nah, I'm in a hurry.' But on rising quick, has to sit back down. 'You okay?' 'Bit dizzy.' 'That'll happen all right, when your head gets in the way of Rat Paul's mate's boot.' 'It's just . . . been a while since I ate.' 'Sorry, can't offer you anything, mate.' 'Don't worry. Might head over to that place across.' 'Keen on taking your life in your hands, are you?' Getting back to his feet. 'I'll take my chances, and if Terry puts in an appearance . . .' 'I'll say you're looking for him.' 'Cheers.' Then limping back out. Mike shaking his head, then cocking it. 'What's that, mate? Pint or a half? Coming up!' BLACK.

INTERIOR. CAFE. NIGHT. Sounds of a greasy spoon coming up in the black. Jangle of the bell. Door open. Door shut. Then a close-up of hot tea in a blue mug. Milk already added. Focus pulling to the trembling bowl of a soup spoon as it heaps four, five, six white sugars in. Stirring clockwise, then anticlockwise. Then clockwise again. Lifting it out to check the last granules have melted. More toffee than tea, it gets raised to his lips. A sip and suck of air like too hot. The other hand pocketing the spoon, right after that. And the liquid's surface blown as the general caff soundscape grows very specific suddenly. 'Oh, no you don't, sunshine, put that back.' Hesitation. Then a shove from behind.

Tea slopping over. Then the spoon returned to the chipped green table-top. 'And don't do that again. I don't want any of that shit in here.' 'Sorry.' 'Do you hear?' 'Yeah.' 'Do you?' 'I do.' 'Good. Now drink up and fuck off.' BLACK.

You scribbling away, but I wonder what you see? Or no. More how, may-be? Is it still yourself up there or now only Danny? A thing undergone from the inside? Or critically and from without? The scrawled notes suggest dis-tance but not the set of your mouth. And not the way you sit. Also, when we're not here, is that different? Has to be but then, what about with Nick? Better or worse with him than watching alone? Or do you only concentrate on refinements? Maybe the writing, and shooting, and the various processes have turned it all into a foreign object now? But, eventually, it'll be out for strangers to see. And maybe love. Or maybe use as a stick. How must it be to anticipate that? And which watch will be worse for you, them or us? Or may-be all awful, just differently? Too many layers here for me to unpick when there's so much left to see.

INTERIOR. THE PARTY SQUAT. NIGHT. Somewhere off the Holloway Road. Rough as guts. Whatever lath and plaster remain, kicked to fuck. Whatever wallpaper, peeling or ripped up. Front door off its hinge. Rotted remnants of carpet. Hole, where floorboards must once have been, and a pink bathroom sink stomped to powder at the foot of the stairs. Music too, up at sick-making levels, like being inside of or seeing instead. At least that's how the POV experiences it. Pushing its way through the awry bodies cast everywhere. Upright in doorways. Horizontal on the floor. Some sleeping. Some fucking. Camera switch-ing over to follow him lankily stepping across. Sometimes not making it either. 'What the fuck?' Trying various shoulders. 'Seen Terry?' 'Bog off!' Clearly growing darker as each not-Terry's ruled out. Swigging from however many bottles, or cans, come to hand. Eventually taking the stairs. A few at a time, in hopes of not falling through to his death, but still denting extremities on the way up. 'What you up to, fella?' 'You *wanna watch yourself.' Some guy on the landing having a piss. Some girl so out of it her skirt's soaking it up. But he does not pass judgement. Only looks and barely sees. 'Oi mate!' He turns. 'Yeah mate, over here. Got any cash?' 'Might've?' 'Want in on this?' 'What?' 'Come and see. Be worth it, definitely.' Close-up on his eyes as they turn the offer over but, clearly already, knowing his answer. Bit of a nod. Half of a smile, and he steps on over the passed-out girl. Into BLACK.*

BLACK SCREEN. Music disorientating and like inside a tin drum. Backwards language and reversing rhythms implying madness or, at least, loss of control.

What is that, Stephen?

Throbbing Gristle.

Never heard it before. Pretty disturbing.

Again, it'll be more filled out   when we do the sound properly but   you get the idea.

It's already giving me the creeps.

Well, good. That's how it's meant to be   inside his head.

Continuing only black but, somehow, rolling too and thrashing like in his mind's eye. How have they done that? How can he know what I'll see? Does he though, or do I just think it and it's different for everyone else? *Then the sound overtaken by the hospital bleeps. Some sort of terrified breathing as the black itself becomes visible, undulating* I can't guess the trick *without ever seeming to stop being blank.*

And look over to ask but am interrupted by

Light. Swelling darkness from his eye, before receding into a more normal daylight and

INTERIOR. BEDROOM OF THE FINSBURY PARK FLAT. DAY. (FLASHBACK.) Same day? I don't think so. Not much after though.

Likely a few days. Maybe a week? *The young woman rushing forward and back. Dumping clothes in a suitcase. Shoes in a bag. Long beautiful hair streaming. Still the same degree pregnant. And she is no longer surprised. She is only angry now. Morning flooding the rotted sash windowpane, burning sun dogs into the action. The camera handheld but stationary, mostly, staring. Primarily concerned with its phony equilibrium and, only latterly, with comprehending. Focus pulling on her as she crosses in front but dissipating straight after to a lazier notice. Falling back to the window and the great outdoors beyond. Seemingly dreaming itself into Finsbury Park where it imagines reality must be less inglorious. From then on, the camera jumps in and out of him. Especially when his eyes alight on the wormy window-ledge pigeons, obstructing his fantasy's pretty park view. 'Shoo!' he says and 'Fuck off!' flapping a hand vaguely too. She stops, dead centre of the frame. Light behind, so her expression's in shade, but discernible nonetheless. Then another voice chimes, unexpectedly, in – well, not chimes so much as thunders at him – 'Are you even listening? I'm talking to you.' Camera shoved hard enough to dislodge his, already unsteady, Point of View. Then his thin frame pivoting to take in a well-turned-out older man* and by quite a bit so, most likely, her dad *with considerably less lovely hair but equally angry. 'Stop gaping out that window. Do you understand what's going on? She's leaving you and not a moment before time. Are you even listening?' 'I am.' 'And?' 'I'll fix it' suggests the young man, on the off chance that statement might yet prove true. The older just snorts 'Will you indeed? And how do you propose to do that?' 'I don't know but . . .' 'But? You listen to me, the only "but" you're entitled to is saying "I'm a worthless scumbag, but I'm sorry."' 'I am sorry.' 'That's enough!' she insists. 'Both of you, stop!' and with sufficient emphasis suddenly a pin could be heard to drop. 'Just take my cases to the car.' So, her father does – though not before adding, via close fisheye up into the young man's face 'I hope you're pleased with yourself. Not only have you ruined my daughter's life, I'll probably be picking up your little bastard's tab for the rest of mine.' Before any reply though, she shouts across 'For God's sake, Dad, shut up!' towering and furious. Both men's heads lowering before it. 'Just take my things to the car, I said.'*

Grace's jaw going left like in tearless smart. You taking her hand.

Gracie, love, don't
No, Dad, it's all right.
He didn't mean it. It was me he was angry about.
Mum already told me this story.
I'm sure she did.

It's the bitter tone makes me look. Bit rich considering? You, though, realise it yourself.

But, Gracie I was   she had it tough and your grandfather was also a
Dad, I know what he was and, really, it's fine.

All her towers falling though, as her father goes out. Legs crumbling beneath, into a sit on the bed. The POV from above – his – and her convulsing in sobs. Then his notice zooming in to her hands working hard at her skirt, as if it all depended on smoothing those wrinkles out. 'Don't cry. Please don't cry.' Young man sitting beside, slipping fingers through hers but hers brushing them aside. 'On top of everything, I have to go back and live with him now. The final fucking indignity, so thank you for that . . . as well as all the rest.' Camera watching closely, in a two-shot, front on. Him honestly wanting to comfort but with nothing to offer beyond 'You don't have to go.' 'I can't stay here.' 'You can and . . . I'll do better, I swear.' Her wiping her face. 'And how will you do that?' 'I'll . . . get clean again.' 'No you won't.' Her hand opting though to accept his then and he is grateful for it. Genuine affection

– 193 –

evident in the mingling fingers. But while she holds his eye, the camera sees her other hand reach over and push up his sleeve. By the time he cottons on, the track marks are already clear. 'Don't do that.' Standing up. The camera tracking away, to catch him trying to recover himself. Then re-covering his arm and how, in his search for an excuse, their brief intimacy passes on. Still, unwilling to capitulate, he forges onward. 'Look, I've made mistakes. A lot of them, I know, but . . .' 'You barely survived a heart attack. You were in a coma, for God's sake, but the minute you got out . . . you went right back and now . . . this.'
I like how Danny, almost physically, shrinks. *'And this is new, isn't it? Or, relatively speaking, I think?' 'Yes, but . . .' 'But what?' 'I . . . thought it would help . . . take the pressure off.' For her, however, this is the living end. 'How dare you lie to my face! You're doing it because you want to. There's no noble fucking excuse. You just like it and don't want to deal with anything else. Am I right?' Her anger hitting now like a slap. Her livid face. Then his, in close-up, trying to conjure an expedient response. But she won't give him time and just reiterates it. 'Am I?' Eyes indicating every intention to wait for the answer he'll do anything not to give. He tacks instead to the side. 'How am I supposed to answer that?' 'Honestly, for once in your life.' Meeting his eyes and not giving an inch. The camera becoming her cruel accomplice – despite the accomplice she really needs being a friend. Unable to choose otherwise, however, she's obliged to witness the lens slowly disclose the seep away of his interest.* Stuck right in Danny's face as formerly in hers. This unforgiving choice, it seems, become a strength of yours. *His eyes go from holding hers to moving across her cheek. To considering her ear. To a strand of hair above it. Then a slow, but intentional, wander off at an angle, behind her and up the wall.* Perfectly judged. Unerringly clear. *That's when she knows, and he knows, there will be no answer because – and despite professing the desire for her to stay – he himself is no longer at home. Not really. Not any more and while there are residues of feeling, most is only by rote. His glance of apology now putting in an appearance, along with*

his familiar *impatience to just get the door.* Danny excelling at how still you get when you want to absent yourself from whatever awkwardness might be. *But making one last effort, she tries to hold him to account. 'Well, if you won't answer that, you owe me this: when you say you'll get clean again . . . do you mean it?' Close-up on him now, biting the inside of his cheek, bridling at her implication and keen to insist. He sort of starts to, then stops. Seems to realise this might be one lie too much, even for him. Close-up switching to her, also realising. So, instead, he takes her last pair of shoes from under the bed. Puts them in the bag. Closes over the flap and, with some care, zips it up. 'Thank you' she says. 'That's what I thought too.' BLACK.*

Grace pressing her palms to her cheeks. You then taking her bony hand and squeezing it. She places the other on top. Like with like. Runs it up and down your forearm. Comfort? Although I wonder if she's also tempted to turn it, to check for what once was there? Even I'm thinking it and I already know the answer. No time for this, however, for

BLACK SCREEN. The chaotic music roars back in again. Throwing us around the dark inside his head. What's happening to him now? I don't understand. Except, certainly, something bad. Beyond the bounds. In fact, something concrete to grip on to would be welcome any time now.

Grace wedging hands again between her knees while, from the corner of your eye, I see you evaluating. Who's all right and who is not?

All right to keep going?
　I'm all right.
　Fine too, Dad.
Okay, but if that changes, shout.
　Okay.
　　Okay.

INTERIOR. THE PARTY SQUAT. NIGHT. Shake. And him shaking awake. Above, the ceiling fibrillates, albeit only briefly in view between the flickering eyelids his POV's shot through. Just innumerable browns that the dark leaches through. Then lowering back down into blackness again. And the music humming. And the music throbbing. Then the music becoming some enemy, attacking from everywhere. BLACK.

INTERIOR. THE PARTY SQUAT. DAWN. Second time up. Thrashing. And hard to say if the person on top is helping with a seizure or pinning him flat. Him breathing hard through clenched teeth, like pain is playing a part. Danny looking so out of it, and so frightened, to me. *Head and eyes rolling. All sweat in the thin, dawning grey. Then back down into it. Blackness again. For one more nasty time. BLACK.*

BLACK SCREEN. But the music changes in this next dark. Into more discernible. Into a song? Of sorts. Not exactly harmonious but maybe *comic?* What it is? What does the voice say? *'What a day, what a day, what a du-ull day.'*

INTERIOR. THE PARTY SQUAT. MORNING. Third time now, coming around. Just enough to be sure there'll be no more going back down. And he is suddenly in such blessed silence, the body heaves a sigh of relief. This in spite of discovering himself in the corner of a semi-derelict room. Windows smashed, some wholly gone. Only a taped-over bin bag between him and the elements. And he is bone-frozen now. Not just him though, is it? All around lie reams of the fucked and bolloxed out of it. Where've they all been to, this last exploratory night? And that girl beside, what about that? Her top pushed right up and a hand in his pants which remain, he is relieved to see, done. Still, he looks at her breasts a while, trying to recall. Thinks about touching them, then decides to pull her top down and remove her mitt. 'What?' she says. 'What? he says, but she's already

slipped. Wonderingly so, he pulls himself up and manages into a sit.
Me bolt upright

    Oh! I remember this.

Grace asking

    What?
    I was on this set. It was the only day Stephen let me visit.

You, turning now

    Oh yeah. That's right. It was the last day of the shoot. The
    only fucking day the landlord would give us. So we were all
    completely frantic just trying to get it done.

*Camera panning the room of clammy skeletons, all twisted like war
although, in fact, only unconscious. Sitting amid, he tongues his mouth,
like for a tooth. Then, somewhat surprised not to find any loose, casts
about as if this is a win. No one looks back though, that he can see.
What he can are the dregs of a bottle of Bushmills so claims it for his
own. But as the bottle goes up, a hairy knuckled hand grips his wrist.
'I don't think so.' And he looks over. 'Terry! Where've you been?' 'Oh
mate, it's you . . . well . . . here, mostly.' 'Mind if I?' 'Go ahead. Save
some for me though.' Which, comradely, he does. Terry, by now, also
sitting up and looking every bit as shit, asking 'What the fuck was that,
man?' 'No idea, but it didn't agree with me and now I'm starting to
get the shakes. Anything on you?' 'Sorry mate, but Jimmy will, back at
the squat, if you can get past his vicious bird.' 'Vicks?' 'No, that fucking parrot. He's trained it to squawk if anyone tries the door. Shits all
over the place too. It's disgusting in there.' Young man surveying their
milieu. 'Still, probably worth a go?' 'Yeah, I'd say so. You can distract*

it while I sneak in.' 'Does it bite?' 'Don't know, sometimes, I think. Definitely got a very fucking sharp-looking beak so . . . you'll want to take care.' But both find standing up less straightforward than they'd expected. And, even once upright, the problem remains of getting out without trampling the still passed-out to death. Stumbling and 'Oh shit! Not this again!' Interfered with also by the recurrence, in split-second frames, of the previous night's other adventures. Not quite forgotten but not quite there. Touching people. Being touched himself. Enjoyed or endured? Hard to say. Both. Maybe. But shying from what those possibilities might mean, he lifts fags and matches from the will-less prone. And, in long strides, at last frees himself from that ill-omened room to disappear, with Terry, out its hacked door.

EXTERIOR. HOLLOWAY ROAD. MORNING. Picking up on both loping off down the street into the Holloway morning gleam. Early enough there's still no one but the camera to see it – which chooses to show what it does without comment. But I read the tattered twosome, handsome and fucked, as wheeling through their lives as if nothing approaches, neither consequences nor time. *The music restarting when the first 172 goes by. 'What a day, what a day, what a du-ull day. What a day, what a day, what a du-ull day.' Until they are quite far away. Then going to BLACK.*

INTERIOR. THE HOME SQUAT. DAY. SQUAWK! Inevitably. *Parrot flapping round his head. Young man's arms up in defence as Terry digs under a mattress. 'Fuck! It bit me!' 'Shush.' SQUAWK! 'Go on, shoo! Shoo to fuck!' SQUAWK! 'Ow!' 'Punch it!' 'I'm not punching a bird.' 'It'll have your eyes out!' 'Then hurry it up, Alfred fucking Hitchcock.' SQUAWK! But as he gets grip of its leg, the parrot savages his arm instead. 'Come on. Jesus!' 'Got it!' 'Go!' Parrot flung. Them out the door. Then SQUAWK! SQUAWK! rages on the other side.*

CUT TO:

INTERIOR. THE HOME SQUAT HALL. DAY. Them on the other side, laughing to retch. Young man, arm out, examining the pecks. 'Fucking hell! This better be some amazing shit!' 'Don't worry, knowing Jimmy it will be. Let's go up and get fixed.'

Hasn't Danny got a thing about birds?

Has he? Never said. If he didn't before though, I'd say now he does.

Poor Danny.

He did really well. That fucking parrot was a nightmare.

Well   children and animals.

I know   I did it to myself.

INTERIOR. THE HOME SQUAT BATHROOM. DAY. Hands again. Terry's, not his. In no way as methodical or neat. Young man just watching, elbows on his knees, back to a rusted radiator and directly beneath a window showing houses elsewhere. Peck marks aside, the cursed bird's forgotten already and he's only waiting now. Perhaps thinking as well? Because, just as it's ready, he says 'Probably wasn't a great idea, getting into this.' 'Probably' Terry agrees, struggling for a vein. 'Ever kicked it?' the young man asks, trying to help. 'There? Will that work?' 'Don't think so but yeah, plenty.' 'So why go back?' And Terry lays down the needle with wisdom to impart. 'Just like it too much, I suppose.' 'I suppose, but . . . still.' 'Why'd you take it up then?' asks Terry, recommencing the search. 'I mean, no one made you.' 'True . . . just seemed . . . logical . . . to slow things down instead.' Terry laughing 'Yeah, completely logical, mate. Just don't get too slow because they say rigor mortis is a bitch!' Young man laughing too then 'I'll remember that.' But as Terry jags between the toes, his eyes move

– 199 –

along the faint-with-damp roses patterning the wall. Camera wending their twists like following thought. And though preoccupied, he hears Terry say, in the first blur of nod 'I wouldn't worry. You can kick it any time.' 'Yeah, I know . . . give it here.'

Again, your eyes wander to Grace. Examine, in the moving light, the side of her face, but it doesn't move from the screen. So, with other things happening, you turn back too.

EXTERIOR. THE FIRST DREAM. NIGHT INTO DAY. The camera, aperture down, as if hung, sways in its passage along. Two foot above the surface of the presumably *Holloway Road. Gliding it. Elegant, even when swinging wide on taking a bend. Skimming its crossings and crossroads, the same. Periodically other tyres spin in, and twin for a few rotations, before turning off someplace else. White lines holding it centre. Yellows warding it off. Litter. Newspapers. Broke glass and fag butts. All necessary to the capture of a city asleep. And strange serenity to how the camera's weight seems borne by air alone. Weightless as it crosses the cusp of dawn and on into day. But if seeking a destination, it fails to find and, by Highbury Corner, realises it's time to return to the BLACK. Persists in moving a while inside that. Then not. Then is, unquestionably, still.*

All in all, the sequence must take two hypnotic minutes but I could've easily done more.

That's extraordinary, Stephen. How did you do that?
>Suspended the camera from the hook of a pick-up truck.
>Pretty heavily weighted so it wouldn't blow about. Then,
>very slowly, drove the length of the Holloway Road, hoping
>for the best – in terms of mad drivers.

Just before dawn?
>Right. We'd been shooting the whole night, so it worked
>out well.

And all in one take?

One false start but we got it after that.

Reminds me of flying dreams I had as a child.

Funny. I had those too and that's exactly how I wanted it to feel.

Then smile purely to each other. An unimportant secret shared, but shared nonetheless, of flight's magic and earth's inescapableness. I'd like to hold and have it, but the film goes on.

INTERIOR. THE HOME SQUAT. DAY. 'Fucking dirty thieving cunt!' BUMP and BUMP. POV up from darkness. A woman's voice screaming 'Stop!' Slap sounds and instinct pulls his body tight as a further jolt indicates his skull might, unluckily, be the source of the bangs. So he looks. Finds it is. And how a man's dragging him by the leg down uncarpeted stairs. The woman behind screaming into the puller's neck 'Stop! You'll kill him like that!' 'I fucking well hope so!' brings him right round. 'Whoah, mate! Whoah!' and to the necessity of intervening now if he wants out of this in one piece. 'What're you doing?' 'Putting you out on the street, you ungrateful, robbing shit!' But when he gets a grip of the banister, the puller – unprepared for resistance – stumbles on the stairs. 'Fucking hell!' 'All right, mate? Honestly, I didn't touch a thing!' 'Then why the peck marks?' 'I was looking for somewhere to kip, so . . . I went in your room and that bird lost its shit, so I legged it. I fucking swear!' Raising his hands like this is a bust. Danny opting for useless and charming at once. *'Well, someone lifted it.' 'Really? That's terrible, mate.' 'Told you it wasn't him, Jim! He's had trouble enough.' And confused by all the opposition, Jimmy gives up. 'Fine, but you're on your last chance. Anything else disappears and you're done.' 'That's fair, there'll be no trouble from me.' Daring to sit now the threat's receding, the young man and girl watch Jimmy descend, yank open a door and bellow 'Now then, Terry, what you got to say for yourself?'*

That was lucky. So, who was she?

Again, wait and see.

INTERIOR. THE HOME SQUAT STAIRS. DAY. His protectress offers a cigarette 'You're lucky I arrived when I did. He dragged Terry all the way down. If his hair wasn't thinning before, it fucking is now.' 'What'll he do to him?' 'Nothing too bad. You, on the other hand, don't look like you could take much more.' 'Yeah . . . I've felt better.' Green looking, though enjoying that cigarette. Camera moving right to left. 'Why don't you have a lie down in my room?' His eyes wandering her and like what they see. 'I could do with it.' 'You, my friend, could do with a whole lot of things. Three-course meal for a start!' 'Any chance you've one of those up there too?' 'Wouldn't I love it but no, how does a cheese sandwich sound?' 'Piccalilli?' 'Don't push it, mate.' 'Then I'll take what I can get.' BLACK.

Jesus, Dad, you got beat up a lot.

Yeah, I was   definitely better at getting in trouble than out of it, back then.

INTERIOR. THE HOUSE SQUAT BATHROOM. DAY. Bathroom window glass. Behind it, sun. Black-and-white tiles. 'You don't remember me, do you?' she asks, sat beside the chipped bath he lies in, fully dressed, and eating a sandwich. 'Should I?' 'Probably.' 'Where from?' 'Drama school . . . for one.' 'Not my year.' 'Year above. Same as that girl you went out with . . . go out with?' 'Not any more.' 'Hardly surprising' – a comment which begs him to enquire but, busy with crust, he only answers 'Just life, isn't it?' The camera watches her light a fag, then wait for him to get there. But, receiving no signs, she gives up. 'Aren't you going to ask if we fucked?' Lowering the sandwich, he scrutinises her, eyes and mouth. 'I think . . . I think we . . . have not.' Then something returns from the mists. 'But . . . you once gave me a blow-job in . . . Gordon Square?' 'I'm impressed.' 'That was you, wasn't it?' 'Yes.' 'What'd you do that for then?' 'Make my boyfriend jealous.' 'And did you?' 'He didn't give a shit.' 'Well, thanks anyway. Here' and hands her the empty plate. 'So where is he now?' 'Downstairs. It was Terry.' 'No, fucking hell! Didn't even know he had a girlfriend.' 'Yeah, still together too.' Him sitting now, tongue winkling the last of sandwich from tooth. 'So, will he still not give a shit?' 'Probably won't but . . . my turn now, isn't it?' He pitches over the side of the bath, just as she lies back. Puts a hand up her skirt, working fingers in, until she says 'Get on with it.' At which point her skirt gets pushed all the way up and he disappears between her legs. BLACK.

You, right away, covering your face. Grace trying not to, but looking embarrassed. Me just thinking I wouldn't mind a spot of that. Then, straight after, what a great thing it is that thinking is private, no matter what company you're in.

INTERIOR. THE HOME SQUAT BATHROOM. EVENING. There again. Later. Music stuttering in. Once more, the young man in the bath. Filled with water this time. The long thin body naked. Unpalatably pale, where not bruised, and hair in need of a wash. Smoking. Looking up on the cherub-faced girl pouring in a kettle of hot. Naked too, saying 'We should get out of here, you and me. Get away.' His eyes working to concentrate. 'And what about Terry? Won't he be needing a break after this afternoon?' 'Oh, he'll just sleep it off.' 'Then what about my girlfriend?' 'What about her?' 'She's having a baby.' 'By you?' 'Yes, by me.' 'How do you know?' 'I know.' 'Well, she can find someone else, can't she? How many dads have you had?' 'No good ones, that's for sure' he nods. 'Me neither, so maybe she'll find someone nice and it'll all work out.' His eyes starting to travel though, away from her face. Into the past? *'Drugs?' she suggests, snapping him back. 'I could use a little pick-me-up.' Smiling, she gets up. 'I'll see what I can do!' Wraps a dirty towel around, then vanishes outside.*

There'll be music seeping up from below at this point. Fast.
Very loud. Also, voices so we know it's full-on below. Parties.
Fights. People coming and going.
    To score?
        That too.
Was that how you ended up there?
    Yeah   essentially.

Neither of you looking at the other, but I see you both nod, like
agreeing to keep this separate from your nowadays lives. Having
heard it all – or in a more sanitised version – less is at stake for me.
Meaning I can be more nosy, which I certainly am.

        Is Terry dead now?
    Long time. Fifteen years.
And her?
    I didn't see her again   after this.
        I could ask my mother if they're in touch?
No   Gracie   why would you do that?
    Wouldn't you like to know if she was all right?

And that's a very interesting look on your face. I probably wouldn't have
been so blunt but, since she has, I'd also like to know. So wait as keenly on
your answer as Gracie does.

    I wouldn't bother. They're not   in touch.
        How do you know?
            Because she killed herself.
        Because of you?
No! Jesus, Grace, no! Later. In the mid-eighties   I think.

Do you know why, Stephen?
She got sick.

Cancer?

No   she never cleaned up, so

Aids or?

So they said and

        Fuck.

    Yes.

    So   is she in it as remembrance?

Something like that. She was certainly part of   the change
for me.

    What did she do?

Grace asks. But I know where we are on the thread, so return to
the film and leave you to it.

    Well   that bit won't be long.

INTERIOR. THE HOME SQUAT BATHROOM. EVENING.
Close-up. A line disappears up a quid. The young man sits back, wipes
his nose, polishes his teeth, then passes it on. Camera tracks the next
from mirror to nose also. 'Fucking hell' he says, as she does, 'that's hit-
ting the spot.' Runs his tongue round his gums. 'Told you!' she laughs,
shaking her wet hair like a dog.

INTERIOR/EXTERIOR. MONTAGE. NIGHT. Everything going
fast. Jumping frames. Music loud. Two of them up on their feet. Kissing
with tongues. Heading out. Laughing down the stairs. Shoving through
heaving rooms of strangers. Terry with a black eye. Her kissing him too.
Young man, unfussed, finds a woman to scab fags from, hair fiddle and
kiss. Take out the back. Fuck up against a hedge. Halfway through,
losing interest. Ripping leaves off a branch, between finger and thumb

– fascinating, just fascinating – then confetti-ing them. Her shouting 'Fuck off' or so say the shape of her lips. Pulling clear. Him falling over on his arse. Long legs splayed and laughing, with a nosebleed in the works about which he doesn't care. Dark and light. Legs loom above. The camera going over him. Front to back. The first young woman offers her hand. Pulls him up and then on inside. The camera takes off alone as he's swallowed by the house. Searching stories for itself from the lives of the crowds. Various debaucheries fleetingly caught. Late seventies music. A smatter of punks. Frayed T-shirts hung from bodies ashen with drugs which youth alone seems to keep on their feet. Rougher looking than we are, I think, but then, ours are different pills. *The camera stays attentive until catching him through windows, heading back up the stairs. First floor – laughing, wiping nosebleed on his wrist. Second – pausing, hand on his chest. Third – losing his balance, then falling against the glass. Her bawling back down until Terry comes up. Gets an arm around and hauls him out of sight. Frustrated, the camera goes to the garden, for one final sweep. Then, still at the mercy of its own interest, returns to zoom in at the windows with hopes of snatching a view. BLACK.*

INTERIOR. THE HOME SQUAT BATHROOM. NIGHT. Handheld view of her tying him off, saying 'This'll be better for you, won't it?' 'What?' he hazards, but then Terry's above. 'You're in need of a relax, mate, so we're going sort you, all right?' The young man's eyes – up to studying if not interpreting – give glazed assent. 'Or' she posits 'should we call an ambulance?' Young man rousing 'Not that!' and Terry is 'Just hold his arm flat. Right. Now give it a slap.' Then takes a stab 'Fuck, Terry' he flinches 'You missed!' 'Shut up. Let me concentrate!' A close-up of the needle going in. 'Better' the young man says, already going. And the camera steps out to catch the look on his face as focus passes from her mouth, saying 'Doesn't look right to me' to somewhere off left, on the floor. BLACK.

Jesus, Stephen, Danny looks fucked.
Stayed up all night to get that shot.
Shows.
All hail The Method, I suppose.

But giving me a quick smirk.

Oh no, if he was shit you could mock, but he's really fucking good.

And your hands up.

Sorry! Sorry! Fair enough.

Grace pissed off with this bicker and unaware of its frequent recurrence.

Will both of you please shut up!
Sorry.
Sorry.

And we are, again. And again, he has done this because of what's coming. But she doesn't realise it, or understand how to him, yet.

INTERIOR. CHILDHOOD HOME KITCHEN. DAY. (SILENT FLASHBACK.) Little boy on his belly on the floor, weaving a dinky car between the legs of a chair. Kicking his own up and much preoccupied by making sharpish turns. Getting bolder. Doing stunts. Then, accidentally, letting go, so it scoots across . . . to get stepped on, and slipped on . . . by his mother. The child's face all instantly horror. Body preparing to prepare. Already on him though, she has him by the hair.

Pushes him down. Practically on top, slapping his head. Then, sudden-ly, SOUND. Screaming into the side of his face 'What did I tell you about that bloody car? Disobedient!' SLAP. 'Selfish.' SLAP. 'Brat.' The child, sorrying for all he's worth, crawling under the table. Almost does. But she drags him back, hissing 'I'm not done with you!' BLACK. SLAPS. Breaths. Something rips. And the little boy tries not to make that horrible, tormenting sound.

You only flex your hand. And Grace only notices once it goes crack. Looks at it. Then turns her eyes back. At times as hard to know as you.

INTERIOR. THE HOME SQUAT BATHROOM. NIGHT. To a less identifiable sound. 'Terry? You here?' 'Yeah but hold that thought.' So, the POV returns to his arm. Focus pulling there as the question forms 'But Terry . . . why's my arm gone black?' No one answers, although the sound's now explaining itself, as if his brain's tuning back in. Just the suck and rub of unathletic fucking.

> Still be pretty high levels of music at this point too.
>> But you'll keep this in?
>> Of course but   probably further down in the mix.

Now I'm the one smirking, to your appreciative look for this technical query, as the noises get worse. Hopefully you won't dis-comfort cough and, luckily, seem to know this.

His POV travels until sight and sound match. Her dry humping poor Terry for all he's worth. Once located, eyed with ambivalence though, before it's back to his arm.

INTERIOR. CHILDHOOD HOME KITCHEN. DAY. (SILENT FLASHBACK – VERY BRIEF.) The little boy examining extensive bruises blackening his arm then too.

INTERIOR. THE HOME SQUAT BATHROOM. NIGHT. He
picks the skin. Tidying flakes. Then getting more into it. Using his nails.
Picks more than he should and the pain makes him impatient. 'What
happened here?' 'Terry' she answers, without turning, 'Missed the
vein.' 'Yeah, sorry about that, mate . . . be fine in a couple of weeks.'
And return to their humping. The camera, to his face. Sound of her
finishing while he, uninterested, worries an old scab that'd be better
left. Lifts it. Peels it back and, displaying some skill, keeps it attached
while continuing to pull, until it's very long. Jaw held like teeth hurt
as blood starts to come, sucking in the pain but pleased with his work.
My own squeamishness relieved when the camera cuts *to her dismount-*
ing Terry, who complains 'I'm not done!' 'Who are you kidding? Your
dick's been broke months.' Then grilling the young man 'What're you
doing that for?' Involved, he gives no answer. Terry too 'Mate, no, that's
fucked.' 'Stop!' she says. 'You're freaking me out!' 'I want it off me.'
'It's a bruise, you just have to wait.' 'No, it's coming' and persists until
the black arm's acquired a bloodied strip. 'That's disgusting! Stop!'
she pleads, snatching his wrist. But 'Don't fucking touch me!' Some
wrangling. Pushes. Blood flecked, she backs off. 'Fuck! That went in my
mouth!' Terry laughing 'Little Boy Blue's finally lost it!' This freaks
and makes him indignant 'What're you calling me?' 'Take it easy.
We're all mates here.' But he's also getting confused 'What's the Boy
Blue stuff then?' So, to soothe his bust compass, she offers 'A joke . . .
about how blue you get on the nod, like you're ODing or something
except it's not . . . it's . . . your heart's fucked, isn't it?' And rank weird
horror fills his face. 'How do you know that?' 'You told me.' 'I did?' But
clearly his flesh creeps over blank. Then a loud hospital BLEEP startles
him inside and

INTERIOR. THE HOME SQUAT BATHROOM. NIGHT.
(FLASHBACK.) Him, naked, curled on the floor. Scratching a 2p on

the underside of the bath. Her smoking, stretched adjacent, asking from nowhere 'Weren't you in hospital before you got here?' 'Who told you that?' 'Just heard it, so . . . were you?' 'For a bit.' 'Industrial herpes?' 'Luckily not!' 'What then?' 'Cardiac arrest.' 'You what? Isn't that for old people?' 'Apparently not.' 'Did it hurt?' 'Don't remember . . . only waking up.' 'Fuck.' 'Yeah . . . it wasn't great.' 'And now?' 'Long as I don't take anything speedy, I'm fine.' Scratching a heart in the flaking paint. 'Are you pulling my leg?' 'No, I even died, they said.' Scribbling it now back into specks 'Fuck! Did you see the light?' 'Think I'd be here if I had? I'd have been off this shit mortal coil in a flash' 'Oh yeah' she says 'I definitely would too.' BLACK. BLEEP.

INTERIOR. THE HOME SQUAT BATHROOM. NIGHT. 'So I knew, when you took that turn, what Terry should do . . . except he fucked it!' BLEEP. 'He's still here' Terry argues 'Despite the little boy blue act' BLEEP. 'Stop calling me that!' 'Why? You were very fucking blue. We even got Mick up to take a photo. Imagine what they'll say down the chemist's at that?' and both fall into jags of reiterating laughter. BLEEP. But losing interest in their skitting, the camera cuts to the young man in close-up, his active horror as before, until his eyes connect with a blue shimmer on the floor. Just staring first, then searching out its source. Up the wall. Across the cabinet with the ripped-off doors. Its lens bearing witness to the moment he recognises . . . distance. Sees there is a beyond. BLEEP. 'What's he gawping at?' But their chat blurs behind the hospital bleeps. BLEEP. And their growing pain in his pulse. BLEEP. Preferring the shimmer though BLEEP he perseveres with it. BLEEP. To where it lifts above. BLEEP. Then in close-up. BLEEP. There it is. A solitary square of blue stained glass. BLEEP. He reaches up to touch. BLEEP. 'Don't' she warns 'the whole thing'll fall out.' BLEEP. He does anyway and the whole thing does. From the rotted frame, all down the rotten house, into the rotting garden. SMASH. Then all at once, MORNING. Like it has always been. Silvery gold and lovely *with mist. All for him, in bleepless silence, beneath a now wide-open sky. 'Wanker' Terry curses 'We'll have to board that up.' Ignoring him, the young man leans out and looks. There it is, amid nettles and crushed lager cans. The camera scrutinising as he realises. 'What you looking at?' she asks. 'That glass' he says 'It didn't break.' 'And we'll be freezing our arses off anyway' Terry says. 'Yeah' agrees the young man 'You probably will.' Wincing then, he rolls the sleeve down his black arm. Turns to leave. 'Wait' she says 'Where're you going?' 'Don't know' he shrugs. 'Well, can I come?' 'No' he says 'Not any more.' BLACK.*

EXTERIOR. THE HOUSE SQUAT GARDEN. MORNING. Coming out, he kicks around in the glass. Spots the blue. Pockets that. 'Mate, you are fucking mental' Terry shouts, but he just turns his face where he's going. Crosses the slippery back garden. Jumps the shitty fence and disappears into the alley behind. BLACK.

Was that that then, Dad?

How do you mean?

For you know turning your life around?

Well, for that leg of it, I suppose   it was.

I wonder what they did after you'd gone.

Same probably   I would've.

So she changed your life by   freaking you out?

More by saying it as it was, out loud.

Doesn't seem like she meant to.

The bluntness was enough or   I was just ready to hear.

Why didn't you take her, Stephen?

I couldn't.

Why not?

Because the minute it got rough   we'd have let each other go back.

– 211 –

EXTERIOR. HOLLOWAY ROAD. MORNING. Out he goes, to the beginning of day. Raggedy coat on. Looking freshly like hell. Spring in his limp though, and so sure he's remade that it's only a while before what's been lost is reclaimed, whatever the lost might be. And Route-masters pass. Magpies ugly sing. Grocers spread acrylic grass then start their stacking. Life renewed, albeit by unromantic Holloway, but he is still here. Abides. Remains. Camera catching its glitter across his face as he turns to take it in. Fine, if tired, eyes and dramatic cheekbones – Danny's good but not quite as yours, I think. *Yet. Underneath. Is it there? Just faintly? Quite far back, the infernal bleeping? The young man entertains other excuses first – internal Morse for Do up your coat? After all, it's fucking cold. So he stops. Does. Top button and . . . Now? Cocks an ear. Shit! There it is. BLEEP. Right then. What's next? He leans on a lamppost for balance then violently shakes his head.*

Why's he doing that?
  In case it's tinnitus   and he can rattle it free.
Why would he think that? It's clearly hospital machines.
Well, he also thought heroin might help his heart condition.
    Jesus, Dad.
  I know, love, I know.

When the shaking does nothing, he starts unplugging his ears. Yawning. Nose blowing. Palm to lug pressures. Yet it remains. Bleeping. What does it want? Danny's increasing confusion outraged and comic. *Unable to believe he's been so easily thwarted, 'What the fuck is it?' he shouts. But this merely serves to draw looks from passing skin-heads with the night's remains of brains still on their boots. Luckily self-preservation also notices and gets him on the go again. But as he limps off, salvation's hitch starts to delve around in his head. Recalling. Remembering.*

INTERIOR. HOSPITAL A&E. DAY. (FLASHBACK.) 'He's failing.' Hospital ceiling. Strip lights gouging sight. Skipping frames. Doctors or nurses. And no self. Disorientation suggesting pain. All else chaos and vibration. Then, abruptly, BLACK. And the varied noises switch off. Wait and wait. Dead in here. 'Clear!' from someplace. SLAM! Slips of light again, embroiled with sound. Then gone again. Drifting nowhere. 'Clear!' SLAM! Yet another. But this time within it 'There's a pulse' and so the bleeping begins.

EXTERIOR. HOLLOWAY ROAD. MORNING. 'Fuck's sake! Dozy muppet!' 'Sorry, mate.' He backs off, hands up, mea culpaing to the dustman whose cart he's clipped, knocking brushes into the litter he'd swept. 'Watch where you're going.' Story of his life! 'Will do . . . yeah . . . sorry, mate' and legs it before the real haranguing begins. Tries to cross between parked cars but steps into an ambulance. Swipe. Camera. No. Doesn't touch. The almost of it though, giving sufficient shock, he sits on a bonnet, to get his breath. Hard to, too. Holding his chest – while pretending it isn't that. Danny's eyes on his own palm's light pat, transforming its purpose into picking a thread. So delicately done you'd easily miss it if you weren't intent on every trick.

> I like that little detail, Stephen.
> Came up with that himself.

But I've seen you do it, so I'm betting he has.

> Just subtle   about his denial.
> Exactly, Eil.

More drama than he'd bargained for, he seems to think. So, for a breath or two, lets himself drift. POV wandering the Holloway Road with disinterest, to the point of growing soft. Ignoring the build-up, alongside, of traffic. Entertaining only the delicate bleeps. Now slowed so, presumably in sync with his heartbeat. Meditative. Until they suddenly stop. Then, coughing in fright, he regains focus. Camera, with great clarity, on the back of his hand, flexing involuntarily on his thigh. Something about it catching his eye. So he flexes it again, of his own accord. And again, exactly as before, as if overlaying a memory upon one that exists. But then BLACK and one so imbued with bleeps we're surely moving into their time.

INTERIOR. HOSPITAL WARD. DAY. (FLASHBACK.) The young woman sat by a hospital bed. Sunlight falling all over from the window behind. Crying in the worst way. His POV working out whatever it can. That orange blur's a Lucozade bottle. Those are her knees. The round of her stomach – not large but definitely. Then his own hand pulls focus, down at the left. Fingers moving like trying to form language from drummings and flexes. But these fail to transmit, leaving her grief a barrier he cannot surmount. Shelving it then, he smooths the bedspread instead and the bleeping takes over once more.

EXTERIOR. HOLLOWAY ROAD. MORNING. He stands up, annoyed at having indulged in this, and prepares to embark by vigorously tying his lace. Though by the state of the sole I'd say what's the point? *The bleeping though, exasperatingly present and seemingly gaining pace. But as he rises, some further remembrance flits his face and even gets a look of 'Oh yeah . . .'*

INTERIOR. HOSPITAL WARD. DAY. (FLASHBACK.) Sitting up in bed. Looking like shit – yet still better than at present. Film present, rather than life present, that is. You look great now, I think.

And smile at you to confirm. Which makes you return it but mouth

What's wrong?

Nothing　　just smiling　　that's all.

　　Okay.

BACK:

Doctor. Clipboard. Doctor things. 'I won't lie. It won't be easy, but people do succeed. It rather depends on your strength of will.' 'Wouldn't lay any bets then, if I were you.' Undeterred, however, the doctor continues 'You need something to occupy yourself with. A hobby might help.' The POV does a recce of its bedbound bone and skin. 'What do you suggest, doctor? Rugby? Maybe tap?' 'Frankly, I'd say whatever works.' The young man looks out the window at nothing at all. The doctor tries again. 'How old are you, twenty-one? Your whole life can still be ahead but, believe me when I say, you've already had your luck so you can't afford a relapse. Your body won't take it, do you understand?' The young man nods towards the glass. 'But do you care?' And 'Not really' the young man says. 'Why?' the doctor ventures 'What happened to you?' 'Nothing' lies the young man 'Just got in too deep.' But the camera shows the doctor realise more is there, obscured but definitely present. 'What's said in this room remains private' he says 'Whatever that might be.' And he seems the honest type. His concern, genuine enough, so – fleetingly – the camera observes the young man consider it. Eyes moving from the window, assessing the face, all the while reflecting on how it might be to say it. Close-up and unsparing as his quandary plays out. But soon as he decides to, emotion overcomes his mouth in the form of a tic. The tic, in turn, disables his speech until he's behind his hands stuttering 'Not not tttthhiiiis' – Danny's face so ashamed I can't look. And the doctor, alarmed by it, panics, misdiagnoses, then overplays 'Is it getting that girl pregnant? You can still do right by her.' But it isn't that. So the young man closes. And the doctor sees. 'Sorry' he says 'That wasn't it. Tell me?' But the young man, recovering himself, says only 'How about you tell me how to get to twenty-three instead?' 'Walking' the doctor answers, also resuming himself. 'I've heard it can help, both with cravings and to clear your head.' Then he suddenly Charlie Chaplin's about, saying 'You know how to walk, don't you, Steve? Just put your feet together . . . and go.' Young man, recognising amends in this, plays along. 'Not Chaplin though, is it? That's Lauren Bacall.' 'Just testing' the doctor laughs. 'And how did I do?' 'On film trivia? Great. As for the rest, well . . . that's going to be up to you.' BLACK.

EXTERIOR. HOLLOWAY ROAD. MORNING. The young man, on the bonnet, has a moment of 'Huh' which distils into thought and finally becomes 'Walking then . . . all right.' On which pronouncement, the bleeping stops, so completely his eyes scan for a cause. Even shakes his head, to verify the broken curse only to find it is indeed done. Then a lightness comes over and he prises himself from the hood – although every action requires some winding up to it. Nevertheless, he shoves bony hands in his pockets and strides on up the road. Tracking back, the camera suggests he's, at last, covering ground. Revitalised, replenished, and also how he's swiped an orange from a grocer's display. Tosses it high. Catches. Glances back to check he's not caught. Then, mid doing, stops and, in close-up, sees himself. First time in a while. Doesn't recognise the face and, alarmed by the figure's proximity, steps back. Then sees it's himself. Just skinny and fucked. 'Christ' he mutters, but as he does a further image starts to overlay. Trick of the light? Except he can't look away. What is it? Shifts his head side to the side. Left, it seems, mostly recognised. Right side, however, is where there's wrong. Just reaching into his eye and holding. Perhaps some unpeaceful resemblance showing that he's never noticed before? Thin hand on his face appearing to confirm. There. Around the eyes and mouth: a troubling likeness. ENOUGH! He forces himself from the glass, announcing emphatically to his inadvertent street audience 'That window needs a clean.' And however banal this observation, it affects

– 216 –

his release. Once again, he is only in the street and, if no longer with a spring in his limp, at least his grand odyssey's back on.

CUT TO:

EXTERIOR. HOLLOWAY ROAD. MORNING. Bin lorries. White vans. People crossing where they can. Just a normal London morning turning to early afternoon. Each image once sealed long ago in its time and, because of you, living again.

EXTERIOR. SIDE STREET. EARLY AFTERNOON. A curl of orange peel drops on the street. A small child, messing in a puddle, grabs it. 'Don't!' he says, but it's already in its mouth. 'No!' he says, stopping to pull it out. 'That's dirty!' The child, however, sinks teeth in and will not be separated from this boon. Eyes browse for a parent but, finding none, 'Right' he says, hunkering down, 'If you give it me back, you can have some orange, how's that?' The filthy face, pleased, releases it – although the eyes follow its toss back onto the street. 'Forget that' the young man says 'Look here' breaking off a segment and passing it over. It is immediately absorbed and followed up on with the famous 'More!' This he gives, before straightening up to squint along the street. 'Where's your mum at?' 'More orange!' stonewalls the face, with a degree of intent unusual in a six-year-old, or round that sort of age. 'All right, keep your hair on' and he picks off more pith before handing over the rest. 'Do you live in one of these then?' But the gobbling takes precedence. And then it starts to rain. He lays off asking. Pulls his collar up, mumbles something profane probably about there not being enough coat left to keep much deluge off *then sets his course to on. The camera, back in a longish shot, watches him walk off. Then stop and glance back at the child standing in the rain. Back with the young man, a close-up shows memory is not being his friend. Is not letting him forget one thing.*

EXTERIOR. CHILDHOOD HOME. NIGHT. (BRIEF FLASH-BACK.) Another little boy. Out in the rain. Under an insubstantial porch. Trembling like a wretched dog. Intermittently knocking the door. But it does not open and there is no answer, although silhouettes move behind its laddered glass. He gives it two fingers for a while but withdraws them when a figure looms close. Buckles his skinny legs into a squat and buries his head in his knees.

EXTERIOR. SIDE STREET. AFTERNOON. His mouth twists. Turns back, almost against his will. 'Okay, where do you live?' 'Twenty-six' a voice says behind 'At the top. But just put him in, he'll take himself up.' 'Cheers' he says, as his informant passes on and, with the rain now fairly hopping it down, sweeps the orange eater up in his arm. Then 'Fuck!' feeling his injury, stops and swaps. Starts again. Twenty-four. Twenty-six! 'This you?' as he climbs the front step. But the orange-smeared child only looks. So he shoulders the door and it swings in. 'Right' he says, angling to put the child down but, unwilling to be, it clings on. A little failed extrication then, after which he sighs 'Fine' and makes on up the stairs.

A parrot, a child, and now a second one too!
Yeah, glutton for punishment, I know.
This one's great too though.
Now he is. During, he was a little shit.
Why?
Scratcher. And his mother didn't care. So, I got a few. Danny got worse. Little fucker.

But laughing, which I like to see.

INTERIOR. BEDSIT. DAY. 'C' on the door. 'This you?' And, though the child still gives no answer it accepts its release, before running on in. 'Knock knock' the young man says, knocking, which only knocks it wide. 'Anyone home? Hello? I think I've got your child.' Nothing. Or no one, so he follows on in. Dark, low-ceilinged, dormer bedsitting room. At his flip of the switch, nothing happens and the meter is, predictably, run down. 'Where's everyone then?' he asks the child, who already busies itself with wrapping up in blankets. Mess everywhere. Dirty dishes. Unmade bed. Clothes neatly folded though in a small case – child's clothes. 'We should get something dry on you' he says 'Before you catch your death.' Remarkably, the child gets up and presents itself. Even holds its hands above its head, patiently waiting to be stripped – which the young man now dutifully does. 'What about this? This jumper?' The child nods so he puts it on. Some trousers. A dry pair of socks. The wet he drapes on the radiator, despite its cold. Then turns to see he is closely observed. Camera noting the child's sunk cheeks and violet shadows. 'Still hungry?' The child nods. So he skims the mis-hung and empty cupboards, finding only burnt matches and a heel of bread. 'Want this? The child very delicately takes it before returning to the bed. He watches this, then looks away, leaving the camera to pan the browns of the room's desolation. Arriving back at the lone window, he gazes out, noting it's still pelting down. 'Fuck' he says 'So much for walking . . . I'm not going out in that.' Eyes falling, however, on a half-smoked pack of fags, he can't help but help himself. 'Don't think she'll mind much, will she, your mam?' The child pays no notice. So he sits down at the crumb-strewn table – saucer serving for ash. 'Anyone else live here?' Again, the child doesn't answer. 'Keeping mum' he says. 'Very wise' slowly stretching the black arm out to the point of agonise. Hopeful, however, of the cigarette's magic, he drags it all the way down. One eye though on the child as it roots under the bed. Camera unsure if he's thinking of it or remembering himself. At last, he asks 'Don't you mind having a strange man in your flat?' But the child's preoccupied with shimmying back out, towing a tattered book with. 'What's that? Colouring? Let me see.' The child spreads *it unquestioningly on his knee, then invents its first sentence. 'Tell me a story.' 'Then you can do more than ask for orange?' The child nods. 'What kind of story do you have in mind?' The child solemnly presses a finger on a red elephant. 'Good choice' says the young man, grinding the fag butt to death. 'Will we get comfortable?' The child nods. So they shift to the floor and he's surprised when the child plonks itself on his knee, as if he has always, natively, been here. But 'Once upon a time, there was an elephant' is all he says. 'Who really liked to eat oranges.' BLACK. The sound of not far off rain. Just above, as it is, but penetrating other realms. Growing louder than it ever reasonably could. Dense and menacing and then, all at once, it stops.*

CUT TO:

EXTERIOR. THE SECOND DREAM. NIGHT INTO DAY. Again, of the Holloway Road. Skimming along, once more above. But, this time, experiencing knocks and dislodgements, followed by the odd metallic scrape. Startling after the smooth of that previous dreamscape where lack of deviation was all. Now even car exhausts interrupt the flight. Cat's eyes. Manholes. All badly managed. Something sickly too in hitting those ruts. This isn't how it should be, not after how it was. Still, it goes though. Still takes to the air. Proof, should some be needed, that a plan yet survives in there. That survival survives in there. Even that there itself is still there and somewhere to want to be. BUMP.

INTERIOR. BEDSIT. LATE AFTERNOON. POV flips open its eyes. Murk. Camera cutting to him realising he's still in this doleful flat. Also, that there's a child asleep on his lap, sucking its fingers, he hears. The room gone cold as a witch's tit, evidenced by his now discernible breath in the, what's become, half-light. And, as his eyes adjust, that there's now another person, another grown-up, over by the door. The camera attempts to decipher but the shadows rebuff. 'Who's there?' 'Could ask you the same' she says, voice high – not with fright, more like unease. 'What do you want?' it adds. 'Nothing' he says 'I just brought this one home. It was pouring out and some passing woman said this was the place, so . . . here we are . . . must've fallen asleep.' 'I haven't got anything' she says. 'Yeah, I've noticed that so, luckily I'm not on the rob.' Then, yawning, shifts the sleeping child off and tries to, undramatically, get up. 'Stay where you are' she says 'I have a knife.' 'I'm sure you do' he agrees 'But I have a cramp' and gets on up anyway. Once on his feet, however, the cramp doesn't abate. In fact, catches him so sharply he has to hang on to the table. 'What's wrong with you?' she demands, backing away. 'Nothing' he lies 'Just not eaten all day . . . my head's gone a bit weird. Any chance you've got . . .' 'Nothing! So get out!' But the cramp has other plans and buckles him forward. 'Fuck' he says 'Fuck' voice gone all edge. 'Get out' she repeats. He sits instead. Has to. And then there's silence while he catches his breath. Right up until he says 'You're the woman from the street . . . who told me where he lived.' 'No!' 'You are. I recognise your voice.' 'So what?' she says. 'I was in a rush.' And though the cramp re-gets him, just at this, he forces himself up. 'I could've been any kind of pervert.' At which she steps out of the dark to the light, or what of it penetrates. Hair dull. Face drawn, if once fine, and winnowed underneath her clothes. 'You're not though' she says 'I know what you are.' 'I know what you are too' he answers. 'Same, right? Except for the tricks. Not that I'm judging. I know how it is and I wouldn't put it past myself . . . if the need arose.' 'I've got nothing' she repeats. 'Doesn't matter. I'm getting clean.' 'Yeah, me too' she laughs 'Every single time.' He nods to the sleeping child. 'But that's not good.' 'My sister's coming for him tomorrow . . . until I sort myself out.' Camera cuts to the packed case. Cuts to the child. Then back through the dark from her indifference to his. 'Good' he says, succumbing to another twinge. 'Fuck me, my stomach hurts.' 'It'll do that' she agrees, and they stand in a silence more filled with practicality than regret. Then the child wakes up, coughing

like a bark. Both skeletons jump. 'All right, love' she says 'I brought you
something to eat.' Produces from behind herself a bag of chips which
the child falls upon, savagely. 'Want some?' she offers, spidering out a
spindly hand. 'No. I think I'm going to vomit.' 'Well, good luck with
it all' she says as he shoves by, out the door. Camera lingering on her
eyes following him go. And, once he is, turning on her soon-leaving son.
Nothing there. Neither dislike nor love. Just apathy, accompanied by
the noise of someone running uncertainly downstairs.

Bleak, Dad.
　Yeah.
　Do you think her sister came?
I don't know.
　Did you ever　see them again?
　　About six months later, I went for a look. Thought I
　　remembered where　but I couldn't find it　maybe I was
　　already hallucinating by then.
　　　Because of withdrawal?
More because of myself　although I'm sure that didn't help.

CUT TO:

EXTERIOR. FRONT STEP. EVENING. Door wrenching open. A
puke down the front steps. Not much in it, despite the vigorous bowk.
Coughing the rest out while losing control of his legs. Bracing the wall
but failing to right himself because cramp has other dreams. Eventu-
ally, he sits, rain wet as it is. Camera on his dour survey of the damp
dark of the street, as well as – we are prompted to think – his damp-
er darker road ahead. Then, picking sick from his lip, he re-gets to
his feet and, in spite of precarious balance, makes down to the street.
After that? Whatever awaits. And the scuffed door swings shut behind.
BLACK.

INTERIOR. GREASY SPOON. NIGHT. Lights advance and retreat, other side of the pane, through the miasma'd condensation of steaming plates, teas, cigarettes. Roy Orbison on the radio. Oil cloth beneath his elbows and his head in his hands, where it shakes. 'All right, love? Get that down you' as the tea slides in from a liver spotted hand in a sovereign ring. 'Thanks' he says, looking up and not looking too well. 'What do I owe you?' 'That's all right, love, you've paid already.' 'Have I?' 'At the counter? 'Member that?' 'That's right' he says, though less from memory than the sake of politeness. 'Anything else? Fried egg sandwich? Bacon roll?' 'No, I'm fine . . . thanks very much' but the smile he tacks on goes somewhat adrift. After a quick once over, she has the measure of it. Her tone less disparaging, however, than he'd have reason to expect. 'You feeling all right, love?' 'I'm fine.' 'Not from round here, are you?' And, as always in response, 'No, up north' he says. 'I've a sister in Manchester.' 'I'm bit further south . . . Sheffield.' 'Like the knives and forks?' 'That's it.' 'Long way from home, aren't you?' 'That's how I like it!' Although he tries taking the edge off with another smile, her eyes note the odd tone, but let it slide. 'Well, good to enjoy a spot of wayfaring in your youth. I lived down south a while myself.' 'Yeah? Where was that?' 'Morden' she says. 'How was it?' he asks, smothering a laugh because, despite himself, he's enjoying the chat – and is unaware she's aware he has nothing to laugh at. 'Horrible' she says 'Just all parks and . . . nah.' 'Horrible' he repeats, for want of greater insight. 'Where you stopping now?' she fishes. 'Here in Archway, is it?' But, as his eyes go down, she sees a nerve's been hit. 'No' he mumbles 'No . . . Finsbury Park . . .' 'Not too far then. Bunking in with some mates?' Her eyes trained on the further sink of his head, until the camera spies under his matted hair. In there, he studies the pool of his tea in despair at this expectation he explain. 'No' he pulls out, sitting back up. 'It's me and my girlfriend.' Camera, holding them in a two-shot – her up and him down – interrogating his effort to satisfy her doubt. 'That's nice' she says 'Specially this time of year. Been together long, have you?' 'About three years.' 'Time to shit or get off the pot!' she decrees. 'That's what my mum used to say.' The camera focusing on how he tries to smile but can't quite bring himself to. 'Mums, eh' is all he manages 'Never fucking wrong.' And sees she's taken aback by the bite in his response. 'Just want the grandkids, don't they?' she mollifies. 'Mine used to drive me up the wall. "When you having a baby? Don't want to leave it too late." "I want to be young enough to enjoy my grandkids."' 'For breakfast?' he jokes, in a weird kind of way, lid barely on his irritation. 'Something like that' she half laughs back. 'Bossy old cow, but I loved her to bits.' Although he laughs along, she sees he's taken something amiss. Starts feeling wary of the strange dislocation in his face. In turn, he too registers her shift. Tries to work out why she's watching what his hands are playing with. It takes some staring at his own fingers to get it – she's relieved that no knife's been laid yet. Offended by, and embarrassed at this 'Afraid of something?' he asks. 'No' she says 'Are you?' 'Am I what?' 'I don't know. You just seem a bit worked up.' 'I'm not worked up, I just . . . why're you looking at me like that? I haven't done anything.' 'Never said you had, love, but you need to calm down.' 'I am fucking calm!' 'But you're not really, are you?' and she starts backing off. He gets to his feet, unwisely attempting to plead his cause. 'I just don't . . . I just don't . . .' 'I think it's time you went' she interrupts. 'Why? What have I done?' Following her. 'Stop following me!' 'I'm not following you, I just . . .' Too late, she's resolved 'That's enough. Out of my caff.' 'Suits me' he shouts, losing his head. 'If I'd wanted your fucking mother's advice, I'd have asked for it!' 'Out!' she roars 'And don't come back.' Camera trapped between as she pushes him towards it. By the shoulder first, then with hands on his back. 'Don't fucking push me. Don't you fucking touch me!' he warns, as two burlier punters present with 'All right, Janey, we're on it.' 'I never laid a finger on you' he shouts, resisting away 'On any woman.' 'What do you want, a medal? Probably not

– 224 –

*even true.' Jump cut into close-up, right into his face, realising it isn't.
And remembering when. Time collapses.* Danny, fucking amazing, *'She
would've killed me. She would've killed me!' he says, transferring the
terror in his voice into a horror on her face. For a split second, Janey
prevaricates but comes down on the side of Too Late. 'Fucking nutter,
I never want to see you in here again.' 'I wouldn't come' he bawls
'You're all the same!' grappling, nonetheless, at the doorframe. This
with no success because he still ends up in the street on his arse. 'Good
riddance to bad rubbish!' she shouts, flicking his very presence away,
before slamming the door and offering herself to the more deserving of
her care.*

*EXTERIOR. STREET. NIGHT. He sits in it, the night-street muck.
Presses hands into it to propel himself up, blind with incoherent rage.
Protesting through the window 'I did nothing wrong!' Then focus pulls
on his reflection in the steamed-up glass. But, even taking the trans-
verse of streetlights for granted, he can see that he is mad. By his eyes
and the bizarre way his body inclines. In the mismatch between his
mouth and what he's doing with his hands – grasping weirdly at some
void. And he gets so frightened. Tries to stop. But can't seem to make
himself. Can't effect change at all. 'I'm sorry' he shouts 'For what I
said' as if a child's approach might forestall the pending mayhem.
Receiving no response though, beyond his madness looking worse, he
tries stepping his whole body back and, despite banging it on a lamppost, manages. So he takes what he can get. Wipes his nose on his rag
of a coat, then pushes off as fast as he can. BLACK.*

Careful now. I quiet my breath out. I know where this is going,
that the only way is downward but still   to see it. There on the
screen. You so confounded and slipping out of sync with what I
know had been so painstakingly made – that boy you'd decided to
be when you first escaped. It just   makes me sad.

EXTERIOR. SOMEWHERE BETWEEN ARCHWAY & FINS-
BURY PARK. NIGHT. Hands in his pockets, he limps along. Breath
vapouring whitely into icy fog. Off the main drag. Now residential
streets. Respectable homes mixed with windows stretched by sheets or
various drapings of tie-dyed scarves. Where they fall short, however,
life happens behind. Dads with their daughters. Grandkids with their
nans. Newlyweds at each other's throats. Dinner-serving mums. Some
show youngsters dressing up for the night. Others, armchair alcoholics
who have theirs already planned. Council flats, above, mostly provide
a better view. But each is thoroughly examined by his confusion in
case it reveals where he belongs. Recognition stays elusive though, so he
continues on. Past lads smoking on the corners. Girls passing in heels.
Bit further back, likely scoring and tricks. Still, he's keeping his head
down. Not engaging with this. What he saw in the caff window still
at the forefront, despite all the rest kicking off in his brain. 'Remember.
Remember. Remember' he starts saying. First only with lips. Then enliv-
ened with sound. Oblivious too to those choosing to wide berth around.
Until stopping, startled. 'Can't be' he says 'This is London, remember
that instead.' This being a distinct sign of not remembering where he is
and, perhaps, even who. Camera working Danny's face on a rotating
diagonal. Top right down to bottom left. Continuing on round behind,
back of his head and the neck. Staring, for bearings, into the dark.
First at the sky, then to the street. To his eyes again. Recognition. And
he turns sharply left. 'Remember. Remember' he says. Another family.
Another window. 'Londoners' he says 'I know that's true because . . .'
then he picks up and throws a stone. From the look of the family with-
in, they've heard it also. Father pressing up to the window, warning
'Hop it, mate. If I have to come out there, you'll regret it.' Young man
holds his hands up. 'S'all right' he says 'Just checking you were really
there.' Unimpressed, the father shouts 'Get stuffed' before shutting his
drapes. Suddenly darkness where light was and silence after sound.
The camera following his eyes, hunting some target. 'What?' he shouts,

but 'Remember this' a voice says from elsewhere. 'Where are you?' he asks, twisting. No one there. A few motors pass. 'Remember what you did?' it says. 'Remember that? Filthy disgusting animal.' 'Stop it!' he shouts, breaking into a run. At which precise instant he's bowled into by football fans. Laughing, in their England shirts, as they down him. 'Sorry, mate!' 'Sorry about that!' slapping the back of his head. Camera accompanying his stumble to the ground. To the brown brick wall beside. His POV in the gutter looking out at the road. Gravel. Smashed Ribena bottle by his nose. No worse mangling though as he gets back to a sit. Just a big joke as they locust off along the footpath. One even turning and rolling him back a can. 'Here, this is for you, mate. No hard feelings, all right?' Rolls right to his foot as a bus goes past – the 210 to Finsbury Park. It's bell even rings and seems to give him pause for thought as he cracks the dented can of Carling. Not too much spray. He takes a big glug of and then, without warning, STARS. Camera refocusing on the night above. But after a plane, and another gulp, the POV labours back up. Starts to walk. Notices one shitty shoe has come off. Turns to see it stranded, not six foot back. Even so, he just looks at it, then at the 210, now disappearing into the distance, and heads after that instead. BLACK.

BLACK SCREEN FOR SOME TIME. Accompanied by the uneven sound of limping along. A single crunch for the only shod foot. Almost nothing for the bare one. His voice repeating its barely audible 'Remember's and the sound of city life somewhere there too.

EXTERIOR. THE FINSBURY PARK FLAT. NIGHT. A scuffed red door that's seen better days, in a block of flats from the 1930s, or thereabouts. Brown brick. Walkways open to the elements. A skinny hand reaches towards, then can't decide. Surveys its bruised black knuckles and nails – dirt and damage. Veins blue against white. Prominent in the loose fist. Goes to again but thinks better of it and lays its palm on the chipped paint instead. 'You in?' his hoarse voice says. 'Are you even here?' But the door, in its obstinacy, does not answer. So, *the young man rests his face on the grain like some kind of remittance might take place. Then again, the fist balls to knock and, yet again, does not.* Courage failing or, by now, the body? *His face exhausted in the unflattering light. As the camera searches its depletion, 'Why are you here?' is asked from behind and the young woman's voice continues on 'I told you not to come back.' Despite what it says, his eyes welcome the sound and his mouth agrees 'I know.' 'Who even told you I'd be here?' 'No one.' 'Then why are you?' But now he turns to her. Asks this too 'Why are you?' 'Landlord's dropping off the deposit, none of which you are owed, if that's why you've come.' Her beautiful face setting stonily against him 'Is it?' He shakes his head, the close-up capturing every shade of his descent. Black beneath the eyes. Red cracks in his lips. 'Then why are you?' 'I want to come back.' And her face wild with disbelief. 'Back to where? There's nothing here. Not any more. Do you even remember what happened now?' 'I do' he says, spinning out his regret, buying time for memory to retrieve itself. Arms crossing her bump though, she's having none of it. 'If that's true, tell me, what was said?' But he has it by then. 'You said . . . the baby deserved better than a junkie like me.' 'Did you argue?' 'No.' 'Why not?' 'Because . . .' 'Because?' 'I fucking agreed.' And though triumphant in this, she takes no pleasure here. He has caused too much pain. 'I'm sorry' he says 'But now I'm clean.' She just shakes her head. 'Don't lie to me. You're not clean. You're not even here. I have no idea where you are or what happened to the man I loved.' Close-up cruel on him. 'Lots of things' he nods. Cut to her, saying 'I know' while making room on the path.* Then Danny – though playing you fucked-up like I've never known you to be – catches something of the labyrinthine shame I've glimpsed, just before it all returns to their past.

CUT TO:

INTERIOR. THE FINSBURY PARK FLAT. MORNING.

(FLASHBACK.) The young man lifts the young woman from the shower. Soaking wet. Kissing her like he's not planning to stop. And she's laughing. Wrapping lean arms around. Accepting his body's every summons. Silhouetting in and out of the morning light. Their happiness outshining the dingy flat as they stumble through to their bed – and the light in there too, absurd with radiance. Memory's nod to romance, I think, or to underscore their starker present? I'll ask you later but interesting, that. *Her head twisting on the pillow as he slides down her front. Long dark hair strewn, and her hand in through his, as he puts himself to work on his knees.* And I see me in her. Him as him. Find electric in my body but refuse it as unfit for this here and now. *The camera cuts away too* – from what we're not permitted to see – *to the reflections from her bracelet trembling on the ceiling. Soundtrack's sound of them getting on through it, just the same.*

Can't help looking at you and see you looking at me – although I don't think we're thinking about the same thing, so I mouth

What?

But you mouth back

You and Danny???

With silent laugh. I pull a face. When Grace looks up though, we both look away.

This is a little gross

she says.

Watching my fake mum and dad.

You acknowledging this truth with a sigh.

Yeah. Probably best if you close your eyes   for this next
bit anyway, love.

And when I glance again, you're not laughing any more. It's
down to lip chewing instead.

*MONTAGE. THE RELATIONSHIP. (FLASHBACK.) Going
back to their bodies. Different time. Another day. Now afternoon light
and all stretched out mid-sex.* Danny's body ensuring her modesty's pro-
tected while his is by her well-placed thigh – not that I reckon he'd mind
either way. *The cunning camera suggesting they really are anyway* – not
that they were. I know that. *Just tight together and soaked in sweat. 'Go
on, say it' she says, and when he doesn't, whispers 'Or don't you love
me any more?' 'Shush' he shushes 'You're putting me off.' But, in recompense, intensifies his efforts. Drowns out her talk with an indecent
kiss. Makes her come then. Comes himself. 'What a fucker you are' she
says, once she can. 'All just part of the service' he laughs 'Which you
sounded pretty satisfied with to me!' 'Fucker, fucker' she repeats. Smiling despite herself although underneath some anxiety may be at work.
While this scene's less radiant than the first, they're still only young.
Most likely in love. Certainly fucking each other for all they are worth.*
Danny, I note, still weighing a stone more and that early happiness very alive
in her. *Then the camera tilts to the ceiling again. This time darker up
there, with no reflections. And a door slams below.*

*Back down. Now the KITCHEN. Now at NIGHT. Same two peo-
ple. Now stood up. Her post- party frayed as he, the worse for wear,
props up the peeling wall. Makes no protest as she pulls open his shirt
– scratch marks on his chest and stomach – just, wearily, tugs it back.
She though, beside herself, hits him a smack. Which he takes, with an
apologetic shrug. Lets her rant in his face. Then runs his hand down to*

*hers. Grips it. But she's not having that. Slaps him again. He persists,
all charmingly abject. Still, she doles out another, and this time makes
his nose bleed. At last compelled from his torpor he swears, and stands
pinching it, as blood runs down the offending shirt. So now she's the
sorry one. Mops his face up. Offers tissues and he is magnanimous.
Forgiving. Even makes light of it until, to her frustration, she's become
who's relented. Is letting him thumb off her tears and kiss her lips –*
how well I know this, plus the double infuriation of being unable to resist.
Clearly a skill you've not forgot. Snagged on this thought, however, I miss the
jump. *Camera back to the ceiling, with a now-flickering bulb, and –* as
I catch up – *returning down again.*

*And carnage in the SITTING ROOM. What furniture there is,
tossed and thrown. Books flung. Bags emptied as, half cut, he* and
Danny having now lost that stone *yanks her by the wrist. 'Where's the
money?' 'Gone!' 'Gone where?' 'I paid the rent.' 'Then they're going
to break my fucking legs, so . . . thanks very much for that.' Wrenching
free, she shouts 'Well, perhaps you should think about getting clean?'
Having already heard this, by now enough times that it no longer gets
inside, he merely concurs 'Perhaps. Or, perhaps, you could take your
sanctimony and fuck off. I'm sure Daddy would be ever so pleased.'
'God, you're horrible when you're wasted' she says. His face then, in
close-up, washed with a self-disgusted rage. 'Well, I do what I can.'
Then his lip twists as prelude to moving this on. 'So, since the money's gone, you can hand over the rest.' 'Of what?' 'You know what.'
'What?' 'What else was in the bag, and I'm not fucking around.' 'Oh'
she mock gasps 'You mean these?' producing a plastic bag bulged with
pills. His whole body stilling. 'Give that here' and when she shakes her
head 'Don't fuck with me.' Yet she dangles and dawdles. Swaps the
bag hand to hand until 'Give them here!' and he dives. She, however,
has a plan. Holds it out the window. Then tosses the lot into the street.
'Oh fuck. Oh fuck' and he's wild with panic. 'What the fuck have you
done? Those weren't even mine.' 'I don't care' she insists 'I just want .*

∴.' – now faltering – 'I just want you to come back.' 'Well, you're going the wrong way about it' he shouts, taking off through the flat. 'If you go after those' she screams 'Don't bother coming back.' 'I'll take my chances!' is all she gets as he slams on out the door. 'That's it then. Do you hear me? I really mean it this time!' But he's already not there, so there is no reply. Even the camera tracks rapidly back, pinning her in there, alone with her sadness. Perfectly still, all of it, except the lamp-shade above her head, swinging in the back draught of his exit. No way to live but   such a beautiful image. *And then the light goes out.*

Dark BATHROOM now. Music somewhere. Apprehension. Running water. Her pale hand pushing open the door. An empty bath. Streetlight through the window and then 'Oh God' him on the floor. Split lip. Black eye. Foamy puke on his chin. And her hard slaps to bring him around. 'Please don't. Please don't.' Dread right through and her awful panic, which the camera dispassionately notes, before tilting off up the wall to the bulb-less fitting above.

Handheld unsteady. One final down. Unforgiving, she rips away blankets. NIGHT. THEIR ROOM. And him, hard at work, fucking some fucked-up girl else. Greenish light loathsome on his body, like death. From above or below? Hard to tell. *Just bruised and skeletal as the young woman pounds his back. Screams at his shoulders. Digs nails into his scalp. 'How could you? How could you? And here!' Eyes rolling in his head, he asks 'What does where matter?' 'Christ, you don't know anything about normal people!' she shouts. At this, he takes umbrage. Vaguely kneels up. 'Like what? You no longer want to fuck? Think I've worked that out.' 'Don't you want to know why?' she goes, with a look on her face that makes him not want to ask. But she waits him out until 'All right. Tell me Why?' 'Because, I'm pregnant! How's that for a surprise?' And it so evidently is, there's a beat before he can get it inside. Thinking it. Thinking it. Oh. It arrives. Skinny hands prise his accomplice from round his waist. A promising start. Except he says 'No . . . you're fucking not.' Once more, she just waits*

– 232 –

him out until 'Oh fuck' he knows it and says 'Get the fuck out!' to the extra girl. As she does, his now-pregnant girlfriend turns on her heel. Camera on how she insists herself up the hall. Head lowered. Isolation embodied. Frames her beautifully in the doorway as she sits on a chair. Its cracked bentwood blending to the waves in her hair. 'Oh God. Oh God' she says, doubling over to cry. Terribly. The camera stops where it is. His long legs brush past before kneeling, naked, in front. 'I'm sorry' he says 'I didn't mean it. It won't happen again, I swear it. I'll do anything . . . everything you want.' For a beat, her awful crying is the only response. Then her fingers stretch to dig in his thin arm. Deep and deeper, until so deep it must cause him pain. 'I'm sorry' he repeats, by now sounding it. And this is when she gives in to his offered arms' comfort, unfathomable as that seems. Allows him to hold her and herself to believe. His eyes travel beyond though, looking elsewhere for light. Then, on finding none anywhere, shut. BLACK.

I can't look around, and the thought of you both   watching this. We're all sitting way too close. I knew though   I already knew every second of it and yet   you were right to see is   different. What you were. What you did.

EXTERIOR. OUTSIDE THE FINSBURY PARK FLAT. NIGHT. (FLASHFORWARD.) Seeing himself as she does, and bereft of excuse, he attempts the apology for which she no longer has any use. 'I'm sorry . . . for everything I've put you through . . . I just . . . I was . . . am . . . useless . . . I don't know what to do.' And she sees he means it but it's all too late. She's now so broken, what remains but to say 'Well, I have nothing left to offer you, so please, please go away.' So any hope left in the young man tramps to its defeat. Head down, he steps round her, as invited. And, though she's doing the spurning, she can't bear to look. Just closes the gate after. Then goes back up the path to wait for their former landlord with the deposit. Cars pass and he disappears. BLACK.

Grace exhales heavily.

> Jesus.
> > Gracie, love.

But she just shakes her head.

BLACK SCREEN. Sounds of traffic then. Maybe a train. Not much else.

EXTERIOR. RAINY TUBE EXIT. NIGHT. (PRESENT.) Now lights advance and retreat on the other side of his eyes, disrupting him to dislocations his POV tries to right. So the camera opts to observe from outside. Even then, not quite as a friend. The matted brown hair. Waxen skin. Bruises and suggestions of malnutrition, all hung in a coat that's long given up. Short in the arm too, advertising the bruise has reached – if anyone was interested and no one is *– down beyond the wrist. Rest of his hands bluish too, cadaverous. Cigarette between joints so prominent, they surely ache in the damp. Not that that interrupts the drag in and out – more dear to him, it seems, than the breath that surrounds it. Knees giving too, every once in a while. Practically through his trousers now. Yet he hauls himself straight, time and again, from some concealed well of determination that's decreed he shall not sink to a sit.* I'd say you know that'd be the end of it. *Rather, his body remains resolved despite no longer* perhaps *knowing where it is. Or what's going on. Or* possibly *caring after all that's happened. Just lots of people pushing by, annoyed by rain and this young man hunched in the entrance. And although he's not begging, someone gives him a quid – which it takes him a second to recognise. 'Thanks' he calls after, but his Samaritan's already gone.* So where will you go? Or even could you now? *He doesn't resemble a man able for thinking too far ahead. Barely manages, in fact, to pocket his quid.* Does he know what he might do with it? Even realise he needs a feed? *Then ambulance light rotates in his eye and* returns him again into real time, if only in preparation for what memory's about to do next.

INTERIOR. SOUND STAGE. EITHER DAY OR NIGHT. (FLASHBACK.) Young man looking thin albeit wired to within an inch of his wits. Sound design, as if within, thick with pulse. Indistinct. People shouting. Scraping. Castors on floors. Hammering somewhere. Behind him, a door. 'Quiet on set, please!' Then, there is 'Set.' 'Rolling.' Markers clapped. The infamous 'Action!' And he opens it. Takes off at full pelt across an expanse. Factory kind or warehouse perhaps. *No matter because, skimming the surface, he just runs and runs it. Just runs it and runs. Right until he unexpectedly doesn't. Can't. And knows he shouldn't stop for his mark's not been hit. But his body's gone to some wall his brain hasn't seen yet. Stumbling forward, grabbing his wrist. Close-up on that. Cutting to blue at the lips. Someone shouts 'Cut.' Someone shouts 'What the fuck!' Thud in his head. The body's balance giving up. Falling. Knees first. Then right down on its side. Eyes going floor to ceiling. Into deep wiring. A right mess of pipes above. Massive. Multitudes. But the eyes keep rolling back in his head. Body convulsing. People running. People kneeling beside. People, urgently, asking 'What happened? What's wrong?' But he's in no state to answer. Mouth only jawing. White eyes alone broadcasting the pain is immense. 'Jesus Christ' someone screams 'Call an ambulance. He's having a heart attack. Quick!'*

You don't think I do, but I see you tug the hairs on your wrist. Tinily. Very discreet. As though small pain keeps the other at distance. And, who knows, maybe it can.

EXTERIOR. RAINY TUBE EXIT. NIGHT. A passing ambulance showers light in menacing streaks across the wet pavement. Cut to his eyes seeing. Then understanding what they see. An ambulance, yes. The light from it. From an odd angle though. So what's the perspective? Oh.

– 235 –

He's on the ground here too. And here too, on his side. Camera above, as the light casts across where he lies and convulses at its touch, in the past.

INTERIOR. AMBULANCE. DAY. (FLASHBACK.) Faces flower over above. A razzmatazz of medical commotion. 'We're losing him' somewhere far off. He doesn't care either way. BLACK.

EXTERIOR. RAINY TUBE EXIT. NIGHT. Eyes click back to clear sight. 'I think he's awake.' 'Maybe he just passed out?' 'Did you hit your head?' 'What?' He, overwhelmed by this bloom of faces above. 'I saw you keel over but . . .' 'I'm all right.' He wrangles free of the pulse-checking hand. 'Easy, fella.' 'Here, let me help' and they pull him to his feet. 'What happened?' 'Are you all right?' 'Alkie cunt!' from way at the back. 'Don't waste your sympathy!' But also 'Watch your mouth!' Circling round. Closing in. 'Give him that, poor beggar needs to eat.' Then a Crunchie's passed through and pressed into his fingers which he, in turn, gazes bewilderedly on. 'You eat that now, son, it'll do you good.' Rubbed up wrong by the 'son' though, 'I'm not' he disputes. 'I'm not yours and I'm not your son.' The giver soothes 'I only meant, put something in your stomach.' 'Ah . . .' and he realises this. Still, continues backing off as his benefactor advances. 'You got somewhere to go?' 'Yeah . . . loads of places . . . loads.' Camera growing uneasy as the bulk of his sympathisers peel off. 'Want to sit?' the man says. 'You took quite a tumble'. 'No . . . but thanks for the Crunchie, mate.' 'At least let me walk you.' 'No . . . I'm sorted . . . I'm fine.' 'It's no trouble, really.' But his tenacity starts to alarm and agitation steers the young man to impossible grounds. Weird thoughts take place. 'Are you my father?' he eventually asks, attempting to look like he knows This Is Madness, even as it's said. 'What do you think?' replies the man, moving close against, inviting the dazed POV into his face. 'I . . . don't think . . . I don't think you are.' 'That's right' the older reassures 'But

. . . why don't you come back to mine? Have a wash? Something to eat?' The young man's eyes though go Rush, and his body hits Flight. 'What the fuck?' he shouts, backing right off, dispersing what's left of his well-wishing crowd. 'I don't know you. Leave me alone.' 'Take it easy' the man says, poised, implacable. So, the younger, trying not to be mad, works to contain himself. It doesn't go well. The tic runs riot round his mouth and down his neck. 'I'm off' he shouts, taking to his heels. The other springs after. 'I'll walk you. Wait!' with such alacrity his composure shows cracks. And the camera, unsure whether to follow or not, lets them turn the corner. Then in their absence, arrives at Should, and pushes forward to join the chase. BLACK.

And I think of your body. What it's been through. Then of how little matter that seems to you. Stiff in the cold. Sometimes. Or the damp. Sensitive on the scars but not about. When coughing, occasionally, holding your chest. Still, and often, neglecting to eat. But do you know how I love it? Love having it close? That others have too, or have wanted too, is hardly a shock. Yet – and although it's only Danny's up there on the screen – I'd like to hide it. Cover and fix it up. Ward the sharks off but, in that water, you were the blood. Even I can see.

EXTERIOR. ROAD. NIGHT. Erratic sound. Images split. The young man runs – not very fast, and not really running but the intention is there. *Features surfacing to the streetlights. Submerging again. The other close after, easily catching up. The light and dark spells condensing to blocks of the young man, then his pursuer, until they are abreast. Man grasping his frayed sleeve. Pulling him back. The arm over his shoulders effecting a halt. And whispering 'Take it easy' in his ear. But the younger keeps struggling and not only against him. His body alive with unignorable compulsions. Twitches. Tics. The say-so of cramps and whatever else is flittering across his mind.* Running his clock down to pieces, feels like. *Definitely breaking, visibly, apart. 'Let go* of me! Let go!' 'Just trying to help.' The man releasing him but keeping pace as he makes off, lamely, down the road. No longer choosing, just accepting where its meander goes. And it goes off the beaten track. To places streetlights get rare and the houses lapse towards dereliction. No more families here. No rich, curtain-hid lives. Closer to squats, like those that have been but further eeried by city silence, which very rarely bodes well. That more than one thing's going wrong now, I'd suggest, but then I know what's coming next. The shoeless foot missteps. 'Fuck!' Again, granting the pursuer helper's rights. 'Here, I've got you.' 'Let go! It hurts.' 'I won't hurt you' the older protests. 'No, it's my arm . . . stop touching it.' The camera steadying its eye on them as he's steadied on his feet. 'What's wrong?' the man asks, pushing up his sleeve and, getting an eyeful, 'Jesus! You'd want someone to have a look at that.' Young man yanks it away. 'Why don't you fuck off?' 'I only want to help.' But the younger, transiently in possession of sense, says 'I know what you want.' Conceding, the older shrugs 'I could help with a fix, if you'd like to swap?' But, for all his mess, the younger says 'No.' 'Really?' 'Really' he says. 'Well then, good for you. Bet you're not feeling great though, so . . . how about a fag instead?' Before more's transacted, however, the heavens break. Thunder. Lightning. The whole dramatic shebang. Rain sheeting so totally the camera can barely track them. There? No. There. On the move. The older backing the younger through a rusty gate. Down a privet-wild front. To a long-disused house. One pulled sheet of ply later and they're in, although the night, with its storm, stays all around.

INTERIOR. DERELICT HOUSE ENTRANCE HALL. NIGHT. This place born for filming and the camera loves it. Broke glass. Ivied woodwork. Floors Tarkovsky wet. A horsehair armchair, disgorging. Evidence of rats, and mould afflicted mirrors to catch the two men shaking off this bad rain. 'Fucking hell' curses the older. The younger eyes his reflection, in the puddle, by his feet. 'Not great, eh?' the older says, *sliding in to view it. Both there. Then lost once the ceiling drips. 'What about that fag you mentioned?' 'Oh yeah, here it is.' All eyes on the pack as it's pocket-dug free and, once extended, accepted keenly. 'Ta.' Younger leaning in, to the left, for the light. Heads close as it flickers. Eye to eye. Information exchanged. Enough that, by his breath out, he's realised nothing's for free. 'Not even this shitty cigarette?' 'No, not even that.' His eyes drift off. Then drift back. 'Okay.' he says, resting his back to the spindle-less banisters 'But that's all you get. I won't do anything.' 'Suits me' the older says, affecting a nonchalance which, it soon becomes evident, he does not feel. Right from the start he's at the younger, tooth and claw. Rains his damp skinny body with work. Hands and mouth everywhere. Obscenities. Hithers. But, while the flesh is available, the rest remains at a remove – infuriatingly, increasingly, until 'Come on, I can tell this is getting you off.' Camera noting this is only the truth. But when even this extracts no greater response, the older curses him. 'You reek, you know that? You're filthy. You need a wash.' 'Well, no one's forcing you' the younger scoffs.* Apparently able for laughter now he's given up? *'Or I could force you?' the older suggests, extending a strong palm across the gaunt face. Squeezing until it digs into the cheeks. If anticipating panic, however, all it receives is a mumbled 'Please yourself.' And when the camera, as the older, examines the younger's eyes, detachment is the most it finds. Leading the half-hearted aggressor to finally twig that, whatever pleasures offered, or threats made, he will never cross that distance. He can't even see that far. The perspective switches then, to look out from the younger. Past the older's shoulder. Above the door. Studying the fragments of stained glass. Seeking something. But not finding, it travels through where other panes once sat. On out to the deluge. And the past.* Into what we cannot yet understand. But very soon will.

And Grace looks at me. Eyebrows a little arch, like asking News to you? I shrug. Not hard to ask about that stuff, any more. Not like asking about her which used to be like pulling teeth. Maybe later I'll tell her that, but   about this? All for you.

INTERIOR. CHILDHOOD HOME KITCHEN. EVENING. (FLASHBACK.) Hand over a boy's eyes, nose and mouth. He is earlyish teens. The hand, an older woman's. Thin fingers. Almond nails. Neatly trimmed. Splayed and wrapped around like muzzling. Which he tries to bear, but the risk of smothering intersperses his stillness with twisting. Making the hand tighten more as her voice demands 'Tell the truth. Where were you?' Then released just enough for him to claim 'A dog got run over and I went to help but . . . it was already dead.' The hand vices again. 'Don't lie.' 'It's the truth.' Nails pushing in now, to the point of cut – the boy's eyes straining down to assess how much. Blood. So   pretty bad. 'All right' he panics. And the hand peels back, leaving tiniest slits his bony fingers rub. Buying time though to ready his mouth, for saying what it does not want, and the rest of him for blitz. 'I . . .' he says 'I . . . walked a girl home from school.' Eyes intent, down left, moving up only to her voice. But slowly slowly, as if forestalling her incandescent 'You did what?' He does not repeat. His eyes just shift back down to the left. Flinching. Waiting. He looks back again and then 'No, don't!' And BLACK. And a sound that makes me jump. *Another. Then to very close up on the woman's hand smeared in blood. Widening to the boy, bending double, spitting it out on her shoes. BLACK.*

Grace's hand tight enough to wring her own neck. So I take a stab at mechanising it.

　　　　He's very good, Stephen.
　　　　Yeah   lovely as well   easy to deal with.
　　　How did you   get him ready   for
　　Talked him through it   what it was like and that's what
　　he   did   talented lad.
　　　　I can see   hard to watch though.
　Already?
　　　　Yeah   really.

– 240 –

I'm afraid there's worse to come.

A choke then from Grace. You reach for her hand, but she

No, Dad   I'm fine.

And I see, for the first time, why you really didn't want her to.

INTERIOR. DERELICT HOUSE ENTRANCE HALL. NIGHT. The young man's eyes, filled with this past, find to the mirror to satisfy themselves that here is now, and not then. Parallels yes, but without much precision. Besides, this hand on his mouth is less sure of its right. Shows it by slipping to his chest. Then down, out of shot. So this being only this, bodies at work, he can stay far away. Separate from the involuntary jerks. Hard breaths in his neck. Expected stuff. Easy! Until . . . he begins to reinhabit himself. Why? He can't know. Wants to? Does not. But suddenly he's taking in this stranger pushing against. Recoiling from the activity between his legs. And, in the mirror, watches his body being done a service it really doesn't want. Alarm goes through. Becomes distress. 'Oh God.' He seems so young again. So young and all alone, despite the familiarity he's experiencing. *Smearing his palm across the glass, asking 'What are you doing?' The older just laughs. 'What do you fucking think?' Then the mirror gets hit. And so hard. CRACK.*

INTERIOR. CHILDHOOD HOME HALLWAY & STAIRS. EVENING. (FLASHBACK.) And the boy pulls back from where his forehead's struck the glass. Barely catching an eyeful before the mirror shatters. Strips tinkling off. Patterning the floor. Just bits of broken him remain, along with broken her – the less visible but, nonetheless, sole instigator. 'You go to bed' her voice says 'I'll see you later on.' Adding, as icing, when his cut face turns, 'I think you've forgotten who owns who in here.' BLACK.

CUT TO:

FRAGMENTS. Hands. Stairs. Carpet. A dribble of blood. Upward motion. Ecru-coloured woodchip. Skirting boards. Fingers. Viscous breath. The sound of pulsing. The radiance of panic. He falls. And the edge of the step is right there. Scrambles back up into a lopsided terror. Just keeping all the pieces together. Up. Up. Carries on. He carries on. Until suddenly BLACK.

And that's the moment Grace takes your hand. Winds her fingers in. Then squeezes tight for all she can. You, a little unsteadied, saying

It's all right, love. It's fine.

Is it? I doubt it is. Right now, I'd leave you to yourself. Know how you'd prefer to keep the distance between that woman and everyone else. As if she could still reach out through time. And do what though? What do you imagine? I'd not let her near and bet neither would Grace. Perhaps you don't know you underestimate us? Or, maybe, you don't want to take any chances. Never mind. Grace'll learn it in time.

INTERIOR. DERELICT HOUSE ENTRANCE HALL. NIGHT. 'What the fuck?' from the man, as shards of mirror shimmer the room. The young man flinches away but is caught by him and, for a few frames, the two men hang. Eyes on eyes, inviting understanding, unwelcomely for one, *to begin. 'Easy' the man soothes, without success. For, despite being the stronger and with more at stake, the younger is agile in his panic. Even more, with his resurrected will. Which chooses to pull him violently free. Close-up of dirty hands grappling past the older's body, making for the stairs. And when 'Don't! They're rotten' the older warns, he climbs them anyway. Might even take six before his foot goes through. 'Fuck!' 'See? Come back. I told you.' But the younger won't now, however many bad steps or splinter-bloodied his ankles* get. 'You'll kill yourself!' the older shouts, as half the banisters collapse. Yet, in spite of all this, the body advances. On hands and knees by the time the first landing's reached. But that landing is a different world.

INTERIOR. DERELICT HOUSE FIRST LANDING/ ENTRANCE HALL. NIGHT. Eyes pan the fifties fern wallpaper lacing its walls. 'You're not here, are you?' he calls. 'What?' the older echoes from below, unaware his prey has arrived at its nth degree by now. 'Need some help?' 'Go away' the younger says, so attracted by the flocked plant life ahead that he crawls towards. Crouches beside. Fingers carefully finding the curling shapes of it out while the older, after testing out what stairs the woodworm's left, unconditionally surrenders. 'All right, look . . . I'm going, but I'm leaving you this . . . do you hear me?' No response. 'A fiver, all right?' Laughter erupting above. 'For what? Unsuccessfully wanking me off? Don't think you got your money's worth, mate.' 'Yeah well, nothing ventured, eh? It's here on the post anyway and . . . get that arm to a hospital soon.' But still he waits. And hopes? Then waits some more. All to no purpose, as soon becomes clear. So, he turns up his collar and heads back out into the now-lesser rain.

INTERIOR. DERELICT HOUSE FIRST LANDING/SECOND LANDING. NIGHT. Camera close-up on the long skinny hand. Little finger pressed to the ferns discovering most delicate ways to touch. Frond tips with his tips. Expecting what? I remember you touching me like that. Secret in the darkness with the reverse of your hand. Stupid thing to think except now Danny, as you, is doing it too. Not that these are the same. Camera showing him now rise to his feet. Fingers assuming a more interrogative touch. Pianoing where the plaster erupts. Prising lath loose. Ripping at flock. Like wanting to see in but lightlessness obstructs. So he takes the return to the second landing and hangs over. That's a drop. Almost giddy but then Stop. The camera on his gaunt face sees *how he suddenly knows that somewhere waits something wrong. Dry lips unsealing when he hears it. What? The whole body resisting as it's walked into the room ahead. The camera hanging back though, as if sensing an end and dreading what it might be. BLACK.*

Grace also biting unsealed lips. How far we've all travelled in this confined place, under such low light, before pictures of a past only one of us has ever been in. As yet, unknowably far, I think. And then

BLACK SCREEN. Strings. Unlike any music preceding. But the weft of its undertow somehow aiding return to that desolate room on the screen.

INTERIOR. DERELICT HOUSE. UPSTAIRS ROOM. NIGHT. Through the glass darkly the camera sees. Through the night coldly he has been. All revolving. 360 degrees. Sunken eyes and wet hair. Dirt smeared on his cheek. Eyes rolling in their sockets with the rush of seeing. Then taking some hold. Backing himself back. Neck turning the head to look, from odd angles, into what might be waiting there in the dark. 'Are you?' he asks, lastly. 'Are you really here?' Camera stock still, but the rush in his ears deafening. Yet even with this, the creak of the floorboards cuts through. Instantly his body wants further back again but, as of now, there's no room left. Then, from the shadow, she comes. His very spit. Hooded eye. Hollowed cheek. And his whole body rejects her existence but is powerless to deny what he sees. 'I know this must be psychosis' he says 'But . . . I see you anyway.' 'And I see you' she answers. 'Everywhere. And always. Remember that?' 'I remember' he says 'I remember everything.'

INTERIOR. CHILDHOOD HOME BEDROOM. NIGHT. (FLASHBACK.) The boy in bed as the same woman slides in beside. Swallowing to keep his gorge down as she kisses his black eye and fingertips his split lip. 'Why did you make me do that? You know I hate

hurting you, love.' And though he only looks at her, he really does. Sees all the way through until she crawls with his focus. Until to muzzle it she would do anything. What? So she pushes a long finger in. Past his teeth. Ignoring his tic. Back far enough to make him retch. Instinct taking over, he grabs her wrist and they meet eye to eye. Camera panning back to reveal how utter her grip because slowly, slowly, his hand withdraws from her wrist and he tries to relax his gag reflex instead. Mouth wet with nausea. Panic on his face. Then she forces it further in. Adds a second. The camera takes her view as she presses his tongue before returning to the outside of him. Back in the two-shot, the boy starts violently shaking his head. She is climbing him now, positioning herself. He says 'No.' Perhaps? It's hard to tell. Objecting though, for all he is able. But she, able as well, just puts her mouth on his. BLACK.

No one looks away. No one even is. Everyone hates this room.

INTERIOR. DERELICT HOUSE UPSTAIRS ROOM. NIGHT. His face jerking away as time overlaps. And while the past has been here, she has advanced. Come close to him now in his paralysed fright. Surveying his body and its broken mess. 'Oh my love, what have you done to yourself?' 'No! What have you come for?' he asks. 'One final pick of the carcass? Jackal. Here's all that's left.' Stretching emaciated fingers into what small space remains between. Before more happens though, she is on him. Has him by the throat. Traps him to the wall. Her body to his. He cleaves so frantically from this that skin could rip from bone. But, despite this, he manages to turn to the wall and hide his face. The force of her against him does not abate. 'It's just withdrawal' he argues 'You're not here. How would you even know me any more?' Her voice though, grows over this. 'I know you, you know that, and what we did . . . you'll never escape.' But he will not accept it. 'Never forget' he corrects. At least denying her claim, if not her touch which, cruelly enough, now presents with more tenderness than any other this night. Finger combing his dirty hair. Laying her head on his

back. Terrifying him to his depths. To losing himself once more. Resist-
ance all dissipating under her pressure until he's a barely habitable
body again. Just hangs exposed to a past back from its hither and yon.
So much now he cannot make it stop. 'I did not' he objects 'And I do
not want.' But gets taken there anyway. BLACK.

INTERIOR. CHILDHOOD HOME BEDROOM. NIGHT.
(FLASHBACK.) Something terrible in the dark which even the cam-
era refuses to watch. A sexual sound going on and on. Breathing. The
boy crying. Intermittent struggle. A 'Don't.' A 'No.' A 'Please' and,
maybe, 'Stop.'

The reproduction so horrific Grace and I clam up while you just
wring free of her hand. Fold your arms. Then decide it'd be better
to unwind. So do and, instead, wag a finger at the screen.

Don't know Eily   what do you think? Too much or   to
the point?

And I understand I have to find a voice. Fast. Just find, fucking, find
it. QUICK.

Not sure   I think   it's right not to see but   maybe do
something about the volume?
    What's wrong with it?
It's just   very overwhelming. Might be asking too much
from the audience   maybe?

Despite everything else, the Director in you is annoyed.

Maybe that's just because you know me, rather than
            Well, I still have ears, don't I?
        Right   yeah   I'll make a note.

Slide a look at Grace. She seems taken aback that this is when we're discussing sound effects. It's for her we are, though. I know that. Just as I know far worse happened that night than any film can show. So if annoying you helps, I will do that too. And you do ask again.

    This next scene then I   I wonder about the placement of the sound.

So I take this bait also because   it is for me and I'm glad to be myself, to you, once more.

    In what way, Stephen?
        Just   should it be over the scene or not? Should it just be a blackout and then the scene after? I'm still not sure. Okay, well   let's see.

EXTERIOR. THE THIRD DREAM. NIGHT INTO DAY. Sound of what's happening in the room everywhere, but the camera on the Holloway Road again. This time it attains neither height nor flight. Just pulled along the surface like a body dragged. Only junkier sounding because metal and plastic, convulsion and pleas bleeding through. Then glass adding notes of the lens being scratched. Grit getting inside. Bashing across litter as she finds where she wants. As she lets herself free. And the boy's Don'ts just disembody. The lens shatters to bits. But, against the pure white dissonance, it captures a few last feet. Though, once splintering starts, it can only bear witness to itself being destroyed. Fragmenting. Finally strewing all down the Holloway Road. Its last mechanisms gutted while the white lines blur. Going grey-white into silence now. And then, in silence, to BLACK.

Jump in! Jump in. Anything but cry.

$- 247 -$

It's   I think   you've judged it well.

Not too on the nose?

It's pretty literal but   the sound alone would   be too
much.

That was my hunch.

And it's already   hard enough.

Yes   I'm starting to realise that.

But I don't think we should matter here, me and Grace. We're only observers of this, who can close their eyes or leave their seats, while you were   I
look to her, hands over her mouth, making no comment at all.

INTERIOR. DERELICT HOUSE UPSTAIRS ROOM. NIGHT.
And she is all around him. The room moves to her pace. His head hung
between aching arms, bracing himself. 'What was I supposed to be?' he
asks. 'After? What am I supposed to be?' That flitch of wallpaper on the
floor his whole world now, beyond which his eyes cannot stray. 'What I
am' she says. 'You'll be the same . . . because now, my love, it's yours as
well. In you, like it was in me.' The camera then wrestling to the outside
of him. Willing challenge but getting only his eyes taking it in. 'On and
on' she says. 'On and on and on. My father to me and me to you and
you to . . .' 'No!' LIFE surfacing. 'I never would.' 'Oh, but you will' she
soothes. 'Or it'll never stop because it knows all about you and how to
get what it wants. My poor lovely boy with your beautiful face.' Reaching
over his shoulder to place fine-boned fingers on his cheek. Him shirking
from but 'Can't outrun it' she whispers. 'It's always been. It always will.
And I'll be there when you become me as well.' All now accomplished
for her. Except. These words crash his last panic-less part. Convulsing
his body so badly he tries to disperse it by shouting 'Never' to not much
effect. Fear instead running that wild, he starts banging his head off the
wall. Hard. Harder. Bringing plaster to crunch. Blood trickling his face,

then attacking himself. 'Get out of me! Get out!' Falling to the floor. Roll-
ing it. Kicking. Yet she does not go. At last, breathless, he drags himself.
Stares down. Then gazes up. Sees her unmoved, as if there is nothing
amiss. As if she can't even see despair burning off him. 'I understand' she
says simply 'But everything that must be, will.' Everything that must be,
will. At that the world stops. Even its air. The rain outside. The dust drift-
ing in here. There is no more time. There is only him as he stands to look
in the window at his mother's son. Or what's left. *And* to what is *he says*
'Then it's the end.' 'What do you mean?' 'It's the end' he repeats, con-
necting somewhere to something she has no idea how to reach. The end.
The END. Become the words that wake time. Danny seemingly not doing
much but burning the screen. THE END. *Her face changes and, in their*
echo, she is   suddenly   less. Left grasping her throat like some mirror
of Grace. *And eerily human, watching her son,* ruined as he is, *back from*
the room. Her anguish obvious. Her terrible longing for him plain. But in
this End, he is deaf to her siren song. So, when he crosses the threshold,
she is left alone to be reabsorbed by the dark.

INTERIOR. DERELICT HOUSE SECOND LANDING/
THIRD STAIRS. NIGHT. Once out on the landing, the night opens to
him. And he is alone again, looking at the last flight of deathtrap stairs.
Already knowing what he'll do at the top of them. Camera following
thoughtfully as he ascends. Up and up. Into BLACK.

Whatever they feel now, no one says. No one says a single thing.
So nearly there, he and us with him, at this finish, whichever it will
be.

EXTERIOR. DERELICT HOUSE ROOF. NIGHT. A small sky-
light opens, already barely on its hinge. Detaching further as he clambers
out onto the steepish pitch. No wind though. No more rain. Time ambig-
uous, but streetlights remain on and the sky an ocean of nothing to see.
Just clouds across the moon. Mist across the city. Camera scrolling the

vault of it before finding back steadily to the young man again. Stood, somewhat precariously, on the ridgepole of the roof. From his now calm, battered face, the now quieted eyes look and map his route across to the edge. 'It's all right' he says. 'It's all all right from here' then moves his feet. Inches them forward along the slates. The shoe-lessness, at last, become benefit, although the odd squelch of moss disconcerts. Then a police siren goes off and he, sort of, jumps. Takes some steps forward far too quick. Finds himself staring at guttering. And further, down to the street. It's so nearly now but still not yet. Instead, the camera takes off, to locate and retrace those roads he's been. Redbrick estates and Victorian terraces, the same. All the same now he's done with them. And strings in the soundtrack. Pulling up and up. Severing ties with that unmatter-ing world. Implying transcendence of its squalor and the degradation of what he's been. A spirit shirking off what mortal coil pins it down, hems it in, with its weight of past and inescapable consequence. Unexpectedly, some part of me even roots for that. *Camera returning before long though, to him in a long shot. High on his precipice. Gazing down. Stone idol above its metropolis, eroding now. The illusion breaking on his taking of a deep breath in and*

You don't though, do you, Dad?

Grace suddenly asks. I look at you and you don't look back because you haven't told her everything yet.

Just watch the film, love. It's almost over now anyway

His toes to the line. It would barely take a sway. Danny's eyes going all the way, right to the bottom, but unafraid. Some clock inside telling him to wait for the very best moment to. The terror gone. Desperation too. Like he understands. Like there's no more confusion and, if nothing else, this affords him, at this finish, relief. His mouth opening a little as he readies himself. A close-up so close up I almost see the clock tick. *See it say 'The time is now. Take it and everything will be done.' So, his body prepares, and just as he is, the sun throws out its very first beam. Pinkish white. From the wilds of the east. And that beam finds right to him. His white famished face. The startle enough for his grey eyes to raise and look to its source in return. Corneas colouring up then with rings of the sun.*

Beautiful that, Stephen.

And you smile but keep going. Nearly there now. Almost home.
He holds to the sunlight as it keeps coming in. Expanding. Fluorescing. Undoing night into dawn. His eyes too, less resolute, as the city comes into view. Teasing glints of light livening and life below, like glad to show its day self again. And then. And then. On the street, just beneath, appears a young woman. Long hair loose. High heels in her hand. Singing herself home from a hell of night. Body limber with excess and unconcerned by broken glass, even underfoot. Caught out by dawn, however, she checks her watch. Then swears at herself. Maybe 'Shit!'? 'Maybe 'Fuck!'? When the camera cuts back to him though, he is engrossed. Pallor intact but resolve eroded. What does he think? Would he like to know more? *And then, the camera, switching to above his shoulder, sees his weight shift from the front foot to back. Still looking down, as if he will. Although, increasingly undecided, he delays long enough to watch her sit. To see her, inelegantly, slide shoes on and do up the straps. Notices her, dreamily, stroke her own leg.* Imagining she's imagining being touched that way? Perhaps. *But he avidly watches her root through her bag, more swearing ensuing, until she unearths her fags. Tears coming into his eyes when she does. And he wills her to get it lit, despite her lack of coordination and viable matches.* Does he share her satisfaction on finally breathing it in? *Instead of answers, however, there's another trick. The camera pulls quickly back up the slates*

revealing we, avid watchers, as her sole audience, and that what had seemed his perspective was not. I cannot pinpoint the shift. *The camera, equally surprised, searches for him. Left then right. Right across the whole roof. And, on not finding, approaches the edge.*

Fears it.

Looks over it.

Then, down.

Further down.

And that's where he is. Not sprawled though or smashed. Emerging from the rusty garden gate. Limping and ruined but 'Hey' *he says* 'Any chance I could scab a fag?' *Far too far gone to be startled, she holds them out.* 'Fucking hell' *she says* 'You've had a wilder one than me.' 'Probably' *he agrees.* 'I was actually going to head up to A&E but . . . I've got a fiver so . . . fancy something to eat?' *She gives him the once over while he, tolerantly, waits.* 'Might as well' *she concedes.* 'Can hardly be worse.' 'Yeah' *he says* 'That's what I thought so . . . let's just see how we do?' *And, with that, pulls her to her feet. They exchange smiles in frazzled close-up. Then, making what chat they remain capable of, set forth on the new morning world.*

And the camera resumes its rooftop perch, keeping watch below until they're completely gone. Once they are, however, tilts back up to its height. Looks out across the city. Light now. Come to life. First strains of 'Sleepwalkers Woman' *weaving in, as it opens out into a panorama of London. Old and new. Still and travelling. Unceasing in its ever on.* BLACK.

First Winter

Silence.

Your quick throat clear.

Silence again.

Technically the song's an anachronism but

Yet more silence.

And there'll be credits as well at this point   obviously.

As the silence continued you turned to me, casting out line.

So   now you've both seen it.

Just before I could bite

Jesus, Dad   Fuck!

Signalling the end of silence. And the forlornness of her so vast,
you just folded her in.

Gracie, love   it's all right.

But it wasn't. So then it was

Grace, don't cry like that.

And when that made no difference

I'm so sorry, love   for everything.

Missing entirely her sadness's meaning, which I knew was for
you, not for her. Old thorn that, guilt, but for you to pick. So gathering myself I rose   before getting tangled in.

I'll just   I'll leave you to it   Stephen.

Although your eyes said wait, they saw also I'd not and returned to what fate then hid in your shoulder. In the mess of her hair. In the rent sobs she made. In your aloneness with them, like it was all you deserved. Or all you expected, at least.

All right, Eil   we'll be out   in a bit.

Nod for a nod. Then I slipped my seat. Left the two of you there in the lap of your history. Secret, terrible and buried, but family. And I could not be part. So turned my trespass towards other air. Your film still at work inside, just differently to her, and I suspected I was a few steps ahead. Interested already in the hows of what you had made and the whys of its variations from what I'd read. Because for all its fidelity there were departures as well. Events shifted to some remove from the actual. Or were those just other ways in? Same truths, different medium? Or, free of the page, had it taken on a life of its own? Become more than you? A story you were also watching? Wanting to find out how far he could get? Evading your sackcloth, and the obedience owed it, to look anew at that past? For why should yours, alone, stay on ice when everyone else's gets tugged everywhere? These my first thoughts as I made on out to the foyer. Just absorbing and adjusting to what you'd let me see. All the feeling on top but the questions beneath. So, I lit up a cigarette, then imagined what might be happening back in there with you two.

And I didn't have to for long.

Ten minutes, perhaps, before the preview theatre doors opened. Except only you came out.

Where's Grace?
Gone to wash her face. She'll be along in a sec.

Wary-eyed, you cast over me. Readying, I thought, for further blitzes of feeling, but I was – and after that film I was many things – not in need of that. Which set us at cross-purposes when you leant in beside, lit up and asked it

So?
So.
What did you think?
It's incredible.
Yeah?
And not easy to watch but   beautiful. So beautiful.
You mean that?
I do.
And you're not upset?
I am upset but   what's wrong with that? I loved how it took hold of me and just did what it wanted. I was so in it by the end I forgot he was you and   what's wrong?
No   nothing, I just
What?
That's what I wanted   for it to have a life of its own.
And it does.
Different for Gracie though.
I'm not surprised.
She's very   upset.
She'll be all right.
You think?
I do   it just might be a while.

Both looked to the door then, then back. West End air not much help. Neither cheering, nor head clearing. Just enforced patience and wait. You fidgeting and so thin in your shirt that, all at once, I took you in. Hand. Then face. And was taken in return.

Oh God, Eily   come here.
It's all right, Stephen   it really is.

So you collapsed in my shoulder. Breathed stress into my hair as I stroked yours and whispered words I thought might help.

She'll be fine. She loves you and now you can tell her anything.

Which I also thought was true. Then got kissed for my troubles like we were alone. Soft and more. Finding to open. Both bodies giving in to their habitual closer. Closer. Until we were there. As if no time had passed or any strange weather had troubled the while between. Just you and me kissing in a foyer like the best of times. Then a break to whisper in my ear

You might have been right   before.
So you've remembered me, have you?
I never forgot   just seeing the two of you together
Freaked you out?
Maybe   a bit.
And now?
I just want to go home.
Well, once Grace comes out we can go.
I don't mean that   I mean   I could do with being alone with you.
That bad, was it?
Not bad but   a lot of the past and watching it with both of you made me realise how much I
What?
How much better it is   when I am close to you.

And there again we were. Useless as fuck. Me studying you as you studied my mouth. Going for it when you kissed it. And all of it like love. Finding back together when

Dad?

I turned first – your mouth needing a wipe before offering her a smile.

Feeling better now, love?
Since you gouged my heart from my chest?
Yes, I suppose   since then.
A little.
Well   I'll take what I can get.

But wrapped your arms round her, relieved at her smirk. Got hugged too, to strangulation, in return and with alrightness, if not absolute, approaching, it was enough to set her back down.

So what now then, daughter?
I could murder something to eat.
I'm sure that can be managed without further bloodshed.
Eily?
God, yeah, I'm famished.
All right. Out to Wardour Street we go.

So, for now, we upstairs-ed to the door – although the night lying beyond it was what I was after. Just then though, as one of the two hands you gripped, I could wait for later on.

First Winter, Later that Night

A long draw of brush down through my hair. Unmaking its tangles into curls. Far as my shoulders. Then further. Concentrating but waiting. Or ending the wait, depending what happens in the miles of this night. Seeming travelled so far to, yet I still heard your voice at its hang around her door. Checking she was fine. Checking she was warm. Concerned for her settle before your last get. But at last you got and the door went click. Me still at my hair when you finally made it. And would not turn to look. Just let you draw near and get your hand brushed.

> Ow! That's my finger.
> Then keep it out of my hair.
> Why should I?
> Why have you till now?
> That's fair.

But unfair as much because my primary interest was shirking down bra straps while, in the mirror, watching you watch. Then reach to the front. All eyes on your long fingers as nails slid down my neck. Into the dents of my collarbone. The soft of all else and every iota of it after touch. Making game at my breast. Who would crack first? Round and round. Round and round till I leaned back against. Wanting, as first off, the smell of your neck. Finding it. But I was not the one who said

> Turn around to me.

Nor did I. Nor would I, however much you asked. Let you persuade with all your charms – which were very much. Just bided that time, best I could and as long as my will would hold out. But

Turn around to me, Eily. Be in love with me still.
    You fucker I am   despite everything.
        I know   I know

Then the grip took us over for all it was worth. The able finding of underwear and yanking it off. Felt for and found quickly. No dance. Just straight in. And that first go, like it would make me blind, made every exhaustible nerve end run wild. You having to curl into me to damp your own sound. But pushing so much we staggered forward and Shit! Hands hit drawers. Knocked the mirror and a tower of books. Both of us going, loud, Fuck! with surprise. Then

    Everything all right in there?

Called through the wall. The telling moment, in which you might stop – which drew and quartered me between expectation and hope. But you pulled me back. And told her a lie.

    Just me being clumsy, love. It's nothing. Night night.
        Night night then, Dad. Night, Eily.
    See you in the morning, Grace.

It barely from my mouth as we fell on the bed.

    Sure, Stephen?
    Sure   and long past.

The very last question before falling apart. Or together. However it should be regarded – that getting to where bodies said Go! And damp skins remembered their fit. How far in you could be. Yet the care for quiet made even kissing the most secret thing. Stopping sometimes to look but always starting again. Having to. Further. Yet, barely resisting, I would not let go. And so, though tempted, neither would you. Just holding then. Me. Close to you. At the foot of disaster.

Come, Eil.
Will you?
With you.
Now?
I will.

Then. Let it run all round you and up through me. Knowing each other and no longer trying to stop it.

Fuck.
Fuck, Eily.

You burying the worst in my neck. Me giving vent with nails to your back. Then sliding hands over to just keep you near. And a grasp for words as you lay on me. Rolling slowly so the sound went numb. Then whispering to each the inanest nonsense only the other could understand. Settling down to our new landscape. Trying not to laugh. Trying to keep all between, and private, at least for now. Slowly becoming too, in the after, what afters always have. Lazed kisses. Finding tissues. Shoulders offered. Heads drowsed on. Smoking fags but, at length, being where I could ask about your film. And you fooled with my hair, answering my every question. Neither taking any favour for granted. Then reset so, we started again.

First Winter, the Morning After

In the morning, she woke us. Tapped on the door. Stuck a head in and knew well the state of us under the covers – probably – but wasn't bothered. After all, she'd had parents before. Besides, it was you who became the surprise. Being content, as you suddenly were, to lay your head against mine and ask what we fancied doing that day?

And, in this way, all Firsts came to their end.

The city, magnanimously, raised its weft and offered us room to turn. Then, on resettling, spread its warp even finer to make it home. And therefore let the two be three, with our links of bodies but even greater of willing. At peace together, looking out at the rain as it ate the snow down to slush on the pavement. London forever keeping its form, leaving us to discover how best to fit ours around. Hers to yours. Mine to hers. Your revised fit to me. Loose with disorder, perhaps, but able when choosing. So, all would be grand then, as far as we could see. Which it was, for a while. Up until the city, remembering its knives and forks, invited itself back in to dine.

Spring

So, after that winter came the next thing. Bit less cold in the flat as the world got green. Grace back to Canada. Me, to classes again. You, to the last lap of your film. Nearly there. Every day until it was. Done! To your palpable relief. Took me out to celebrate it with pints and chips. When I watched it again, I only loved it the more. For its ferocity. Its unforgiving soul. Its beauty too, although I knew what darkness it had taken, and, in turn, taken from, you. But there it was now, forever, your reimagining of that time, as well your escape from the life of being looked at, into the one of being an eye. No. The eye. From beginning to end. And when I stared out into that wide space you'd claimed, I felt   not envy but   want for myself. Like something inside me had been changed.

At the off, just like whispers but, in increments, more. If not quite aloud, with some voice. Pushing. As suspicion. Sometimes dreams. Or at night. Pressing what had been settled in me out of joint.

Gone, all knowing. Gone, my sure. Replaced by what though? No, too much to know. So I got the fear and, to hide it, talked myself out of any desire of which Acting was not the name. But the yearn kept landing anyway, in places I did not expect. In fact, when least expected, showing itself without offering up any whys.

Start of the term, for example. The very first day back while I was checking the noticeboard for my casting.

Amazing!

Alison shouted.

Lead again, you jammy bitch! How'd you manage that?

And I   saw that I had. Dream casting until   the under voice said

Yet another young woman who is lost in herself.
Will there never be more than this?

The second I heard it; I made it stop. But the split one before had already sown doubt and, no matter how thoroughly I ignored it, it never left again. You are being ridiculous, I explained to myself – as everyone else in my year surely would. Because what would I do if I didn't do this? Hadn't I always sworn I'd never be anything else? Made my future so certain that it already was. Is. Is what will be. And in this blunt fashion the voice was dismissed. Found itself banked as mid-Second Year jitters. Or pre-Third Year anxiety about the saleable self I'd soon have to become. The one to be devised from pragmatic appraisal of my looks, of my talent. And once that package had been decided   I'd become it   for years   on repeat.

And never let myself imagine doing what you had done – make beauty and life from all the fuck-ups. Mine. People's. Whatever interested me. Never find myself full of thought, but at a loss, and then discover intention through work and more fuck-ups, more fuck-ups and work, until   a thing got made. Right from the bones up. The whole of its skin. Not just to imagine myself inside, interpreting. Being its face or constructing its voice. But making it all, from the start.

No.

Too much risk in those thoughts and what dismantling they'd mean. So I drowned out the voice, gratuitously. Gave you all holy hell before going to sleep. Gave it to myself in every class to blow at the old spark. Rewatched the films that first burned aspiration in. Studied each choice of their actors and how those bred up excitement. Or sat in the theatre, whenever I could, to feel again and feel part of the worlds there created. Worlds that circled outside me and were made for the eye. But then also read books which turned my mind towards other things. Incomplete worlds. Worlds suggesting how they could be built. Which really didn't help. Which led to imagining how I'd fill pages myself if I ever would do such a wanton thing. But in spite of these efforts, that future I fully believed had to be, still broke. One logic at a time. Worked for its own collapse on the other side of my mind. All because the new want wanted its wicked way. So I walked into summer, blind, willingly. And, once there, slid to further mistakes.

Now

Although all of that happened, still we are here. As mapped by then? Maybe, but mostly me. Under the rain outside and gloom of our kitchen, through fag smoke, piccalilli and the desperation in him pinning down my arm. Tracing the vandalism. Asking why? While I squirm and wish it off. This sight, and these last months, right back to the moment of such bad choice that nothing's been breathing right since. In the light of cannot though, I close my fingers. But he just closes his grip. And there it is, in all its glorious five inches, up the inner of my arm. Return to the moment of my

    Stephen   I

And his

    All I want is why, Eil, because   this just fucking scares me
    so much.

Visible now and undeniably. In the spirit of this, I survey its topography. Patched savaged skin. Rutted with punctures where stitches have been. No longer a match to its smooth friend there on the right. By my own handiwork become forever lopsided. Will I always walk in circles now? Either way, our eyes trek it up and down. His almost unreadably, so I take first jump.

    God   it's ugly.
   Not really and   it'll fade.
       Will it?
    Of course   in the end.

Recalling me to the scarred circuits of his. All of which I have, over time, traced and kissed. Enquired into. Been told about. But never felt complicit in, so is that what's going on? Perhaps. And fuck, tonight it's all going on. So I'll just go shall I go? with it.

    How long will that take, do you think?
     Not sure. Depends. Does it hurt much?
     More   sensitive   it doesn't like being touched.
      Sorry. Sorry   love

And takes his fingers away. But keeps them hovering as if he may yet try it for a tune. Knowing, however, it carries none, I turn it face down on the Formica veneer. What's been seen though's been seen, so cannot unbe. And where this will go now, I cannot read in spite of my various skills.

Don't worry   it's all right   just feels odd.

Trying to signal END. No such luck. Having got me this far, he has to ask

But why did you do it?
I don't want to talk about that.
How can we not? There must be an answer. Some answer.
There isn't.
Eily, come on   you can say anything to me. You know that. You must know that   after all I've said to you.
I've said plenty to you too.
Exactly! So   was it on impulse or
I don't know   I just did it.
Because of   me?
No.
Why then?
I just did.
Eily   please try to say.

But questions only sink me to where I've been striving from. The abject flounder of this last autumn, summer and, before it, the spring. None of which contained the tight-lipped logic he seems to imagine. How he looked at me and I would not look back. How he kept offering a hand I wouldn't clasp. How he wanted part and I wouldn't allow him in. Making the arm one problem but his real

- 265 -

question something else: why had I sealed myself off and chosen to go it alone? Except that's easier to ask than know, even for me.

Stephen, it was
It was what?
Just

Just. Just. Light another cigarette up. How to describe having done something he'd probably want? But at my own instigation and for my own purpose. Then flipped the switch off once it was incarnate and advancing towards the world? How now it sits like glass between. Not the leafy kind either or tinted saintly with stain. The distorting one, that proves only a body is there but gives no hint of who. Useless. Then do something useful Christ! Try harder to say.

I was just   lost   I
   I don't understand why that was.
And you were so far away.
   Eily   I wasn't   I didn't go anywhere.
   I know   I just couldn't
Couldn't what?
   Say it   out loud.
     Because?
   I don't know.
     Jesus! It's like   you don't trust me   at all.

If this was a film, the floor would open and I would fall through, to travel revelation until I was renewed. But it doesn't, because this is only me and him, and the kitchen sink. And the blood-stained lino. And the vinegary stink. And what he is saying, I already know. I just didn't then. When it was dammed by other revelations which I couldn't climb or lead him through. Instead set off on the brittle path without. Left him, if not exactly twiddling his thumbs, unanswered as to my goings on. Funny, it's easier to parse when thinking it a film. Revisable cuts to context and time, helping. Less easy from within our actual then. But much as I will us back to spring's laxness again, unspoiled by this smother of touchable pain, more is coming, I know. Because this is the evening for undreamable scenes to finally meet the air.

Second Summer – June

'So feeling less shy now or more sure I'm a freak?' 'Both!' I said. 'Both!' he laughed back. 'Well, there's no pleasing some people.' But at least he was laughing, that's what I thought but, nevertheless, going on to the next bit in my mind's eye. That bit when he would maybe kiss me again and make all the alarms start going off, once more, in my head, making me get even worse than I already was. Still, it would be worth the effort

Unlike this, which is clearly total fucking shit! And rip the whole page out. For Christ's sake! Have you not enough to be going on with without pretending you'll ever be able to make something of this? Flip back the foolscap. Shove it down in the drawer. But then, like an act of mercy, the phone. Thank God. Grabbed and wangled its cord around. Hello? Oh hey, how are you? Looping as rings and braceletting arms, I sagged to the floor and occasionally ummed while Grace asked how I was?

Fine.
    Sure?
    Why do you ask?
    Just   is everything all right?
        With Stephen? He's grand.
    I know that. It's not him I'm asking about.

And I thought of lying beside, as you slept, while locks unpicked inside my head. Images becoming sentences that made no sense but would not go away. The feel in me then of something strange which, if let, could peel. Could be shed. Once stepped from though, what after it? A quick elation. And a rush of fright. But also how I'd seen you be it – very lately, changed. From all those cinema seats I sat on across that June. Showings and screenings. You at a podium, or panel onstage, from your unimaginable past choosing to say

Pretty autobiographical, yes. Fictionalised to some extent but essentially   the same.

Leaving no room for turn. Or place to back off. No one saying You can't ask him. Just them asking. And you answered. And when I asked, you answered me too.

Doesn't matter to me, Eil. Not like telling you   or telling Grace. I made the film, didn't I? And not just for myself so here it is   out in the world and I'd be lying if I said it wasn't weird to   know people know   or that they can guess   and have all kinds of fucking opinions about it   but   making it   even showing it   it's   generating distance and I don't mind that change.

Words to seep into the crannies and cracks. Suggesting place for more, and of a wider type. An opening up. A letting the world right in. And you could because you'd made something of it. Or because, at last, you'd understood it from without. Meaning your past could no longer run like rats, biting away at your insides. Were you now a man with wiring that worked? And therefore suddenly admissible to the ordinary world? I know you'd once dreamed of it. But, back on the phone, I played deaf to her friendly hints I could always tell her if there was ever something was wrong.

> I'm all right, Grace   there's just a lot going on.
> With the film and
>   Yeah   with everything.

And stayed quiet on how, in that long mirror of you, I glimpsed the start of running in me. A want for other solutions to my faulty wiring. How else explain this discontent with what had thralled before? Or the draw to questions about which direction I should be looking at the world from? Still, I kept to the leaky safety of was and had. Unable unwilling? to look at myself as   a person who might   have made a mistake? A person who might   have misread herself? A person   whose mind was suddenly running far faster than the place she was. Who had realised it could run as fast as yours and would love it to take its chances out in the originating world but if I did who would I then be?

Second Summer – July

You went to Canada and, again, I missed before. Not everything but   the bedsit off the Camden Road. Dinners of chips. Sitting feet to the gas fire. Itching chilblains from it. Or its closeness last summer, before we moved. Smoke trapped and past crammed but still infinite enough. That look on your face when all you wanted was me. And how sure I was of how everything would be, from then on to forever. Forgetting already how much that room had shifted us. Down from arm's breadth. To hand's length. To fingertip's touch. Then no distance at all. Just pieced broke bits to broke bits over nights. Over months. Sharp sometimes too, but then after it, us.

But then after that, Grace.

But then after there, here.

But then after then, this.

Time, this summer. So much on my hands. Rife with impulses that I could not bear to chase down because   I know myself. Know myself. Or is that knew? To settle this running then, I chose to just stop. To not arrive at the conclusion something was   off. Too much to accept. Too hard to change. Too humiliating to admit. Too much effort to throw away. But at the root, too much fear of being a person again to whom unexpected things could occur. Who was just there, alive, defenceless against life and whatever it happened to throw.

And when I was away it still followed round inside. That vast space and all the white mornings I spent there. The far mountain now only heather and stones because all of me wanted a way back. As if even the memory of that time could make marks on my skin. Blazed sometimes it even felt. Because I preferred that tinier place with only room for two. That let no other words in from the time before. We made a beginning and liked it better than the others we had actually lived. He being a full glass carefully carried within while I

But why would I even bother with that? Loneliness. That's the sum of it. Because I'm here while you are not. And I should throw this posy rubbish out but   something in it is   making a sound. Even the rereading makes something happen inside   like I could get outside of the world. Rip it up! And cannot. So just put it away and maybe   maybe at some point someday   I could try making it more. STOP. That's more than enough of that   for now.

Which led, two weeks later, to lying under sheets, appreciating the return of your unfussed nakedness. Jetlagged. Lovely. Middle of the night. Bearing gifts. Love from Grace. All the sex we'd not had requiring redress. Done with more pounce than precaution but so insistent we were soon ringing with it. Besides, no harm done and I'd soon sort that out. After lighting fags. Catching up. You slinging me slices of toast before running the shower. Making tea while waiting for it to get hot. Emptying your case. Inveigling into a kiss. And then. And then. Unable not to again. Your body always bringing traffic enough for practicality to be quieted by other stuff. Not least the re-joining lines of speak and touch. Even though I've made my bed so must lie in it crossed my mind, You can change direction argued the secret want, while still remaining no master of my fear of it. So, the fear bedded in as a lie of It's all right. To escape it, I asked after her

What'll Grace do next year, Stephen?
    Gap year, I think.
    And then?
I don't know, love. Anything she wants.

Anything she wants. My soft envy of which bred a neglect I chose not to fix. In this way, I led myself to deceitful August. To my very last day of nineteen. Just asked chaos in. So, by the time you returned from that shower, it had begun to begin and would be made real in no time at all.

Second Summer – August

Hot lake drifted under us, on our backs. Sky-eyed we relented into all the sun had. Even the bald bits of swimsuit letting it in. By evening I blotched red. That night you said I was scalding as we lay beneath one white sheet. But for now, licked the salt from each other's lips. Sizzled and fried in the August heath heat. Ate sandwiches. Ice creams and watched London beneath pass itself through each turn of the day. A.m. smog-filthied. Afternoon blue. Later on, tower blocks diffusing gold windows. And when unwelcome words worked in my head, flitted them off to be only what I recognised on this lovely baking day. As it dimmed though, we collected ourselves for the visit. Time to be again with your past and the man who knew you in it. Fondly. Rafi.

Even of your antics from the black and blue life of before – that one I dream magic apertures for, through which I could see you then.

You really don't, believe me, you wouldn't want that!

But I really would so, as second best, tend to use each St John's Wood visit to wheedle out whatever I can. His house alone a trove of When was that? and What were you doing there? Silver-framed pictures mostly but, likely as well, wild hearsay as the night runs in. Us beginning it though, by his front hedge, however many times the same.

Do I look all right?
  Lovely, Eily. How about me?
Very nice.
  Smart enough?

Always, but only, such efforts for Rafi. His widowerhood anointing him conduit, apparently, for showing your oldest, now late and much-missed friend David – somewhere up in an ether you don't even believe in – how your life has changed. That it was worth him saving you from the worst of yourself, way back at the end of the seventies. After you'd jumped off that roof. After you'd been plastered up. After you had been sectioned for   being mad, as you described it. Took you in. Got you working. Got your ex to let you see Grace, at least for her first few years then. So, though David's gone now, Rafi gets the civility of a clean shirt whenever we go around.

Definitely. Let me just pull that thread.
  Thanks.

And a kiss behind the privet before we enter. Then get further

kissed, hugged and decadently welcomed before even a threshold's
been crossed. Rafi just taking the proffered bottle. And ushering us
forward, with

Come in! Come in! You both look well!
You too, Raf.
That's beautiful, Eily, new dress?
No, I just haven't worn it for ages.
I think it will go well with my birthday present.
You shouldn't.
Of course I should. You only turn twenty once!

And then off

When did you get back from Paris?
Thursday.
And how did it go?
Well, the build was fine . . .
Oh, one of those . . .
Yes, but . . . let's have a drink first.

And

Which play next term, Eily?
Wonderful. Belvedira?
Yes, worse luck.
But it's a beautiful part, especially for you.
That's what I keep telling her but
The folly of youth!
I'd have preferred Aquilina, that's all.
Why's that?
Bit more of a challenge.

But Belvedira will probably help get an agent   she's your casting after all.

This I know, so shrug it off. And that he is right, whatever I might prefer. Which is?

Stephen, heard back from the festival yet?
        Yesterday afternoon.
                And?
Been accepted.
                For?
        The main competition.
                Amazing! Congratulations!
Yeah, we're all pretty pleased.
                It's a great piece of work.
    Well   it is what it is.
            I agree with you, Rafi, and so does Grace.
            And how is the lovely Gracie these days?

A taste, that's all, for our tumble of this. Each time. Every time. Catching up on the quick. Details to come once we're all settled in. Even more after the glugging of wine. And then, perhaps, more of both after that. I'll certainly be rooting around.

            Where do you want us tonight, Raf?
Outside. Under the tree. It's so warm – at least for the Irish and English.
            Somehow both thoughtful and scornful at once!
    Well, you're such pasty creatures.
        Blame the Vikings.
                Excuse me, Celts! Do you need any help?
No no, you both go on. The table's already been set.

So you led me on in through this garden I knew. First seen in like profusion. But too in snow. Admired for its early buds earlier and now, once more, summer passed over again. Another night in, only. Intended to be. Yet tides turned there that would take some undoing, and time to play out.

Why don't you take the bench, love.
Ta, did you say Rafi got a dog?
Hey Raf, d'you get that dog in the end?
I did. I'll just let him out. But he's nervous so be calm.

Then out he shot, the scant what of him. Grey shivery but enthused and sniffing.

Ah gorgeous! How old is he?
About twelve weeks and . . . Stephen, no! No feeding him crisps!
But look at him, Raf, he must be ravenous.
He's an Italian greyhound. He's fine.
He's a what, Stephen?
Fancy whippet!
I beg your pardon, Italian greyhound, if you please.

Who gets a fair few crisps for his troubles, as well as the odd Ay up!

I don't think it's that kind of whippet.
Ah, bound to be the North in there somewhere.

And it does follow you faithfully everywhere, probably though just for the snacks. Funny, that matched skinny. Such comparable ribs, but it's yours I think of stroking while you're busy making him jump. Tearing myself from it only for the presentation of

Happy birthday for tomorrow! This is for you.
   It's beautiful, Rafi, thank you. Stephen, look at this.
   Nice scarf, Raf.
   I'm glad you like it.

Then demonstrating various methods to elegantly tie it before setting about his traditional grill.

It's months since you've been here. Did you get your weak ankle sorted out? And how was that scene study? O'Neill, was it? Right, and did you finish the Eco? Jury's still out for me. What about the new Mamet? Oh no, that's a pity, but the designer owes me a favour so I can probably get you both comps. House seats, at least. And what about the apartment? All right then, flat. Has that sink been fixed? He is utterly hopeless. I'll come take a look this week. Probably just a washer or some such.
         That would be great!
   In the meantime, tell him stop feeding blinis to Hervé!
   Is that his name?
      It is.
   Rafi's right, Stephen. You'll make him sick!
   He likes pancakes though.
    That's not the point.
    He's hungry.
   No, he isn't.
      You're hungry.
   Yeah   that's true   so   where's the food?
    Well, if you'll stop supposing my dog is you, I'll start serving up.

Can't argue with that. Sorry, Harvey, you're out of luck!

I just laughed at your houndness and drank more wine. *Hervé*'s stomach abandoned for return to Rafi's civilising. Us invariably though making shows of ourselves. Bad with cutlery. Napkins. Finger bowls.

I can only imagine how feral you are in that flat.
Maybe   a little.
Probably   yes.

Chips on our knees. Foils of Chinese in the fridge and not so much else. Milk. Milk! Always for tea. Loaf of bread too. Pre-sliced white from Sainsbury's. Tins of spaghetti and tomato soup. Weetabix for me. Piccalilli for you, and Mr Kipling's strawberry tarts for dessert.

And that's why we appreciate the fine dining of St John's Wood!
Speaking of which then, eat!

Then eat, with all relish, the treat. Dog getting in on the act with your sub-table fingertips. Me more hardened to its plaintive knee licks. Rafi having none of it at all.

Hervé, no! Under the bench!

Hence a sad whippet skulked as we evening'd across. You two with your recounting and, for me, rich findings out. Lax limbs allowing loose tongues. Laughter liberating more of those histories I was so envious of and filled with a glamour of which you seemed unaware. Your memory weighting instead to the emptiness of hotels – foreign and not. Wet walks home. Jetlag dulling New York. Rehearsal room infuriations. But I won't buy every part and know, if I wait – beyond dessert, more wine, cigarettes – blood-curdling tales of you will habitually start to show, because

> Not every hotel room was empty, was it? Not all wet walks made alone.

Rafi convulsing into his napkin until he almost chokes.

> Oh Stephen, she knows you well.
>> I know. No flies on her!

And this, a laughing jag, the very best for

> So were there girls?

Though, of course, you'd never give in easy as that.

> Yes, Eily, there were girls in France. They have a few, I believe.
>> You know what I mean.
> Even if that's true, what could I do about it?
>> What did you, more like?
>> Just played my part.
>> Which was?
>>> Looking pretty sexy while smoking Gauloises.
>> Is that right?
> As a matter of fact, it is.
>> Okay, then let's see it.
>> Certainly, Rafi, please pass your pack?
> Eily, it seems we're in for a treat!
>> Yes, I, for one, can't wait!

Passed and struck!

Well?

　Okay.

Okay what?

Okay, pretty sexy.

　Well, you could be more enthusiastic. Rafi?

Oh yes, I think you're very sexy too.

　I'm wasted on the pair of you!

Dismissing with a brandish of said cigarettes, but then lost grip and they flew. Poor Hervé gave a yelp.

　Oh no! Sorry, lad.

But the dog lets him off for a quiet dropped sliver of cheese. So, on night. So, on stories. So, on time and again of these. Nothing too drastic in this one either, it seemed. Just red wine sipped till our teeth turned blue and I parched for kissing, alien-mouthed, up in the guest room where evenings like this always end. And as always too, starting to ponder how long until bed? Rafi started to clear but you sent him ahead.

　Go on. You cooked. We'll do this.

　You sure?

Even we can manage the dishes.

　There's a dishwasher, Stephen.

So there is, and we can probably manage that too.

Kissed then, once more, and left.

　See you in the morning.

　Sleep well.

Make sure Hervé's in before you lock the back door.
  We will.

And, as ever before, staring him off up the stairs.

    How do you think he was looking, Eil?
      Tired.
      I thought so as well.
      Good form though.
    True, but I worry about him in this big house alone.
      It's not like he's old. Plus now he's got Hervé.
      I know, I just wish he'd meet someone, that's all.

So, from the last of the clearing to one last cigarette. One last quarter of hour and garden at night. Stretching your skinniness out on the bench. Then getting at the Gauloises again.

      What are you looking at, Eily?
        You.
          Tired of me, now you're twenty, almost?
      Opposite, actually. How long till you're done with that cigarette?
        Not long. Why don't you come help me finish it?

Cast a quick brazen up. Rafi's light going off. Your fingers humming of Fairy, from scrubbing the pots, when I took the fag and drew.

      You're pretty sexy too with one of those in your mouth!
        Oh, am I indeed!

Lips now closing where yours had been. Damp at the indent. Chewing it over to the side, just to show I could. And keep hands unoccupied as I stepped across your stretched legs. Watching how you watched me and let. You liking this taking it upon myself. Preferring even for me to set and have it my own way. For me, it's your stoic impatience while you wait. What am I going to do? What's she going to do next?

Give us back that fag.

Snatching it and daring me to make a complaint. Not realising I was already ahead. Far. By a country mile.

Smoke it if you like but   isn't it about time you   put those in?

You sarking

Where?
Me.
But what?
Your fingers.

Slow smile starting up

Thought you'd never ask!
Well, don't make me have to again.
Oh, sorry   let me just
Oh fuck.
How's that?

But all at once, heavy pleasure derails with its weight and I am no longer good at this game. Any game, ever, I now clearly recollect. Besides which, games are no way enough. What I'm after is just all of you. Touch the arc of your eyebrow. Down to your cheek. On and then in between your lips. To lick a little before the kiss. And you, forward to meet but, on repetition, caving to it. Persuading me down on. Stingy with space. My hands on yours and yours on my face. What point of room when none is wanted? Besides, you're as useless as me at the sport of archness or wait. More like climbing the walls to get us beyond it. Untame with mouth. And, on finding, bite. Blood then. A little. Yours or mine? Both and either. My nails chipped on your belt. Gauloises, knickers too, fucked off into the hedge. Until nice dress pushed right up and pressed suit zip unzipped.

    Fuck! Cold fingers, Eil!
      Would you rather I didn't?
    No I   I did not say that.

Then with you and finding our ways once again to get lost, fucking lost, just like this. Mouths fast but hot-heeled by everything else, searching out the unerring to bring it to finish. Letting us have this together like some mercy, I think. Or perhaps curse. But even my grazed knees I took as proof – along with the small drops of blood on your shirt – of how love got moved between us. And so it moved that night too. Terrible want. Work. The relief also terrible. Kept close together. Later a price. But back in the garden, and still innocent, we just tidied up.

    Stephen, can you blow those candles out?
      Pass that last wine glass. I'll stick it on the counter.
        Is Hervé in?
      He's in his bed.
    I'd say he got a quare education tonight.
      I wouldn't worry about it, Eily, he seems discreet.
        Thank God! Door locked?
      Yes, and look.

What?

It's just gone midnight. Happy birthday, love.

Then from your pocket a little case. And from the case, a little bracelet. Thin and old silver sliding it on.

Where'd you get it?

Vancouver. Grace helped me choose. I hope you don't mind.

Why would I? She's got taste.

That's what I thought.

How old is it?

From the twenties, apparently. I just thought you'd like it.

What does the inscription say?

Then catch it myself in the light.

'Eily, always, Stephen. August 1996.'

Did Grace choose that too?

That was all me – can't you tell by the absence of poetry?

I love it, Stephen.

Good and   you know   it's true.

Is it?

Ah Eily, who could there ever be but you?

Some skinny actress?

Well, just stay on the Gauloises and I reckon you'll be fine.

Fucker!

I won't deny it. Now give me a kiss.

By now, foot of the stairs. On the first, I reach right up and so much happiness. Your fingers curling through mine, almost shy with it. But feeling soon reached elsewhere for its favourite hideouts and the kissing ran out of control. Here? Landing? Any supporting wall.

Fancy just going again now?

You corpsing though.

    Upstairs, hussy. That's what bedrooms are for!
     We just did it on a bench. In the garden. In front of a dog.
   He wasn't watching. Up you go.
    Oh, come on.
   Up! Then I'll see   but we've not all just turned twenty!
    Ah, you've plenty of go in you yet.
  Thanks for the vote of confidence. Now

After one more kiss

    Go on!

But even after another, as we settled in bed – sunburned some and still trembling legs – I found myself listening for out there in the world. As if, somewhere beyond Golders Green, the weather had turned and thunder now might roll in. In a while though, of wakefulness, it shifted again. Listening to the house. To the room. To you. Then   from that unwanted within the want again. Making echoes of itself all around and undiminished by the evening's chat. Even by liking being people like us, talking about the life we are already in. Get away! Get thee behind me, Satan!

    Stephen, are you asleep?

Which, it seemed you were. So the habits of an older Ireland took me instead, off in mind towards fright-riven prayer. Let this cup pass? Isn't that what he said? If at all possible. And surely it is?

But then your arm slung over and your body went round.

> What was that, Eil? Think I just nodded off for a moment.
> Nothing. Nothing.
>   You sure?
> Too much wine, that's all.

And is all. For, right after, I got very sure again that here with you could only ever be haven, whatever the other part of me might be at. Watching for stars through the skylight above. We'll be woken by dawn but, in these hours, worth it for the city light soft on your face. Where are we? St John's Wood. Lovely, but not our place. Camden. Where we belong. Where what will be, still will, at least in a world of our own. Eily, always, Stephen. August 1996. Eily always. Stephen August. 1996 but at this, eyelids start going down. Or seeing the stars above behind them. One by one going out. Then turning completely black.

Summer – August, Next Morning

I slipped from the skin of myself, that's what I did. Relied on denial to do the lift. Sure, what would I ever want to be that wasn't this? Even when I'm afraid, am I? Always better to ask than know for sure I am. So I refuted all misgivings, one disquiet at a time, before turning back to the world. Often you'd notice, so'd poke until I'd say. Very often even, just not that day. Distracted as we were by the beautiful Sunday. Preoccupied, perhaps, with me enjoying my birthday? All certainly basking in this familial medley we've somehow assembled here. Maybe also assigning quiet to hangover, which I'm inclined to do. Besides, there was sitting around. And petting the dog. And answering questions about what I'd do now that I was the great 2-O?

I don't know. It's the third year so   hopefully get an agent
and a job after that.

    You will.

  How do you know?

    You will, Eil.

  You didn't.

    Well   that was a whole other thing, and far as I know you
    don't have a drug problem.

  I wish!

    What do you mean by that?

  Then I'd be free, wouldn't I?

 To what? Be a fuck-up? Believe me   it wasn't much fun.

  I'm just messing   never mind.

        It's natural to be nervous, Eil. It's a big year coming up, but
        I'm telling you it will be fine.

    Stephen's right. So, what would you like, if you could choose?

        Anything   something good   Chekhov.

  I can see that. She'd make a great Masha, don't you think,
Raf?

    Yes. Nina too.

        Ah   the old Seagull.

I look at you.

  I wish I'd seen you as Konstantin, you know.

And wonder, briefly, if I wish that more than to be in it myself?
Than I wish to be in   anything   really   if I'm being honest. Which
I'm not, so don't think that.

        Well, Eil   it was a very long time ago, so I'm afraid that
        ship has sailed.

But both you and Raf then stared into the past, leaving me suddenly longing to be happiness. To bring it. And who knows, I might? I know what would, and would change both our lives. For this moment though, I've only a rag of

    At least I have a lot of that.
     What, Eil?
      Time.
     You think it now, but you'll find it passes very quick.
     Oh stop, it's my birthday, morbid fuck!

Back to laughing.

     Sorry!

And lighting up. Not Gauloises though – didn't want to cause strife! So just a ye olde Marlboro Light. Tasting strangely gross but, nonetheless, I carried on.

Into Autumn

And so I was twenty. This was the world. Last settle of summer and startings of Third Year. Final year. All that would be. Then all that would be after it. Let this be the line drawn on the secret want, with its pushings and shovings, with its images tumbling and the words it would use to describe. Chose to take to my casting with thanks instead. Chose audition pieces to work on. Chose my 10x8s. Prepared for choice and the choosing of what my most choosable self would be. So, with choice implied everywhere, I brought the future back to heel. Made it again what it was always supposed to be and no longer a runaway train. This is who I am.

This is who I am, with none of my plans on the turn.

But it grew in me anyway, dread. First only by day. Then took the night for itself. Slowly made each a wrestle, to the far side of sleep, allowing none of the middle's expected respite. On this one I lay, passing it off as Too hot. Not unjustly. We both lay on top. Bare legs itching out drips of sweat. But the rest of me kept suggesting Notice That! Which I had no desire to   so I wanted you awake and kept on saying a lot.

    How can it still be so fucking hot?
   Just London, Eily. It keeps it in.
  Is that window shut?
   No.
Are you sure?
  You know what? The talking's not helping.
Are you telling me to shut up?
 I am begging you to. Go To Sleep!
   I can't.
Well, I can   so   good luck and good night!

Your hand though, laid on mine. Back of it taking the sweat of your palm. Love in it. And comfort. Then came silence and I realised you'd gone over, without waiting for me. Undone by your knackeredness. The hot dark trapping it. But I could not follow, for more twisting yet. While, under your breathing, I listened out for worse – inklings   wardings   from my own within. Listen. Listen. Did and tried to find what I could not bear to hear. So thought better of it because some thoughts are better off left. Still though

    Stephen, don't sleep yet.
     What?
     Just stay awake.

Eily, I'm
   Please try.
   Why?
   Just try.

And, as proof of good faith, lolled a long arm around. Even worked a few drowsy mumbles out.

   Is something wrong?

Could I though? Even know it enough to say?

   There   might be   something
      What?

But in the midst of the effort to pull yourself up, I reconsidered. Then buried my hunch. Decided, in silence, I was making it up   or looking to worry about something because? Because I was very fucking neurotic about what the next few terms would bring. And this version preferred itself to other reasons. So that was the dishonest next.

    You know what, don't worry about it.
     No   if there's something on your mind, Eil?
    I'll tell you tomorrow, all right?
      Tell me now.
     No   it's nothing. I'm just too hot to sleep.
      Are you sure? I don't mind if
     No really it's all right.
    All right   well, night   love.

Then I watched you float to the safe of sleep while I swam

on, wide-eyed, through pools of the night. Under Camden Town streetlights and faraway stars. Rebelling, if only in thought, against your terrible surprise. Your foreseeable joy. If, only if, it was true. But on whispering IT MIGHT just to hear the sound instinct closed my mouth – grasping I think how it might be best if the possibility of talking myself into, and out of, all of this, remained. If I kept open places where choices could still be made but crucially didn't have to be   yet. That's when I chose that this much, for this night, was enough. Released my lingering unquiet to the low pulse of traffic. Let it soothe this hot autumn's last heat and bites. Turned to the serene sweat of your sleep, stretched against mine, and aimed for the same within. And, though I couldn't help wanting you up in wakefulness with me placing some hold on my gathering unreason your body just slept and slept. So, I had to leave you in there.

Nipping that night's heels though, there was soon more. Lowly cubicle in the Girls' toilets where I threw my breakfast up. Then said

Hangover

with some justification to whoever asked. When Alison did later, she only got

Never mix the grape and the grain.
Think I already know that!

Her agreement letting it slip away. But I was glad when the weekend came and I didn't have to keep on repeating it. Far rathered your news and our life in which these more interesting things could occur.

Thought you were done with acting?
Yeah, I thought so too but

What've you been offered?

Doctor Faustus.

No!

Yes.

Well, you have to do that.

You think?

You've always loved it.

I have.

Then you should.

You don't mind? I'll be out a lot   at night.

I think I can cope.

I know you can   I just

Wanted to check? And now you have, so

So I'll say yes.

That's good.

So Saturday I ate cereal while you reread. Liked as I always have to watch you concentrate. God, and still do but now from such distance. Not like then. Which was far ends of the sofa but legs intertwined. Gaming ourselves for how much'd get done before we arrived at the interruptive fuck. My intentions pure, with regards to work. I'd my own script to paste in. Beats to mark. Couple of questions I wanted to ask about when you'd done it, years before. Just the shatterless stuff of an afternoon at home with two people who were largely content. Or until some whistle asserted itself. Drew attention to the matter I'd been giving a wide berth, at least at the forefront of my mind. The one that was

Shit! Am I really   late?

That's all. That's all I thought. And late had happened before. Of course it had. And been all right. So this time too   but   this was not so like that. My summer lack of precaution summoning back. But in mitigation   I did feel like I might be about to start   any time. Same soreness. Tiredness. Same wanting to jump your bones. And yet   wasn't I feeling like this last week also? Which   would be strange because, in the great grand scheme of things, two weeks is double the usual run-in. Then I got stoving and freezing, all at once, while denial took a quick beating from sense. You can't just think this one away. Yet still attempted it by taking solace distraction in staring at the bamboo unravelling on that chair our landlord left. The one you can't sit on because its lowness makes your knees ache. I'm less fussed because, obviously, I'm shorter than you so STOP IT. Stupid. Stop it now! What if I am? If I am? It had to be thought. So I moved the idea around but at a stand-off. Saw, when I glanced up, you making a note by some line you   didn't think worked? And who would you discuss that with? Christopher Marlowe except What if I'm pregnant? he died centuries ago. I know that but what if I am? Pub fight in Deptford, I'm fairly certain. I'm just daring myself aren't I? To imagine it's true? Stabbed through the eye. Except   I am a body too. Died instantly and its workings suggest

All right there, Eil?
Why are you asking that?
Just looking a little embattled. Something   on your mind?
No   I'm trying to study   be quiet!
Okay! Just asking. Christ!

You went back to your script. Me, to my regret at having trapezed along the sharp edge. At having closed my eyes   somewhere in space and this summer   let go. Meaning now I must catch hold wherever I can because, apparently, only the secret want had formulated a plan. Fuck! And it's found a way. Of course, it wouldn't have to see your terrible surprise. Your foreseeable joy. Then how you'd make yourself pretend to no opinion at all, beyond whatever it was I'd want. Which is? Now I think of it. Stop! And went no further than Anything But This Awful Impossible Place. Which danced me around panic, until panic chose to say Hang on! It still might not be true. So true. Permitting me lie to myself again and, to you, that I was – so we were – unchanged.

Now

        I did trust you though   I do.
    Then why didn't you tell me   before it got so out of hand?
    I wanted to.
           So why didn't you?
      I was afraid of what   of
    What?
    How you'd look at me   what you'd say.
        Jesus, Eily, why were you were afraid? What did I do to make it like that?

Unbearable sometimes to be so loved, yet still pass through the eye of the needle enough for blood to get left, very literally, on the floor. I'd throw off the yoke but doubt I'd get far before looking longingly back. Pointless anyway to be at that when it's my own manoeuvrings have brought this storm. Wish we were through it by now, but he's seen my arm and closer than I've ever allowed. So, we're beyond his taciturn glances towards it and my covering it up. Or the sliding by each other via our various escapes from the sadness infesting in here. Given. All a given. But how to lay bare what I'm still so unwilling to own? Offering only

    Nothing, Stephen. You did nothing wrong.

Syllables tiding but not helping us. The waters just pulling us down to a depth. To the murk of below and its airless press. Him, despite his tiredness, still casting a net. This time it's

I knew   you know?

Hard though, to hear. And take.

    How?
  First, something about your skin but then   in yourself.
    What?
   Just that something was different.
    Why didn't you say?
  I wish I had but   I wasn't sure, so I thought it was better to wait for you.

All this going beyond what protection pure silence affords. Not that what was afforded didn't end up costing more, once all the totting was done. Clinging become cleaving. But I know which night I had chosen not to see that he could.

This Autumn Gone

Unnatured my body as I stood looking out – at furthest, of doors but nearer, myself. Until, as best of both worlds, at my reflection in the evening dark glass of our room. Wandered its traitorous outline. What have you done? Like I wasn't already far beyond that. Better sport was the exodus from the Odeon across. A nine o'clock showing? Didn't have on my watch – suspicious of time bolting, as I was – and preferring to inspect the lives of others just then. Were those twos and threes off on some spree? Were the solitary misanthropic? Or just finding relief from the many musts of life? Like me before you   no   leave the past. Then dropped my towel so drops of shower ran the gauntlet. Hair to breast. Knee to foot. Would anyone notice a change? Could I even see it? After two weeks spent agonising, I was almost there. Could almost have said   but chose to look at the rug instead, down where I stood and the carpet got damp. Should've dried my feet better back on the bathmat. Not just thought Will I tell him? as you undid your fly. Stepped from your trousers. Turned the water up high. Even, as you hopped in, asking

>Before you go, Eil, is that green towel me?
>   Yes

I said, but nothing more. So just pulled the bathroom door. Went my way down the hall. Came to stand at the window, looking out. Then looking closer, at it. Then at my reflection catching the light, or what of it lasted while I asked Can changes already be glimpsed? No. But I wished you'd come in, see and say it. Make the choice to. Bear the weight. But you couldn't do that for – however close – you remained on my outside. I had to be the one. At that, I heard you in the hall. Chattering teeth despite the warmth. Will I say it now? Go on. But

>I think that bloody heater's gone again. Did you get any hot, Eil?
>   A little.
>I'll call the landlord tomorrow.
>   Yeah   do.
> It's getting to be a fucking nuisance.
>   It was the same all last week. Sometimes off, then on.

So. That. Was that. I did not say. Only nodded and dried. Tied up my wet hair. Gawked down at the shouts of Watch yourself, mate!

– transport-based fury of the traditional type. As for cinema leavers? Dispersed and carrying their newfound images off. All London coloured by what was now in their heads. 'Things Explode!' or 'Desperate love!' or 'Idiots at large' or 'Just deserts!' A few happy hours on the outside of life and I wished I could do that. Then saw you, behind, watching in the glass.

    Everything okay, Eil?
   Why do you keep asking that?
  You seem distracted lately. School all right?
    It's fine. I'm just tired   getting used to being back.
     Well, don't get run down.
    Thanks for that, Dad!
  Fine! I'll shut up! But an apple once in a while mightn't hurt.
    Says you, the man who lives on beans on toast.

Thus undone, you shrugged but did continue to look. Up me and down me. Tempting me to speak. Some part though still refused and held out for my self-deceit to be true.

    Stop staring   you're freaking me out.
    Sorry   you just
     I just   what?
  I don't know   seem   different.
      How?
    I don't know, Eily   don't mind me.

But I did mind and so did you. So your eyes kept working until you did you? I thought, perhaps, you did? Saw. Did see. And for the first time we were facing in the same direction. You, willing to step out into it albeit with caution, saying

Eily   I think we should

Then I pulled your towel away.

No   hang on a sec   I

Ran my hand right down to   mouth as well. To the very last bit. To the very end. The one you could never

No   Eily, wait

Resist. But I didn't. Or for a second stop. And you held out not much longer than that. Let me hide in your body, knowing you knew. I hoped forgivingly. Hid thoroughly though. Or thoroughly enough that once I was done, your only question was

Your turn?

My body after gave over to its own content. Made itself for wrapping around and dozing against. Stroking you back awake when, for an instant, it fancied there might be more. But after the Camden night hit its peak and revellers found to last tubes or the earliest night bus, leaving only ne'er-do-wells contending on – roaring from the Lock to Mornington Crescent – only then, and when you didn't hear any more, I finally made the choice. Time to step from this game of Let's Pretend. Tomorrow I will buy a test. I even swore to it then, whatever the fallout would be.

Now

Well   if you knew   you could have said.
    Well, you did know, Eily   and you didn't.

I didn't know how to tell you.

You never tried.

That's not true but   I realised

What?

How you'd react.

Oh, did you? And how did you know that?

You told me once   about that girl you got pregnant and
how you felt when she got rid of it.

That was years ago, Eily, and   different.

How?

She wasn't you and   I was a mess.

Exactly!

No! Not exactly. Fuck!

I didn't want it, Stephen.

I've gathered that much.

And you would've.

That's not fair. You never asked.

Because I already knew!

How? By fucking osmosis? You're not the only person in this
room.

I know you, Stephen.

And I thought I knew you. I've loved   you so much, Eily. I
did then, and I do, but I don't know what to do. I don't even
know where you are any more.

Don't say that   I'm right here.

Not really though, are you?

What do you mean?

Well, for a start   what've you done with what happened?

Nothing.

Something.

That can't be true. I'm in bits and it wasn't me it happened to.
  Don't be in bits.
How can I not? Every time I look at you I feel so much
fucking guilt.
  What for?
Well, I'm the one got you pregnant, who you couldn't bear
to tell. What does that say about me?
  I couldn't even tell myself.
So it never occurred to you I might've agreed? That it wasn't
the right time but I'd take care of you in it   that I'd want to
do that   whatever you decided?
  No.
That's what I mean. Why the fuck not?
  I just   I felt guilty it'd happened at all.

And he wasn't expecting that. Guilt touching to guilt across the
kitchen's expanse.

  But it wasn't your fault, Eily   accidents happen.
  Except   Stephen   it wasn't.

All exhaustion then chucked to by the by. Eyes finding right up
me. Concentrated now.

  What do you mean?

This Autumn Gone

Your first day of rehearsal. So different to the film, with its pains-
taking rush of pressing images into time. This was return to an
older life. Still, you seemed restless somehow.

You nervous?

It's just been so long. Nearly three years now. I don't even
know if I'm an actor any more.

But you still want to be?

Don't know that either. So much has changed, maybe I
don't need to be   someone else any more.

Well, you'll probably know by the end of the run.

Yeah, probably.

In the meantime, you're acting like you're not going to do
those dishes, so

Oh God, you're good.

And you did them, while I made entry to the thought I was acting too – the distraction artist. Fairing weather which was getting
rough. Leaving you with no part. When you asked last night, why wasn't
I honest? By now we'd be over the hump and onto the rest, whatever that
would be like. Getting your coat on, you kissed me by the door. Just
a Bye kind. In a while, kind. But then, with eyes narrowed

You've been quiet lately, Eily, but   if there's anything you
want to tell me   I'd really like to know.

I didn't even pretend not to understand. Nodded. Took your
hand. Said I'd walk you to the tube before heading to school. As
we walked down Parkway, you slipped in

Might give up the fags   what do you think?

And I thought it was a good idea. Aloud anyway. But once you'd
gone into the station, I lit one up, then went across to Boots.

From there

Bought the bloody test.

Went on home.

Went in.

Went down the hall.

Went to the bathroom.

Went to the cracked window and opened it all the way up.

Opened the packet.

Ripped the foil.

Took the targeted piss as sweat ran wild.

Looked at my watch.

Planned minutes out.

Felt I got to notice all the mechanics of our decrepit bathroom.

Last replaced: I'd say 1960s.

Last painted: circa '92.

Last saw a plumber: first summer here with you – for the hot tap, when its tread snapped.

Last saw a boiler engineer: coming up, supposedly, some time next week.

Last saw disaster: Well, Jesus in about three minutes that would be here and now.

Icicles bore down the instant there was no escaping back. Even false doubt had been better. But there it was. Blue lines imparting all the knowledge they had, whatever the bridlings of my phony impasse. Or my efforts at squinting. Or at tilting my head to make the reading unread itself. New deceptions, however, got swiftly refused and so, the present forever changed. For I was now, apparently, a body engaged upon a very different task. I saw it all in a moment. Even into months ahead. How the fuck had I got here, and yet I knew it was the want had affected this change just the wrong fucking kind because of my   silence   intransigence   fear.

That was as far as I could go. No further. So I closed the doors.

Now

And I owe it. Know it. Even make the shape. Then find I did
what I did but can no longer explain. Not to that look in his eye.
Or bewilderment of his tone. So stand graceless and tongueless in
a brine of shame. What'll I? I should I? What can I say?

Eily you can't say that and not explain.

So now I am there, in it, again. Remembering everything.

This Autumn Gone

Crying in the corner. Banging my head on the bath. Thinking of all
undoings, here was the worst. Forewarned since forever and yet what
have you done? Faithless body pursuing its luck in spite of in spite of
everything I knew. Despite, on those nights, knowing too there lived,
inside, a sliver of risk. Took it anyway and now this. The incalculable
thing. All alien from the romance of back in the garden. Two of us in
it. Making one of our own. With your long fingers and my forgivable
nose. If it even happened and I'd clearly half thought it would not.
The other half mostly imagining how happy you'd look, how surprised you'd be. Not that you'd have questions or I was unready. And
how safe I'd feel then from my secret want. Just pitched forward to
change, freed of having to choose. Of having to say out loud I don't
want to be what I'd imagined. There are other things in me. Except
here it now was. And I didn't feel free of a thing.

Now

He looks so hard at me. Right in. And I realise this will be the
last night I pretend that I am the one who's been waiting for him,

when he's been the one waiting for me.

> I wasn't on the pill.
>> What?
> I stopped.
>>> Why'd you do that?
>> I don't know.
> You wanted to get pregnant?
>> Not really.
> Then I don't understand.
>> It's hard to explain.
> Please, Eily, try because   that is a lot to take in.

This Autumn Gone

Came down that whole day in sticks and stones. Shelterless. And I found myself a woman with a body, doing what it does. When it's let. Because I let it. Because I would not own what I really wanted. And that this was the place I was probably going to from the moment I chose to hide. Then I knew I could not see it through. Every bit and bite of me refused. Wanted to run from myself, far as I could to a world where I hadn't done   what I did. While inside, so much loneliness. The furthest I'd ever gone from myself. Knew too, right away, that what must happen next might take me the furthest I'd ever been from you.

Hours then.

I remember learning the bathroom mat. Its redness, through fingers but through tears, kaleidoscope! The colours of colours making no sense. The dust in its fibres, our cast-offs as well. Or so I reminded myself, in lucider seconds. All parts of us fall away. Then stumbling up to the kitchen. Bin under the sink. Stowing it deep down in the rubbish. Right to the bottom where no eye would see and I'd be the only one thinking of it. Of what I'd done. So that was the day I was and wasn't. The day I waited for you. The day spent chain smoking on a breakfast bar stool. Staring down at the lino. Going down too. Going down. Very far.

Now

Now. Now. Now. Except the past remains against. Neon flashing through our window, black and drenched. Having found my courage, I lose it again. Answers drifting from grasp just as the storm had. But my silence leading our storm inside to lift from a cold one into active hell. And I look at him. And his eyes ask again. And I look away.

This Autumn Gone

As you came in that night, saw you see it again. Now the first thing about me. Not unreasonable, considering. But the look in your eye suggested you might ask, so I veered to generalities about the day's dids and nots.

How was being back in rehearsal?

Interesting. Strange. More absorbing than I was expecting.

In a good way?

Yeah, just a lot's changed since I last felt like that.

And how were the others?

Nice enough. I know a few of them from before.

What did you do?

Just a read-through, you know. Talked about Marlowe. Where the problems might be.

Doing Faustus at last though. You must be

Yeah I am.

Can't wait to see it.

Well, that's a while yet   anyway   how are you?
   Fine   just classes today.
   And how were they?
     Same.
Not rehearsing late?
 Not yet.
   So   what do you fancy for dinner then?

In this way, we crossed evening and on into night. Spaghetti
Bolognese, which we are both bad at but keep trying out anyway.
This time you. I was on garlic bread.

     Bit soggy, Stephen.
   Maybe the soup was too much?
   Or maybe tomato soup isn't Bolognese sauce?

Laughing at you and you going

   Well, next time you make it   fucking Delia Smith!

But ourselves in that moment. Push it on pause. Ourselves in that
moment but not long after, you going

   Look   I want to talk to you, Eil

And that's when the phone rang. Blessed phone. I legged to it.
Snatched it from its cradle and

     Hello? Oh, hi   Grace.

Never so happy to hear her voice, I assumed the position of a
very long gossip. And when I saw your eyes ponder my stomach,

I pushed the yapping on and on.

How's the gap year going?

And

When will you be over here next?

And

Be glad you missed Stephen's Bolognese tonight.

Eventually though, you stood to take it.

Here, hand her over to me.
He wants you now, Grace, but I'll speak to you soon.

Fingers slipping fingers in the exchange. Now was the moment of escape, except you kept hold of my hand and mouthed clearly

Wait.

But I yawned back

Nah, see you down there, all right?

And whether it was, or was not, took my grateful leave.

So, in the lee of my lie then, I went to our bed. Left you to her, however long that might take. Instead of rest though, I lay listing in the dark beneath labyrinths of future until reason got lost. Became running. More running and stepping across, to wide places of fear. Into numb ends of shock. Clamps of remorse growing tight round my neck. I strained from but, strangled by its now fast approach, felt I'd nowhere to   nowhere to   nowhere to

Oh.

A white gleam of first light at the far end of abyss. Except not light. Not really. Really, something much worse. Now I can scarcely believe I devised this.

What if   I made you do the work?

Simple in its logic and made for spreading blame even if one of us wasn't so guilty as some. But to fuck with that. I left it behind for theories of How I would. Could? Here again the gleam evolved into the shit of What if I made you   not hurt me   or maybe   hurt me a bit? And only enough to act as goad towards making it like it had never been. Or been but resolved by nature's own intervention, over which no one even you could grieve. At least not for long. Or if long   not very deeply I hoped. So there was a plan. All set up and clear. Until realising I still had to account for   the other hows of it.

How unwilling you'd be.
How you never had.
How, the one time I'd asked, you'd said I won't do that.

Firmly enough too to leave no room for doubt. Lucky you   to know who you are. So, not hurt. No. Too wild to work. Rough   however? Rough   perhaps. Rough was different and definitely in there – as witnessed in the fractures when more feeling than you were able for breached and came flooding through. Therefore   rough could be and   considering the practicalities of this   I remembered whereabouts to press.

Settled in the lee of my lie then, and our bed, I waited for you. It took you an age, but The stars move still, time runs, the clock will strike! Heard you hang up at last. Flick through your script. The kitchen light go off. The kitchen door shut and the front door key turn in its lock. Heard your teeth get brushed and you have a piss. A nicotine patch taken out. Peeled and stick! Listened to you walk down the hall. Then. Ready? You came in and were I think surprised by the dark.

> Asleep already, Eily?
> No   not yet   come here.

My hand reached, and yours took, before you could guess that the blackness had a purpose. Just came open to me because you wanted and I wanted it. Yet sharp enough to ask on feeling my grip?

> What's   going on?

And looked like a boy put to work in some vast machine, wary it will cut but not knowing when. Capitulating though once I began to take that caution apart. But your body wasn't all fooled. It remained alert for other mechanisms that might be at work. That could weigh on your long arms. Or your legs as you knelt. Where I pulled you to the place and became instrument myself.

> Crunching cogs.
> Slicing iron.
> Hammered discs.

Yet still restrained by yours. Even as we kissed. Even as your mouth found to my breast. Making me the one struggling not to forget what I had come there for. Hard to, just then. Then got released somewhat by your hand stroking my stomach. Feeling for a rise there? I clutched it back. Forbade it what your fingertips begged knowledge of. Part of me wondered too maybe but KNEW I must not. Because there was no place for this, between us, without risk of my saying

I will.

Or

Stephen, if you're ready I'm ready as well.

Which would have been as is evident now an even more terrible lie. No, I steered clear of those sweet treats, with their inevitable rot. Kept the lee shading me and the next part on track. Kept your body doing what it thought mine would like   because it always has. A little on the out before going in. Which it does like. My body. And cannot resist. So splintered my plan into the smell of your neck. The touch of your tongue on the top of my lip. To your breath in my hair and what you'd mouth next. The weight of your body on   No! I clawed back. Knew I must. Found that vein in your arm I love the run of. Had so often traced the length of with fingers and tongue. Have been known to stroke my face against while we fucked and this time   instead   I bit.

Eily, Jesus!

Sunk my teeth further in.

Ow! Fuck. You're breaking the skin!

Trying to pull back but me not letting. Me doing the feeling instead. Teeth letting release. Tongue finding the wound. Above your elbow. From the trickle of blood. Then while you watched   I licked.   Metallic.   And clang.   Until it bloodied my lip.

What're you doing?

But I just bit it again. Less hard. And that time   the change in
your breath. The look in your eye when ours met. Giving in. Giving in as I licked all the rest. Up your arm. Your chest. To the vein
in your neck where I heard you on the inside think Don't! And I
didn't, but threatened the risk   as the fuck got rough. Then rougher. Then very close to Fuck this. With only one hesitation – when I
forgot to not flinch as it started to hurt. Your body doing one thing
but your mouth saying

    Will I stop?
     No! God, don't!
    Maybe we should ease off? I   don't want to   hurt
    anything.

But that would be useless. So I got you beyond easily actually by
hurting you more, and not forgetting to mask my own. Made my
body take everything. Until I went white inside with panels of pain.
Regretting too when you shifted and made pleasure again, which
was very hard to refuse – like nights when you'd get lost in me and
the two of us knew there'd be hard times ahead but we'd have to
go through it. There was no other way. And that's where you went
now. Lost in me. Lost in it. While I encouraged blindness. Added in
where I could until even you asked

      Eily   is that too much?   Maybe   I shouldn't?

I'd only to kiss you though, for you to give doubt up and allow
your body put to what uses I wanted. Your attention allowing me
briefest checks only. Wet? Plenty yes. Blood? No. Or not yet. Or

not that I could see in the dark, however promising the pain and hard your work. But only so much of you left, now we'd gotten this far. Pin you in. Pull again until you were at going over. So I let you. Gave you that. Kept my body on, at its own devices, all the way until you were done. Thought I'd kept space from pleasure but then you dragged me along. The pain not even stopping for it. Suffering it through. Suffering to let you hold me until it was finished and I was   done. Then collapsed. You on me. All of you on. The lovely weight and slope off of pain. Only its memory slipped out into the muscles of my legs as they, unchecked now, shook. Tiniest spasms that I felt all down you too. Hoped mine might soon have more meaning though, even if I didn't know what to expect. But now we were on the far side   the fear came again. Of what I'd done. Of what might be in the offing. I wanted you then to know everything   to help me somehow. The one person I hadn't, and yet owed, every part of the truth. Still, we still met on the sheet. Bodies shocked by pleasure. Appalled by it. Before you, seeing all the darkness by now I suspected, slid from me, with

What the fuck was that?

Then just looking   and lying beside and   for a short while nothing more. But the stretched quiet could not last. For, as my body saw yours, yours saw mine back. Knew it snapped with pain like twanged elastic and would or could not endure to ignore. So you touched my face. You traced my jaw. Said

Eily let's not go round this any more. I'm getting afraid and I think you are too.

And the night grew large in me. Fit to burst. Knew the whole of its guilt and let it into my voice.

        Oh God, oh God, what have I done.
          Eily, what have you? Just tell me, love.

Then you gripped me. And I wanted to but shame chose instead, of this offer of your arms and the good hideout they make, to set forth upon the wastes.

        Let go of me.
          Eily, don't go   please

Quick as you were, though, I nimbled it. Foot to the floor. Out of our bed. Out of our bedroom. Into the hall with its dinged bare carpet and wear-smeared walls. Rubbed against. Tea-splashed. Suit-case-hauled. But I don't see them and they don't matter now, all those symptoms of life.

        Eily, wait! Fuck's sake   this is serious, love!

Almost reached me but your long reach not quite long enough. So I made it to the bathroom. Shut in and locked. Laid my back to the door. Let in the pain. You hammering on the other side of it, begging

        Eily   please, love   let me in.

But glass purls in the window had me by then. Suspended in the On lights and Off lights of night Camden. Signalling places of the mad most easily found by those running madly away. And I would   to any another   with its any other shape   from this one I no longer knew how to make. In which I'd become, even to myself, some inventive, unanswering thing. A thing fixed on fixing to a moment in time, from which nothing would move forward or

get left behind. Still wanting what I wanted though, so approaching from the side, like I was doing nothing. Like I was a liar. All the
fear getting me then. Asking why this bad game? What instinct let
it out and let it lead me this way? This one way with its no good
end? Unless   nothing did and,   never mind the secret want, there's
no one in there at all. I am. What if I am no one inside? No! No!
And yet   now might be the time to   to find out.

Eily, please. Eily, please   open the door.

The fucking lights out there just going on and off though.

Eily, open the fucking door   whatever it is   let me help.

But then   the lights did   instead. Wherever they came from
or whatever at. Just stopped their flickering. Put themselves out.
And in the flashless cool after, the next came to pass. You still calling, of course, but somehow further off. My whole body there too
but   turning odd. Growing airy with a twisting pain and   like it
might now be getting its way. Or simply outrunning. I knew how
to outrun. And I was tired of that. It was time for making certain.
Was there an inside me? And if so, who? Liar? Actress? Woman?
Doubt? The mirror, as always, told its own tale but I was getting
beyond reflections just then. So I opened the mirror for the cabinet behind. Not for Anadin either. Or your new nicotine pack. Or
the tube of toothpaste. Or your shaving brush. Its accompaniment,
however   with its replaceable blades. Except you, predictably, had no
replacements. Had forgotten them last Saturday so grumbled all week about
how blunt it was and   nicking yourself. Nevertheless, I banked on its
sharpness enough while taking, with some care, its apparatus apart.
Mindful too to avoid all unnecessary cuts   before making the one
that was. And feeling not so great now. Light. Somewhere wet. Or

that, at least, it might be time to check   but first things first. See
that skin that covers myself? What's in it? For certain. Surprise!

Eily, come out now   I mean it   or I'll come in.

Exhaustion tugging me down but sense saying Placate him.

I   I   I won't be long.
Eily   you're really scaring me, love.

So I did it then, rather than keep doing that. Blood shocking
from its vein as I unsealed it for   investigation only. Rather than
death   although   maybe   it seemed that way.
Funny though funny? Wearing its hurt   while also   feeling
further off   Both inside of my body and out of at once. Con-
firming however   verifying there was   some   will   definitely
within. An alteration   a woman that   or wanted to
except   then she was turning   Or the room went round. Split
tiles veering the upswing while the cabinet slung wrong. Alice in
Alison. Floors listing down   so her feet   couldn't find any
footing as mine and   after   soon   very after   Tip.
Some sound too. Then without any lights   just from very far
down   looking very far up   a far flue of piled stone and
calling above

Stephen! Stephen?

To you. But it shut itself then   a lid went on top   so I didn't
call again and   it got very dark. And it was cold down there and
I was on my own   thinking about how much I wanted   just then
just   to see your face.

– 314 –

Now

I remember. I remember. From out there to back here. The deep keel of autumn from which we have not recovered. Some for shame. Some for guilt. And for want of defence my tongue dulls to useless. What it cannot though, I still hear inside. Even try fitting words to its silence. Not many, or well, but all I can find. So here in our kitchen, late in this night, as he, who is you, says

If it's just, Eily   I'm going to bed.

I, at last, say

No, Stephen, wait. There's something I   want to show you first.

Then here we are at

Show me what?
It's only   I'll just be a second   all right?

And he shrugs because   nearly more effort to not. Sits again in the armchair. Lights another cigarette up. Grey with fatigue as I dig this something out. All right then. All right then.

Here.
What is it? A diary?
No.
What then?
Well   maybe   eventually   something.
Like what?
I don't know yet.

But   you wrote it?
    I   tried.
How long have you been working on this?
    Since the spring.
        All this time?
        On and off.
And all this last while   since?
    Yes.
    And it's about
        Some of it.
    Why didn't you tell me before?
        I didn't know if there was much point.
    Why now then?
Because   this is where it went and maybe even   started it
and   I want to explain so   will you read it?
            Of course I will.

Can't take eyes off his first leafing. Both sides of the page. Foolscap. Dubious? My heart going crossways but now is the time because
if not   there might not be any more.

        So   all of it?
            If you can bear it.
        I'm sure I will, but it's late so   let's see how I do.

Dropping his eyes, intrigued then, from mine as I stand, anxious
sentinel.

    If you're going to watch, Eil, it might be a while so why don't
    you sit and I'll shout when I'm done?
        Yes   all right.

This is perfect sense   still I wait for his fingers to turn to the page before returning to the window. My preferred perch. Pull back the curtain and sit into its ledge. Last of the last of the night reached already. And of what storm has been. Camden now whistlish with cleanliness as the streetsweepers along, spraying guck from the gutters, surprising damp drunks. Old fox crossing against the lights, back to Regent's Park. Could we be back too, at a different start? Except there's no starting again. Only here, these hours later, once more looking out on London. Then into the near glass up close at myself. Then behind me to him, doing his best with my horrible handwriting. How appalling it is and probably obstructing what little sense I've managed to scratch on the page. Will it make any difference, that part-legible tale, with it still spinning logic and faltering steps towards   what? Too soon to know it yet. But if I sit watching his reflection's every twitch, I'll surely die of madness before he is finished. So, instead fetch another fag. Light it up. Name it my last distraction of this transfigured night. And because of its many forerunners know, whatever the upshot, in a few hours there will be another day.

This Autumn Gone

Oh fuck! Oh my God   please wake up!

As if I could remember as much. As if I heard any words through the pound in your chest. Your voice so far behind as you held me to it. Grappled with me or   something. Except even that can't be true. Because   back above   in the world   I was out cold. Didn't come around either until an ambulance somewhere. Halfway to the Royal Free, you told me later. Then though, there seemed only expanse. High. Without actual time moving about. The nearest reality you, gripping my hand so hard and repeating

Eily, can you hear me, love?

And then

She's awake. She's looking at me.

Which I was   though mostly at the blood. On your arms. And
your cheek. Reason taking time to pull its origin free. Slowed on
the uptake no doubt by the pester in between. Other lights in my
eyes and immediate questions. Plus their

You've hit your head but you're going to be fine.

But wanting only your hand as I thought words into my mouth
I

I'm sorry, Stephen   I am.

And must've seemed it because you started to cry. Then tried
not to and said

Don't, love. Don't be sorry. I am. It was me.

Not much after that. Window scraped by a branch. Down hiss of
double-decker somewhere alongside. Boy racers racing, must've been
up in Hampstead. Then I passed back out   I think.

Things. Time. Movement. Noise. All against. On the inside and
outside at once of   my head   which was   collecting   those
but   not thinking too much.

The next bit then was day. Sunlight. Strip lit. An all-viscerating ache. You asleep. In a hard chair. By the bed. Blood scrubbed off your face but elsewhere in evidence. Knee of your jeans, and what of your shirt showed through the soiled folds of your coat.

Armageddon under there, I'd say!

And laughed to myself, thinking I was so funny. Then rued that right off, remembering it was probably certainly my blood. What did I do that for then?

Oh

And found another hitch, up on my forehead. Some numbness but

Ow!

Bandaged hand went to investigate and how did it get like that? You waking as I pressed it and must've groaned. For long limbs stiffened. Eyelids batted. Then you remembered. Jolted forward. Took my hand again.

How long've you been awake?
    What happened   to my head?
Think you hit it on the sink   when you   passed out.
    I fainted?
I don't know for sure but that's how it sounded so   that's when I put the door in.
    How?
Shoulder.
    Does it hurt?
A bit but   never mind that how do you feel?

I don't know.

That's all right. You're bound to be   confused.

Taking this as gospel, I glanced to the window, with its bright high day and tops of some trees bending, not breaking, in a civilised breeze. How nice a day   then the whole of it   of it all   all then came in. Swamp. And how you were looking at me. Angry? No. But very something. Like you knew. So I had to ask

Stephen?

What?

Am I   still?

Not   any more   you lost a lot of blood.

What does that mean?

That you need to rest but   you'll be all right   thank God.

Two things, right then, happening at once. Relief at being in my body again by myself. But in rank parallel   extensive regret for every single thing I'd done wrong.

I'm sorry   I didn't tell you.

And saw you were too. Would die before admitting it though. Or so I read it through my guilt. Now   I'm not sure. Now I think of it, maybe you just meant what you said.

You don't have to be sorry for anything, my love. All you have to do is sleep.

To which every part of me agreed. After which you kissed my elbow. After that, my cheek. And though you smiled, I was scared by how scared you seemed. Because you shouldn't. After all, it had only been me, making a mess of the world.

Now – In One Hour

Snatch a window glimpse of him looking at me. About to   what?
Then long legs go click as he stretches. Again, as he gets up. Then
another somewhere below the click of his back. And I can't resist
asking

    Well?
  Not finished yet.
   How far in are you?
   About halfway, I think.
   And   how is it   so far?
  Interesting but   I need to take a leak so
   Oh right   well   off you go.
Would you stick on the kettle? I could murder a brew.
  Grand.

Very bastardly opaque and on purpose I'm sure. Either way, I am
now the one waiting for you and helpless to do otherwise. So, I
brewed the tea while you pissed. Took your thanks and, after it,
sat back down by the much-becalmed view. But studied you in the
glass until I couldn't. Each page turning in me as you did and ached
for reply to Does it make sense? Do you like what you read? Or
is that heavy sigh your embarrassment for me and my rubbish like
this? In short, every form of torture presented, but I must admit
this is a game of guts long overdue to be played.

This Autumn Gone

When you took me home, it smelt of wash. Of bleach. Cleanest bathroom I'd ever seen. And the strangeness between us. Moving around each other like not to touch, these walls or ourselves, for fear of damage. There could be no further breaks. Me as glass and you at pains to show you knew this to be true. Except I wanted to be held by you so tight I snapped and all of these days also shattered. But I couldn't ask. So instead drank tea and ate nothing of what was set before me. While you watched. Watched and watched me. Right up to when I said

Stop!

Worse then, with your pretending to not. And, because you loved me so much, I knew it anyway. Slow passed the long hours of that day, dragging us forward until bed, when neither could tell what to do. Just pulled up the duvet. Did not speak. In confusion, turned away and dreamt of sleep. Then lay awake in the horrible dark. It was the first night of that. But, in this manner a mould was forged for how we'd get to be.

In the weeks after, I hadn't a moment alone. Despite you getting off the phone to say

They won't expect you back this term   unless that's what you want?
   I don't.
     I didn't think you would.
  But also   they've suggested you see
     No, I don't want to do that.
    Might help to talk to someone, Eily   on the outside.
     I don't want to talk about it at all.
    I know but
    No!
      All right.

So you left it, although it was not. Instead set in place a rota of purgatorial oversight. Rafi. Alison. Even Danny roped in – for when you had rehearsal. Never left the flat when you didn't. And tried to coax me. To make me eat. To invite me to

Let's take a walk up the Heath.
        I don't want to.
    Park then? It's just a few streets.
        I don't feel like it.
    Cinema?
        No.
    Go out to eat? Wherever you like.
Stephen, just leave it   I don't want to go anywhere.

And I wanted nothing in this latch of my mess, where guilt was only increased by kindness. Yours. Or their concern. I wanted to stare at a wall until it could all be undone. Ultimately I settled though for dispersing the audience.

Tell them not to. I don't want them here all the time.
    They're worried about you and   I can't leave you alone.
        I won't do   anything.
            How do I know?
    Because there's nothing left to do.
        What does that mean?
                Nothing.
        Explain it to me.
        You were there.
    Yes, but   why the secret? And once you locked the door
        I don't want to talk about that.
    Eily, I just want to understand. I feel   so

            Stephen, it wasn't you.
                Then why not tell me what was going on?

    And there we were. Snake tail devouring back again. Standstill.
Stood so still. While it still made no sense. Just putting blame somewhere, then trying somewhere else. Knowing only what wasn't. And
then and then, time began placing thoughts. Sharp at incision. Soon
extending beyond. Giving prods, not to certainties but where start
might be found. Start of. Things put. Gave and took – without a
body taking the brunt. A place full of places inside. Suddenly I knew
what that was and that now was time to let   the want   have its
way. So I waited for you to leave for the day. Then I returned to it.
And opened. And it roared in my ears. For a long time just roaring.
Nothing finer emerged. But after that long nothing of roaring, the
start. Words after another. Sentences, in a while. Pages becoming,
over weeks, alive. Full with all of it. Everything there. The annoying
harmless and harmful as well. Reimagining its logic when lost for
sense or the rest of me fell short. But told it best as language could
and with the truths only fiction allowed. Hard ones. Now and then.
New ones, that kept understanding grinding. Wide ones, that forced
the world right in. Free ones, that told me, this was a beginning. If I
wanted it to be. And there they are now, sat on your lap. The very last
secret. Shared not least in hopes it might catch what's been creeping
forward with us and release it back into its time. As for the rest? In
its scribbles and lines, that is wait and see.

The End of the Night

        Eily   wake up.

    Face cold to the glass. You thumbing my cheek. Then sitting
down across.

Are you finished?

Just now.

And   what do you think?

Pretty close to home.

Does it   bother you?

That would make me a hypocrite.

Does it though?

It makes me sad   the parts that are us.

It's fiction though   mostly.

I know, but inside   I still see you.

And?

I know what it is to not want to be changed.

Turns out it happened anyway so I just made it worse!

Smiles interfering then though, to help us across.

But you found something too.

Maybe.

Not maybe at all. There's so much beauty in what you've
written, Eil, sad as it is, and that's no little thing.

You think so?

I do.

And   do you forgive me?

There's nothing to forgive. What I wanted was this   to
understand.

Then I'm glad I showed you.

Me too.

I've missed you, Stephen.

And I've missed you.

So now?

We're still here, aren't we? If you still want?

Breathe out.

    I do   very much.
     Eily, so do I.

Cold fingers under the bangle. Turning it slowly on my wrist. Eily, always, Stephen. August 1996. Then you let them fall back to lace with mine. Their grip and old magic. New badness too in your eyes.

    You realise I'll be chasing you now, for the second draft?

I like and laugh at that.

    I'll start in the morning!
    Too late. It's already here.

And true, the dawn is turning out there. Finding in, across my face. Tired eyes opening to it and

    Snow!
     What?
    Snow. Outside.

Which there suddenly is. Falling everywhere like a first in the world. More just rarity though and we know that. So, after only brief marvelling, finally get to the kiss. Long lost lover-like because a long time missed. But devious too about not giving up. In our re-finding each other and wanting close, until at last you say

    Fancy heading to bed?

And I, kissing the side of your mouth, admit

Sounds good to me.

Both then stretching to get from the ledge. Hop-staggering on the nuisance of gone-to-sleep legs. Hand in hand as we skirt the carats of glass lately ground in our lino by the troublesome past. And beyond, on out to the troublesome hall if only troublesome for want of a new sixty-watt bulb. Now a passage towards, not an exit from, in our haste to get to our troublesome room – chill with curtains left wide to its new winter scene. But, once we're in there, it can snow all over London. On each stone of its streets. Every rooftop. Our bed. For what do we care? We're returned from the dead. Quick now with rekindling, and reclaiming residence, back here in our troublesome life.

Acknowledgements

Many thanks to my editor, Alex Bowler, for his tenacious noting and to my agent, Tracy Bohan, for her support. Thanks to Chris Wyatt for his very useful memory and to everyone who worked on *A Very Short Film About Longing* – you all helped me in more ways than one. Most of all, thank you to William and Éadaoin, who remain the very best people around.